Further Praise for *Hold Still*

"Haunting.... Strong's characters are achingly detailed, and undeniably real, as they all struggle to make sense of Ellie's fracturing. ... *Hold Still* is a heartbreaking look at the damage parenting can do, passed down like genetic code anyone would do anything to break. Is loving as well as you can ever enough? As this unsettling debut shows, the answer might only be maybe."
—Caroline Leavitt, *San Francisco Chronicle*

"Ms. Strong has a highly sensitive awareness of the special kind of disappointment—and the painfully undying connection—that comes with family. There's mercifully little armchair psychology about Ellie and no blatantly obvious reason that she should be so damaged or careless. She just is, and in that way feels authentic."
—John Williams, *New York Times*

"Brace yourself for the heartbreaker that is *Hold Still* (really, go hug someone). This wildly evocative novel, which focuses on the repercussions of a terrible mistake, is Lynn Steger Strong's debut—although we're scratching our heads as to *how*. Strong renders her characters' emotional lives with such depth and precision that this novel-writing thing seems like it'd be old hat for her."
—Elle.com

"*Hold Still* drills down on emotions, and the lack thereof. Throughout the novel, one emotion that Maya owns, and owns powerfully, is her love for Ellie. ... In *Hold Still*, that tortured, grounding love serves as the necessary glue between mother and daughter. And that, perhaps, is the bottom line."
—Martha Anne Toll, *The Millions*

"Strong excels at building place and time, creating a solid sense of locale for her characters to ricochet around, and depicting emotional distance—words that cannot be forced, a hand reaching and then falling back—as she marks the many moments lost by her characters."　　　　　　　　　　—Neal Wyatt, *Library Journal*

"A tender novel. . . . It is gripping without ever reaching toward the spectacular; and its lyrical, undulating prose never calls attention to itself, nor screams out wishing for you to applaud after each hard stop. In these moments, *Hold Still* is at its most accomplished."　　　　　　　—Meredith Turits, *Electric Literature*

"Strong brilliantly captures the significance that unmade decisions can have on a life, and her study of the relationship between mother and daughter is nuanced and heavy with their history. . . . Introspective and intricately plotted."　　　　　　　—*Booklist*

"[An] assured, illuminating examination of the complex ties between mothers and daughters, the ways we can go on living in the face of unimaginable sorrow, and how the stories that have come before us can help."
　　　　　　　—Gina Webb, *Atlanta Journal-Constitution*

"Stellar."　　　　　　　　　　　　　　—*Publishers Weekly*

"*Hold Still* is an unblinking examination of family, the mother-child bond, and the storms it must withstand. Lynn Steger Strong pulls no punches in considering not just how deep, but also how misguided a mother's love can be."
　　　　　　　—Elisa Albert, author of *After Birth*

HOLD STILL

HOLD STILL

Lynn Steger Strong

LIVERIGHT PUBLISHING CORPORATION
a division of W. W. Norton & Company
INDEPENDENT PUBLISHERS SINCE 1923
NEW YORK / LONDON

Copyright © 2016 by Lynn Steger Strong

All rights reserved
Printed in the United States of America
First published as a Liveright paperback 2017

For information about permission to reproduce selections from this book,
write to Permissions, Liveright Publishing Corporation,
a division of W. W. Norton & Company, Inc.,
500 Fifth Avenue, New York, NY 10110

For information about special discounts for bulk purchases, please contact
W. W. Norton Special Sales at specialsales@wwnorton.com or 800-233-4830

Manufacturing by LSC Communications, Harrisonburg
Book design by Brooke Koven
Production manager: Louise Mattarelliano

Library of Congress Cataloging-in-Publication Data

Names: Strong, Lynn Steger, 1983– author.
Title: Hold still / Lynn Steger Strong.
Description: First edition. | New York : Liveright Publishing Corporation,
a Division of W. W. Norton & Company, 2016.
Identifiers: LCCN 2015051170 | ISBN 9781631491689 (hardcover)
Subjects: LCSH: Mothers and daughters—Fiction. | Domestic fiction. |
Psychological fiction.
Classification: LCC PS3619.T7785 H65 2016 | DDC 813/.6—dc23
LC record available at http://lccn.loc.gov/2015051170

ISBN 978-1-63149-265-5 pbk.

Liveright Publishing Corporation
500 Fifth Avenue, New York, N.Y. 10110
www.wwnorton.com

W. W. Norton & Company Ltd.
15 Carlisle Street, London W1D 3BS

1 2 3 4 5 6 7 8 9 0

For Peter, Isabel, and Luisa

HOLD STILL

Prologue

Maya wants to go in with her. They've been out all day, their last in Florida. Ellie's eight and wants to swim just one more time before they go. The sun has fallen past the dunes, and the sky is pink and blue and purple. Maya's daughter stands, smiling, sunny, salty, sandy, and promises that she'll be fine, that Maya doesn't have to go in too. Maya's already pulled on her pants and sweater. She's almost always cold, even here, where, even in winter, it's warm right up to hot. She stands up to where the waves come in thin films of foam over her ankles, her sweater held tight around her, her toes curled into the sand and bits of broken shells, and Ellie bounds away in front of her, past the point where the sand drops off, her tiny body quickly swallowed up. Maya watches Ellie let herself fall forward, arms reaching up and shoulders rolling: she dives down beneath the waves and comes up twice, and, all at once, Maya wants her daughter next to her: warm and wrapped up tight. But Ellie's vertical again and treading water. Her head is small and dark and her curly hair is matted tight around her skull. The water dips as the pressure builds beneath her, and Ellie's shoulders pop up and out, light brown now, with a smattering of freckles. Her bathing suit is yellow with tiny purple dots. Maya calls, "Come in, El," but Ellie doesn't hear her. The water settles. Another wave forms a hundred feet away. The curve of it grows, and Ellie's still and small and getting smaller. Maya's chest and neck get hard. "El!" she calls, as if she'll hear her. As if somehow her screaming will keep the wave from crashing down. Ellie's head is there and then it isn't. And Maya breathes in once, then out. And then she's running, diving, swimming. She kicks, and gulps of water fall into her throat. She has to keep her eyes open so she can see where Ellie is and they sting sharp, her vision blurring; she grabs hold of her close to the bottom, and the round hollow of her chest and the slick softness of her bathing suit are held tight in Maya's arms; she's still wearing her sweater, which is heavy now with the weight of water, salt, and sand. "El," she says and thinks she sees her daughter smile. Maya holds tight to Ellie and drags her up to shore. Maya pants and Ellie's breath is even. "Ma, I'm fine," she says. Maya will not let go of Ellie for the next hundred years.

Winter 2013
(Afterward)

"Maya, where the hell are you?" Boots on stairs, and she can hear the cadence of his breathing. She drops her pen and reads the letter one more time before she slips it in the book she's brought with her to bed:

Sometimes I say it out loud to myself or type it, the thing you did. I write it down and stare at it, try to figure out how to fit it, what it looks like in my brain. I try to imagine a world in which I hate you. I try to see if I'm capable of letting you go. This is not a thing that people are supposed to think about their children, but all that stuff about how and why and when to love is all wrong anyway. It doesn't take into account the specific impulses and capabilities of all the thousand million different people who love and are loved. What makes me angrier than what you did is the impossibility of the idea of not loving you because of it. I'm

irrevocably attached to whatever it is you've done or
do or are, because loving you makes me a person who
could rationalize anything that you've done, as long as
I can know for sure that you'll survive.

M

She curves her neck, chest to chin, as she listens for the last stair to creak beneath her husband's steps. She sets down the book, the cover's edges furred and softened, the back cover ripped. She sits up, her back straight against the headboard, and grabs hold of one of Ellie's tank tops. It's one of the few her daughter didn't take with her to Florida when she left.

When she left because Maya made her go.

Maya fingers the book's spine one final time as Stephen shoulders into their daughter's bedroom. She's stayed herself for his arrival. Still, she starts when she sees him; she slips the book, the letter safe inside, beneath Ellie's duvet and looks up at him.

He wears glasses, thick-rimmed, rounded. He wears his coat still, wool black pants. He's thin, with a face that's pale with creases at the mouth and eyes, gray hairs peppered through what was once the color of wrought iron. He's still handsome, distinguished: a professor of philosophy, widely published, head of the department. He is, even now, the most capable man she's ever known.

Ben comes through the door three steps behind his father. His dark hair is shorn close to his head. She is always conscious of the breadth of him. He's five inches taller than his father, all strength and sinew. She unfurls slightly and turns toward him. He is, perhaps, her favorite thing on earth.

"Ma," Ben says. He looks as if he's told on her.

This is the first that he's been with them in over a year. She wants to beg him not to leave, to stay close and with her; she wants to ask him quietly to stay far enough away from her in order that he not be ruined too.

"How long have you been up here?" asks her husband.

Hours? Maya thinks. *Years?*

She sleeps in here most nights. She starts in bed with Stephen; then wakes up here—often on top of the covers, often with the large wool blanket Stephen gave her years ago—not always knowing when and how she's moved.

Her son won't look at her.

"We're going out, Maya," says Stephen. "You're eating actual food."

Maya wraps the thin shoulder strap of her daughter's shirt tight around her index finger, till the tip of it is white.

"Get your coat," says Stephen, speaking to Ben. Their son looks back and forth between the two of them. His eyes are his father's, his nose and mouth some combination of the two. The sleeve of his sweatshirt is pulled down over his thumb and the bottoms of his fingers; Maya keeps her eyes fixed on the edges of his sleeves as he walks out of the room.

"Maya," Stephen says again once Ben has left them. Her husband can say her name to make it mean a million different things. This one, the tone low and firm, his eyes big and accusing, means she's acting in a way that makes him want to scream. But he will not scream because he has control. He will cut much more deeply and precisely by staying reasonable and firm.

"You have to stop this, Maya."

"Stop what?" She knows what, but she wants to hear his version of it.

He looks at her in the way he's always looked when he thinks she's asking needless questions.

"This, Maya." He spreads his arms. "Staying up here all the time. You're scaring Ben."

She wishes she were the type of person to stand up on this bed and yell at him. She wonders how often anger manifests itself as sadness, how it's so firmly taught to a certain kind of woman that it is better, more productive, to cry instead of scream.

"I'm doing what I can," she says.

Her voice is firm now. She hopes he's quick enough to catch the anger underneath.

"Just stop doing it to Ben," he says.

She looks down at her bare feet and folds the tank top. She places it on the bed, and stands; she pulls back the duvet, the book a bump beneath it still; she leaves it there. She walks past her husband into the room they're still meant to share and puts on jeans and socks—there's a pile of folded laundry sitting in front of her closet. She can't imagine who has thought to wash and fold her clothes—a long-sleeved shirt and an oversized cashmere turtleneck. Everything she owns, all small to begin with, looks oversized these days. She has long dark hair that she unknots now, only to pull it up and tighter, higher on her head.

She walks down the stairs where Stephen waits while checking email on his phone, and Ben stares at her, his coat on but unbuttoned, his sweatshirt still covering his hands.

"Shoes, Maya," says Stephen. She wants to place her hand, palm spread, thumb and forefinger firmly on his collarbone, and put her face up close to his and tell him not to treat her like a child.

She pulls on boots.

Summer 2011
(Before)

Ellie hasn't seen him coming, though the coffee shop—where she works, where she doles out coffee and pastries every morning while every other kid she knows is enrolled in some college she has somehow failed to get into—has a large window looking out onto the street. It's almost ten and the early morning rush has emptied. She's had no warning, no time to prepare; she stands stock-still, a black apron tight around her waist, short shorts, two coffee stains on the hip and shoulder strap of her white shirt. She's half listening to a girl from down the street who talks in front of her, something about new neighbors, a book she's read.

Ellie smiles at whatever the girl's saying, but her eyes stay fixed on him. He's taller than he was when they first met, broader, the sleeves of his shirt newly taut across his arms.

The girl, round-faced, soft-spoken, hands Ellie the money for her order, takes her coffee. Ellie doesn't turn to him until she's gone.

Dylan's hair has always been long, but it's short now, clipped down to a nub around his head. The whole time she's known him it's flopped down heavy in his face; he would toy with it incessantly, one large hand palming up over his head. Now, the sharp lines of his face and the largeness of his features shock her; he has big dark eyes, a long straight nose, thin lips. She can't imagine what he does now with his hands.

He wears a gray T-shirt, jeans, and what her brother would describe as "douchebag loafers." As he stands there, hairless, so much bigger, she has an image of him, fifteen, in Prospect Park: both of them stoned, no clothes and cold, his arms planted straight, chest hovering, thin but broad and firm, angling himself slowly, till his length had swallowed hers. He'd cupped his hand over her mouth and she'd bit the base of his thumb hard until he winced, still silent; he'd let her go. Ellie'd laughed out loud then, Dylan still on top of her, and she'd thought, *Finally, I'm just like all the other girls.*

He takes a piece of the free sample brownie. He swallows without chewing and takes another piece.

She can taste his breath: cigarettes, Mexican Coke, and ginger chews. She can feel the brush of her tongue along the crooked jumble of his bottom teeth.

He still calls her sometimes. Mostly she's able to ignore it: his name flashing over and over on her cell phone as she sits curled under her duvet not able to sleep. But sometimes she answers; sometimes she slides open the phone and lets him talk: she needs too much sometimes to be reminded that he's out there, that there's still someone in the world who's wanting her.

She tries to look at him sternly. "What do you want?" she says.

"Nothing," Dylan says.

She feels Joseph—short and sweet, her coworker and only friend here, her only friend at all right now—he's right behind her and Ellie wishes Dylan would just leave them. Instead, he leans in close to her: the smell is brownie and the hand-rolled cigarettes he smokes only when there are people around to watch him roll them. The rest of the time he smokes his mother's Parliaments. "You," he says. "Always, always. Pretty, pretty Ellie."

She feels her body leaning toward him. She holds tight to the countertop with both her hands.

Winter 2013

"Where will we go?" Maya says.

"Indian?" says Ben.

"Sure," says Stephen. "The closer one."

There's a better place in Crown Heights, but Stephen hates driving the car.

"How was campus?" asks Maya, because Ben's next to her and the silence gapes. They walk down Garfield to Fifth.

"Fine," says Stephen. "Usual early semester jostling."

"Things in order?" she says. "What are you teaching again?"

He pulls at a thread on one of his coat's buttons and pretends not to hear her. He's been teaching the same classes every semester for the past ten years.

"What about you, Benny?" she says, turning to him as they keep walking. She loops her arm through his elbow and thinks she feels him wince. Across the street on the next block is the coffee shop Ellie worked the few months before she left. All three of them are silent for a block; Ben and Stephen look back toward

Sixth Avenue; Maya looks up at the brown awning with the too-bright white scrawl: GINNY'S, it says.

"Calc 2," Ben says. His voice is flat, disinterested. "Western Political Thought," he says. This is Stephen's domain and his back straightens.

Stephen starts to speak, but their son stops him.

"It's a requirement," Ben says.

"Of course," says Stephen. "Speaks highly of the school, then."

Ben's in school in Ohio, bucolic, foreign, a soccer scholarship. Maya was jarred, baffled by the choice when it came.

Ben nods, and Maya leans in closer. "What else?"

"Spanish," he says. It's January and frigid and she wants to tell him to put his hands inside his pockets. She wants to bend down and button up his coat.

"I might have to retake English," he says, turning to look at her.

Stephen stops and faces them. He takes his hands out of his pockets and folds his arms across his chest. "Retake?" he says, lingering on the first syllable in a tone that Maya knows too well.

Ben turns toward Maya. He curls his hand into a fist.

"It's not a big deal," he says. "The class was really early in the morning. I just sort of stopped showing up."

This is her son whom teachers have been calling "gifted" since preschool. Her son for whom there has never been space enough to be a problem too.

"Sort of stopped showing up," says Stephen. Like he's trying out the feel of this idea. "Does your coach know?"

"It's fine, Dad. I'm covering it."

"Covering it." Stephen has been reduced to only able to repeat.

"Fuck off, Dad," her son says.

"Excuse me?" says Stephen, keeping his voice steady, though he looks like he's been hit.

"I'm starved," says Ben. "And cold. Can we keep walking?"

Stephen turns and walks ahead of them. Maya holds tight to her son.

They get samosas, tandooris, rogan josh, and spoon rice and creamy sauces on their plates. No one's speaking and Maya's grateful each time the waiter comes to cut into the quiet.

"All right?" he asks. He's older, with a thick, clipped accent. Maya nods, smiling at him, trying to think of what she might say to keep him there. A Bollywood musical plays on low behind them on a large flat-screen TV. Blues and oranges and purples all mixed up with lithe brown limbs. The waiter walks away.

"I heard Kenny Lambert made the Olympic Development Team," says Stephen.

Maya drops her fork and glares at him. They've agreed not to talk about the soccer. The coach called weeks before to express concern about Ben's "lackluster" involvement at practice in the fall.

A girl on the TV behind Stephen does a back bend, revealing a slick, perfectly flat midriff. Stephen never played or even cared about sports until their son suddenly proved himself a prodigy. By the time Ben was in high school, he was being recruited by a handful of colleges and Stephen knew the stats and names of every high school student in the state.

"Jesus, Maya, what? He's a friend of his."

"How do you even know this?" Maya asks him. She's caught him a few times, trolling the Internet for scores and statistics, obsessive for the sake of it. Ben's quiet. He lines his water glass with the index finger of his free hand.

The waiter comes and clears Stephen and Ben's empty plates

and they stay silent. It's almost closing time and he's removed his apron. Stephen sips his beer. "I'm interested in what our son is interested in."

"Kenny's not my friend, Dad," Ben says. "He's kind of a douche."

Maya's lips purse toward Ben and he smiles at her. She passes her plate to him and he consumes quickly all she's not been able to.

At three a.m. Maya sits in the nook in the kitchen, her arms wrapped around her shins, in running tights, a sports bra, and a jacket, waiting for morning to get close enough that she can leave. If she can wait till five she'll look less crazy. She's decided it's sufficient to hold out till four. She's dressed quietly in clothes she keeps in Ellie's room. She's always kept socks and shoes close to the door.

Pans hang over the island on which there are six stovetops and lines of spices. Instead of cabinets, they have large oak shelves along the walls, the dishes, pans, and cookware on display. They're embarrassingly wealthy—Stephen's parents. He's the only child and they've inherited everything. They have the brownstone in Park Slope, a block from the park, on Garfield, instead of Manhattan because it was what Maya wanted. Because there was a time in their lives when he made gestures as grand as moving to a side of the East River on which he had never previously set foot because Maya liked the trees.

She pulls on socks and shoes and ties them slowly, bends her left knee, and pulls her shin up against her face, then switches to the right. She laces her fingers and stretches her arms, one and then the other, pulling on her forearms. The lock clicks and the door creaks as she leaves.

Their block is shady, two- and three-family brownstones. They were some of the first gentrifiers, when Ellie was a toddler, Maya full-bellied with Ben. They'd felt a little pioneering, with the squatters and the lesbians still peopling Fourth Avenue, the less-than-stellar public schools they let their children attend the first few years. Maya brought up Sophie and Otto Bentwood at least once a week. (She'd even wanted to take in a stray cat that had loitered in their garden a few winter months the year they moved in. But Stephen was allergic; she'd had to bring her to the shelter instead, knowing full well what would probably happen. She was most shocked by how quickly she'd forgotten about it.)

Now Park Slope is more sought-after than parts of Manhattan. Their street is lined with Subarus and SUVs. Maya's always been a little bit embarrassed by just how much she loves this. Academics are supposed to laugh in the face of creature comforts, but she's grateful to Stephen for this: their lovely tree-lined lives, the ability to keep the house in Florida, vacations she would never have dreamed of till meeting him. Now the nicer, more progressive rehab in which they've locked their daughter this past year.

They have the garden in the back that Stephen maintains and Maya's office window overlooks. When the kids were little they would sit out in the dirt as Stephen weeded or trimmed the bushes. Sometimes they'd use the smaller shovels he bought them and help him put in a new tree or plant. He wore khaki pants that were frayed at the bottoms and old boat shoes—he would never not be Upper West Side, Collegiate prep, Princeton, and Oxford—but he's always been more interesting than that. And Maya would sit in her office, surrounded by the walls of bookshelves, all her work laid before her, and think this must be what people meant when they said *joy*.

She's only a block from their house when she sees him. She's headed toward the bridge instead of the park. The park's only three and a half miles around and that seldom feels long enough for Maya now. He sits on a stoop, elbows resting on his knees, head lolling forward. She feels her breath catch in her throat; the stretch of muscle from her shoulders to her neck begins to tense.

She says her son's name.

He pauses too long before he looks at her.

His eyes are glazed and his clothes the same that he was wearing at dinner. She sits on the step below him and looks into his face.

She thinks maybe he's not sure it's her, can't figure how or why he's out here. She wonders where he could have been. She rests her hand on his calf. There's something sweet coming off him; weed, she thinks. She wishes he were small enough that she could pick him up and bring him to his bed.

"Benny, what are you doing out here?" she says.

"I went out," he says.

"Out." Her cheek is even with his knee and she rests it briefly on the denim of his pants. "With whom?"

"Friends," he says. Like she doesn't know the boys he's been friends with since he was barely walking, kicking a ball in Prospect Park. Even this way, he has always been more predictable than El.

"I was in the city," he says. He keeps his head down as he talks to her. "What does it fucking matter anyway?"

In the past year, she has spoken to him mostly once a week. She calls on Sunday afternoons when she knows he's expecting her and they talk anywhere from ten minutes to an hour. Their conversation is hardly ever of much consequence. She knows he writes to Ellie too, but he never brings her up with Maya. Maya never asks. He tells her about class or friends or soccer. Sometimes they catch on something sure—something that he read that caught his interest, a movie they both saw, a moment in the news that feels both ripe for conversation and neutral enough to level back and forth.

"I went out drinking with some kids from high school and then smoked their awful weed."

Maya holds tight to her knees and doesn't answer. He's nineteen years old. She hasn't felt she had any right to scold her son since he was twelve.

"I'm fine, Ma," he says. "Don't worry."

A few times, waiting up for Ellie when Ben was still in high school, Maya caught him stumbling in just before curfew, cursing as he pulled off his shoes or let his coat drop to the floor. She considered confronting him then, making him stand very close to her so she could smell his breath. She considered enforcing some system of punishment that she and Stephen could hold fast to. But it always seemed to her even his attempts at rebellion were laced somehow with good.

"I know," she says. She looks up at him. His head lolls back and his eyes are closed, his mouth half open. He has a little Ellie in the fullness of his lips. "Benny . . ." She wants to give him something solid, something that will keep him safe.

She turns toward him. "I'm sorry, Benny," she says.

"Don't say you're sorry." His words fall into one another. He's so large from far away, but up close he might as well be ten years old.

"Well, what do you want me to say, then?"

"I don't know, Mom. Something angry. Something that shows me I'm not the only one who's noticed that we've basically all turned to shit."

"That's not true, Benny."

"Well, what's left, then?"

"Us," she says. "All of us are here." She stops, folds her hands into her lap to keep them from reaching for him. "The rest we'll figure out. We're still luckier than most."

"Than Annie?" he says. "Jack?"

"Yeah, Benny. We're luckier than both of them."

"But are we? If it's our fault? How could we be better off?"

"It's not your fault."

"It's all our faults."

Maya stops.

"El knew you didn't tell her."

"Didn't tell her what?"

"You didn't tell Annie. She didn't know how fucked up Ellie was."

This is true, but Maya hasn't thought of it so clearly. She told Annie that Ellie was in trouble. She'd thought their kids could help each other all at once.

"You shouldn't have let her go," her son says. "We should have told them."

Her son stands up. How tall he is, it shocked her even as she watched it happen, how even physically he was so much firmer than the thing she'd always been.

"I'm going to bed," he says.

She should go after him. She should walk him up the stairs and tuck him in.

She stays seated on the step until he's unlocked the door, and she thinks she hears it click, nearly a full block away, as he goes in.

Summer 2011

"Fancy job, huh?" Dylan says. He reaches toward his ear, but there's no hair there. He looks briefly as if he's not sure what to do. He runs his hand along the back of his neck instead. "You like it?" he says.

Ellie's not sure if he means the job or his new hair.

She nods, looking around for Joseph. She spends almost every afternoon with him in the backyard of his apartment share in Bushwick, talking, doing nothing, but he knows hardly anything about Ellie's life.

"You miss it, though, right? You miss me?"

She misses looking forward, looking toward. She misses knowing something different, other, better might be coming, even if most of the time it was just a flat line of not quite feeling for hours that stretched on.

"Fuck off, Dylan," she says. She wishes she were brave enough to punch him in the face.

He grins and she tries not to look directly at him, but she also doesn't want to have to look at Joseph now. She turns so she's facing the window that looks out on the street. She sees her mom—hair pulled back, dark blue sheath, black flats—as she walks slowly across Third Street, trying to keep her shit together. She's nowhere close to either crosswalk, is nearly hit by a town car and must stop short. She has her too-big bag over her shoulder, was probably headed up to campus to finish grades or use the library. It's summer but she still goes up a couple times a week. There's a 2 train five blocks from their apartment that's a straight shot to campus, but almost every day her mother goes to work Ellie sees her walk past the coffee shop to the R, which means two transfers and at least half an hour more.

"What are you doing?" Ellie's mom says. She's through the door and the bag has fallen to her elbow. Her arms are tan and thin from all the running. She has freckles spread across both shoulders and tiny dark blue flowered earrings in her ears. Ellie watches her mom wince as she pulls her bag back up onto her shoulder. There are like ten books that she won't go anywhere without, and Ellie's dad always yells at her for carrying too much stuff.

Dylan's back straightens and his face gets hard and happy as he sees her. "Prof," he says.

It's possible that Ellie's mother mutters, *Fuck*.

"Can you tell me what you're doing here?" she says to Dylan.

Her mom is frantic, nervous. Ellie wants to ask to hold her bag.

"This is not part of the agreement, Elinor," she says. Her parents have set down rules as of a few months ago. There was an incident. Ellie disappeared. But she was fine when they found her. They found a single-track mark and freaked out. (She might have been too fucked up to remember to hide it; she might have forgotten where she lived for a day or two, but what her parents seem incapable of understanding is that fucking off sometimes does not make one an addict, that there are whole gradations of just trying to have a little fun that don't end in tragedy and homelessness.) But now Ellie has to be home by ten and has to keep this job or there will be *Consequence.* She has to begin to *Make Some Efforts Toward Figuring Out Her Life.* She's not supposed to have any contact with Dylan. Otherwise, the deal is, she has to leave or go to rehab. Except she knows the idea of rehab scares them more than it does her. The idea of Stephen and Maya Taylor, Vaunted Columbia Professors, Generous Thoughtful Caring Brilliant, having to attend visiting hours and explain to their colleagues where their fuckup daughter's off to now will probably keep Ellie free of any kind of "program" for at least another couple of years.

Secretly, Ellie finds something kind of thrilling about the new restrictions. She likes appointed times and rules and structure, even when these are mostly things she likes to break apart. It's still better to decide things, still better to know there are places she's supposed to be.

"It's not like I told him to come," Ellie says. She should have said it better, nicer. She never means to sound so angry, but she does.

"I just came by to tell Ellie about school," says Dylan.

Education's her mom's kryptonite.

"Really?" Like magic: her mom softens. Ellie isn't sorry for her anger anymore.

Dylan grins and looks suddenly smaller than Ellie remembers. He has a whitehead on his left earlobe.

"About to start my third year at NYU," he says.

"Right," says her mom. "Ellie . . ." But she stops.

Ellie doesn't do much of anything, just this shitty coffee shop, hanging out with Joseph, lying on the couch or on her bed, listening to her mom's old records, staring at the ceiling, when she's home. When she doesn't have work and can't be in the house any longer she rides the subway back and forth for hours. She brings headphones sometimes, but mostly she just likes to sit and watch the people, to walk the long transfer at Fourteenth Street from the 2 to the L, then back again. She looks purposefully ahead of her and walks quickly, as if she has somewhere she's meant to be.

She feels Joseph behind them, watching. It's the lull after the morning rush and the shop is empty. A woman comes in behind Dylan and her mom and orders tea, a muffin. Joseph nudges Ellie out of the way; Ellie grabs the tongs, a paper bag, and hands the girl her muffin, as her mom and Dylan linger, neither of them willing to be the first to go.

"Well . . ." says Ellie's mom. Her hand clutches so tight to her bag, Ellie wonders briefly if the strap might break. "I'll see you tonight?"

"Sure," says Ellie. She winces and keeps half her eye on Joseph as Dylan grins back and forth between her and her mom. Her mom's whole body jerks and shifts as she hoists the bag, holding it with both hands as she shoulders her way out.

Ellie watches her brown leather boots hit the pavement one and then the other as she walks with Joseph to his house. The toes are squared. The leather's scuffed nearly to white across the front. It's too hot for boots, but she likes wearing them. She likes the sound they make against the pavement, the feel of hard heel against concrete, the clack and then the echo that it makes when she's indoors.

They get on the G train and ride in silence. Ellie leads Joseph through the gate along the side of the apartment and back into the yard. Three lawn chairs sit around a pit in which they sometimes build a fire. Joseph and his roommates have parties out here every weekend, and every weekend Ellie says no when Joseph asks if she might like to come. There's a small film of rainwater from the day before across the seats of both the lawn chairs, and Joseph wipes the seat of Ellie's chair with the bottom of his shirt. Ellie nods thanks and sits. Joseph reaches into the back pocket of his shorts and pulls out a bag of lovely-smelling sticky leaves and crumbles bits onto a sheet of rolling paper. He rolls the joint and licks the thin edge, presses carefully with his index finger and his thumb. He lights it, puckering and pinching, then puff-puffing, his eyes closed, his head lolling back.

Ellie holds her breath.

"So, who was that dude?" he says. He leans forward again, the joint still in his hand. "Your mom was pissed?"

She'd somehow convinced Dylan to leave just after her mom. He'd promised to call her, leaned across the counter, and she hadn't pulled away as he kissed her lightly on the lips.

Ellie nods.

Joseph pulls on the joint a second time. "You look like her."

Ellie shakes her head. "Not really." People used to say this all the time when she was little, but not now. Ellie's small like her mom, with dark hair and eyes and features that look shocked and too sharp most of the time, but somehow they wear these things too differently for most people to notice how similar they are. Ellie seldom has the courage to look too long or too closely at either her own reflection or her mom.

"I realized, watching you, I don't know anything about you, you know? When I've spent all this time going on and on about my shit." Ellie noticed early on with Joseph, if she was very quiet and very still, if every once in a while she asked a question, he would keep talking and she could just listen, take him in.

He's twenty-six, recently finished law school. He'd never meant to go, though. He works at the coffee shop, plays music, ignores his student loans.

Ellie's favorite thing about Joseph is that they have so far not so much as touched.

"Oh, you know," Ellie says. "Just aimless teenage shit."

He nods toward the joint, more for decorum's sake than anything. Ellie has so far, each time he's offered, managed to say no.

"And your fancy ivy-covered parents don't care you're not in school?"

"They just . . ." The joint burns as he rests his elbow on the armrest of his lawn chair. The rolling paper crackles and smoke lingers just above his hand.

"No one's that nonjudgmental."

Her parents have learned to be quite good, actually, at lowering the bar. "I had some issues," Ellie says.

"That dude, yeah?" Joseph finally takes another hit.

"Dylan. Yeah, sort of."

"How bad?"

Ellie wants to ask for the joint in order that she might be free to tell him something small and honest. She wants to stay completely sober, tell him the whole thing from start to finish, and have him still want to sit and talk to her.

"You know," she says.

"Not really." Joseph shakes his head. There's an ashtray in the center of the table, and he grabs it, stamping out the joint and letting it rest. "I know you're too cute to sit around all day and listen to me whine."

She feels her face turn red and wishes that he hadn't said this. "I'm . . . that's not true," she says.

"One thing?" he says.

She leans closer toward the table: the little bit of weed that's left.

Ellie nods toward the joint. "I used to like that sort of thing too much." This isn't quite right—she wishes she were something as straightforward as a drug addict—but she wants to see this version of herself on him.

"You should have told me," he says.

"It's not . . ." She looks down and shrugs. "It's just weed," she says.

Ellie burrows her boots into the dirt until the toes are completely covered; she waits for whatever will come after this. She sees Dylan standing at the counter, her mom frantic. She imagines her mom sitting in her office now, doing everything she can not to call or text Ellie. The yard next to Joseph's has a large maple tree that leans heavily, and its branches brush above Joseph and Ellie's heads. She grabs hold of one of the leaves and rips it off the branch. She tears it into brittle strips between her fingers, and, as Joseph watches, Ellie doesn't speak.

Joseph angles his chair close to hers and Ellie doesn't back away. She knows there's a moment when she could sit back with her arms across her chest and today could end the way the other days have. But, as he leans in close and lets his index finger linger on her knee, Ellie just stays very still and doesn't speak.

Winter 2013

Maya stands and runs. She heads straight to Bergen, down toward Court Street, past Atlantic, brownstone, brownstone, brownstone, big park, courthouse, crossing over the Brooklyn Bridge. One foot, then the other: it's the simplest thing she does all day. She never listens to music and she almost always runs alone. She likes the sporadic snippets of the city's sounds before it's fully risen. A baby screaming through an open window, a car horn, a garbage truck backing up the wrong direction on a one-way street. She likes the smells, exhaust and baking bread, the unidentified chemicals as she crosses the Gowanus. The water is so thick with waste that the trash doesn't float, half submerged: it just sits solidly on top.

It's the sort of morning that she loves and lets herself hold tight to, the air just cold and dry enough to catch sharp inside her lungs. The inclines change incessantly. She's up and down and then her arms are swinging harder. Her body doesn't give her what it used to. She's slower now, but no less determined to push and push. Her legs are long, almost as long as Stephen's, though he's at least six inches taller than her—their hips hit at nearly the same point—and they stretch out far in front of her, the ball of each foot hits the pavement, her knee bends, her foot rises nearly to her ass. The pedestrian path on the bridge is wood and creaks beneath her feet as they land, spring up, and land again. Her breath slows and steadies as she looks past the bridge to all the water underneath.

Once in Manhattan, she heads south on Broadway to the bottom of the island, to the seaport where boats are docked and sloshing in the Hudson and the smells are strong of rotted fish, then west and through the steep slate of the memorials in Battery Park. This stretch along the Hudson is usually filled with runners and tourists in line to take the ferry to Liberty Island, but she's so early she has the whole thing to herself: the space of cobbled concrete and small parks, the sailboats, the volleyball nets lined up on rubber courts.

Just past a set of docks with sailboats in a row, Maya stops and slips her shoes off. The wind bites through the tights she's wearing, gnawing sharply along her skin, and her bare face smarts; small drops of water reach her as she walks closer to the edge. She wears no gloves, and the fence that separates her from the water is cold and sticks to her fingers as she holds on and climbs up over the top. The water's gray slate, with tiny whitecaps forming out closer to New Jersey. She can see Liberty Island, boats knocking against their moorings another hundred feet away.

She settles herself carefully onto the other side of the fence, half hanging over the water, her hands holding tightly to the metal bars. Cold drops splash up onto the balls of her feet and around her ankles. The water feels warm at first compared to the whip of the air. She looks out toward New Jersey, the Statue of Liberty almost completely obstructed by the early morning fog. The ledge is brick and the edges catch against the bottoms of her thighs and she feels her tights pilling. She has to alternate the hand she uses to hold the fence behind her, as the sting of it is only bearable for small stretches of time.

Her whole life she's been a strong swimmer. She thinks: if it weren't for the nearly inevitable hypothermia, she'd be able to get to New Jersey before the sun is up. And, just for that moment of going under, those few seconds after the initial shock of the cold, when the water has reached just above her neck and she's about to pull her whole self under, it might be worth whatever else might come as a result.

Ellie, seventeen: Maya would peek over her shoulder. She would grab Ellie's phone and checked the text messages when Ellie went into the bathroom or once she'd gone to sleep. She would hack into Ellie's email and her Facebook. There were rules and boundaries about trust and fairness and giving children space that she believed in, right up till she didn't anymore. Until *trust* felt like a silly word that was just standing in the place of actually doing something to save her daughter, a privilege reserved for people with lives much less complicated than theirs.

She knew Ellie was at a party. She had an address, on Fourth Street and Eighth Avenue (Dylan's, she'd learn later; both his parents traveled for work, and he was, like Ellie's dad, an only child; he often had the house all to himself), not far from where they lived. She thought she'd have to knock, but had no real plan for what she'd say or do when someone answered. Except, when she came up to the door it was ajar and she could hear people talking and the thrum of music knocked her brain against her skull. She walked in still not knowing what she'd do. She expected to see him, maybe find him in some back room with her daughter. She steeled herself for the possibility of catching her daughter fucking someone while a party raged outside the door. It didn't take long to find Ellie, though, and she wasn't fucking anyone. At least not right then. And Dylan was quiet, the only one in the room who didn't seem to be enjoying himself. Maya stood in the hall looking into a great room and watched her daughter. There was nothing preventing someone walking past and seeing her, this middle-aged woman—hair tied in a knot, bare-faced, in jeans and a fraying Harvard sweatshirt—snooping on these kids. But she stayed still because she had to. Once she saw her daughter, she didn't care who found her there.

Ellie was drunk, something worse than drunk. She was in her underwear, beige and laceless, simple, something Maya had probably bought on sale. There were two other girls who stood with Ellie, but it was clear, based on their posture, based on the shock of her daughter's beauty laid out so bare before her: Ellie was in charge. When it came to the commodity of beauty, her daughter was so rich with it she could parse it out to anyone who chose to look. Maya watched the other girls, confined by the need to be self-conscious. They shaped their faces and twisted and turned in ways they hoped might complement their best attributes. But there was no part of Ellie not worth showing off. And Maya wished for the millionth time that her daughter might be slightly less attractive. The eyes, the hair, the way the legs shone as Ellie dipped down to the floor—it was a dangerous commodity to bestow on anyone so reckless and so young.

There were a handful of boys, some men, around the girls. Music played and the girls danced and the men watched them. Dylan sat back on the couch close to the kitchen and sulked as Ellie held court.

Maya's daughter's hips jutted out from underneath the satin string that connected the front and back stretch of fabric that still covered her. She stood up on her toes and dipped down nearly to the floor. She walked over to one of the other girls and placed both hands on her shoulders. She came in very close to her and their breasts touched and Maya held her breath. Ellie took one hand off the girl and ran her fingers down the length of her, lingering once at her breasts and then her belly button, dipping her body farther and farther down. She bent her head back once she reached the girl's knees, her hands wrapped around the girl's thin hips. Maya took her eyes briefly from her daughter and watched the men around her. Their eyes stayed wide and rapt. They were quiet, sipping beers and smoking but hardly moving otherwise, as Maya's daughter dipped and twirled.

Summer 2011

"I'm sorry," Joseph says after, though the whole time he was careful, kind. He's the smallest, skinniest boy she's ever fucked.

"I just." She wants to ask him quietly to please not touch her. She wants to be outside again, sitting a few feet away with her arms across her chest, talking about his student loans.

Winter 2013

Maya drives up to campus, which she rarely does. She loves the subway but does not feel up for all that interacting and is grateful instead for the hour she spends in the car. Over the bridge, the water, she watches a tugboat slip underneath as the traffic inches toward the FDR.

The building's empty when she gets there. It's classic university brick with tall windows on every floor. Out front is a small lawn where, in summer, kids throw Frisbees, and some of the more intrepid girls lie out in swimsuits. Now the lawn is covered in a small film of snow, and the three trees that cover it almost completely in swaths of shade in spring and summer are all bare empty branches that look sharp to Maya and too thin to hold the wealth of leaves she knows will return soon. There's a café on the bottom floor that's not yet open. A small man with a perfectly trimmed mustache mops the tile, with the silver metal chairs propped on the matching silver tabletops. He smiles at Maya and nods as she walks past and up the three flights of stairs to her department office. There are papers and books—*Mrs. Dalloway*, Lydia Davis, a collection of Keats's poems, Barbara Johnson's *A World of Difference*, and an old copy of *Being and Nothingness* she borrowed from Stephen a couple years ago—spread across the desk.

Maya's just sat down and opened the Barbara Johnson when she hears shuffling in the doorway. "*Lollione* was in today," says Laura. She's Maya's oldest, closest friend: French literature, Duras, de Beauvoir, Cixous, all curves and those sort of floral flowy dresses that Maya felt too old to pull off at twenty-two.

Laura wears maroon lipstick; besides that her face is bare.

They've been friends for twenty years, lumped together early. Maya, the Woolf scholar, and Laura with all those Frenchwomen and their feelings, all that sex. It seemed everyone in the department was hoping the two of them would keep each other occupied. And they have, mostly. There are few people in the world with whom Maya would rather sit and talk.

"She's not even taking my class!" Laura says. She has a student nearly every year who maddens her, whom Laura whispers about even as the girl (as she always is) follows Laura doggedly around. Laura sits on one of the chairs opposite Maya, slips her feet out of her shoes, and crosses her legs. "I think she changed her name from Jessica while she was an undergrad." She twirls her right foot in slow circles as she talks. "I heard her talking to a boy before class the other day, a young one, very bright. He was asking her how old she was when her family left Korea." Laura fiddles with her earrings as she speaks. They're silver, long layers of leaves that reach the length of her neck. "They mistake her lisp for an accent," she says and laughs a little, leaning her head back; her hands cup her neck now and her eyes roll up into her head. "The girl grew up in Queens."

Maya nods toward the door. "Either stop or close the door before she hears."

Laura jumps up, and Maya watches her dress flutter, brown with reds and yellows, around her ass and ankles—then walks back to Maya's desk and pulls the chair close. "Oh, she wouldn't care if she heard me. She'd misconstrue it as a compliment."

Laura sits down and puts her elbows on the desk and then props her chin up on her palms.

"She's a child," says Maya, leaning back in her chair and reaching for a book behind her, not pulling it from the shelf, just running her hand along its edge. "She's just desperate for you to like her. They all are. They worship you. "

"Oh, and I *pretend* to like her," says Laura. "I listen carefully to all the hackneyed things she says." The earrings glint under the lamplight and weak swaths of sun come through the window as Laura shakes her head. "And I want to scream at her to please just go to law school like her parents want."

Maya leans forward again. "You don't mean that."

"Please, Maya," says her friend. "You can't possibly not hate at least one of them a year." Hands to earrings again, then back to neck. "They're so entitled, some of them," she says. "As if having an opinion is enough to make them *interesting*."

Maya smiles at Laura, shakes her head, and looks down at her hands folded on her desk.

"I have some I wish came to office hours less."

"Oh, Christ, Maya! Tell me! Just one. Tell me one."

Laura leans forward farther and her shirt falls down to show the first few inches of her cleavage. The skin across her breasts folds, then quivers. Laura will be fifty-three this year, five years older than her friend. Maya wonders how either of them has managed to let herself become so very middle-aged.

"Oh, God," says Maya, sitting back in her chair, "Alexandra." She breathes out as she says it. Both she and Laura laugh. "She did her undergrad at Brown and thinks she's much brighter than she is."

"Please," says Laura. "Please go on."

"She keeps raising her hand and telling us stories about the deconstructionists. She *had a problem* with the shifts in point of view in *To the Lighthouse*."

Laura laughs and puts her feet up on Maya's desk.

"Oh, they all have problems. They have problems with anyone who makes them work or think."

"That's not fair," says Maya. "Plenty of them think quite well." The truth is Maya loves the lot of them. She loves their energy, their brains. Laura does as well. They're both the sort to stay after class for students with questions, to take on extra advisees, to answer frantic emails late at night.

"Boof," says Laura. "Plenty." She runs her hand up through her hair. "Some."

"Enough to keep you coming back."

"Money is what keeps me coming back," Laura says, then shrugs. This isn't true either. There's money that comes from somewhere, whether it's the ex-husband Maya knows was present briefly, or the family out in the Midwest that Laura almost never talks about. But she lives in a full-floor apartment close to campus that no one surviving on just the salary of a French literature professor could afford.

"I'm just a sideshow act to all of them," says Laura. "The crazy French one." She sometimes seems to have an accent, but she's from Minnesota. Though she did spend almost a decade in Paris just after she received her doctorate. "It's exhausting," she says. "Putting on the show."

She stops, her hands palmed at her mouth and her chin rising, angling her head down again and straight toward her friend.

"But then, you're so *earnest* all the time," says Laura, "so *fervent*. You must be even more exhausted than I am."

Maya nods, not wanting to answer. They were doing so well too.

Laura pulls her legs off the desk and sidles to the edge of the chair; her hands reach across toward Maya.

"Honey," she says.

Laura had gone with them. Stephen still didn't know. Maya had never meant to tell Laura Ellie was pregnant, but she'd been so relieved the minute her friend knew.

El was sixteen: they went to a small brightly colored office on Fifty-ninth Street and Tenth Avenue, where they sat quietly in the too-tightly-packed-in chairs with plastic armrests and waited for their turn. Maya tried to hold Ellie's hand, but Ellie freed herself of her mom quickly, so Maya had just leaned in very close to her, brushing up against her. There had been an initial screening to which only Maya and Ellie had gone the week before. The day of, Ellie let Maya stay with her as she changed her clothes and was prepped, and then she sent Maya back to sit with Laura, both of them staring at the yellow diamonds spread across the dark blue carpet, waiting for her daughter to return.

After, Laura took them out as if this were all cause for celebration. They shared a bottle of wine among the three of them. No one carded. It felt like the last thing to worry about then.

"I've had four," said Laura. She was forty-nine then and regularly slept with men ten and fifteen years younger. There had been the wedding in Minnesota when she was still an undergrad that had lasted right up till she left for grad school at Yale. Laura had only ever said her husband had been too sweet to stay with past the age of twenty-two.

Maya watched her daughter finger the rim of her wine glass.

"I wouldn't recommend that many," Laura said.

Ellie pursed her lips, then sipped from her wine glass. She wore jeans and one of Stephen's sweaters. She looked twelve years old.

Laura pressed her palms against the corners of the table and leaned in closer to Ellie. "Things stopped working after the last one." She turned to face Maya. "Uterus like a pinball machine." She shrugged.

She was quoting someone, and it took Maya a moment to place it. She could tell, though, the way the words seemed wrapped up to keep Laura safe—they weren't her own.

"Sophie," Maya said after a moment. *Desperate Characters.*

Laura smiled and turned back to Ellie. She tipped her head toward Maya. "That's why your mom's the best."

Maya wasn't sure if this was right. Should they be talking this way, smiling? But what else was there to do?

"You wanted kids?" asked Ellie. Their food was set down before them and only Laura reached for her silverware. Maya fingered the napkin on her lap.

"Who knows?" said Laura. "I'd probably completely fuck it up."

Maya laughed then, though she hadn't meant to.

Ellie shook her head. "You'd be really good." She sat up a bit straighter in her chair and picked up a piece of asparagus with her thumb and forefinger, taking a small bite, then setting it back down.

Laura smiled. She twirled pasta around her fork and swallowed seemingly without chewing. "Thanks, El. You're lying, but you're sweet."

Ellie tore at a piece of bread and rolled it with her fingers till it was small, smooth, and round, then dropped it. "No, I mean, you're a little crazy. But I think that's good. Less pressure on the kids."

Maya was trying to figure out what this meant about her as a mother. She was either crazy or not very good. Whatever she was, Ellie had told her, thankfully, about the pregnancy. Even if it had taken Maya begging. Even if El seemed to have been stoned when she'd finally come to Maya three nights before, Stephen out of town. She'd cried, crawling into Maya's bed, only mumbling the lot of it, six tests to be sure and no mention of the father; after Maya had begun to cry as well.

"Well, thanks, lady," said Laura. "I think, though, my real talent is as the crazy aunt/friend."

"You're incredible at that," Ellie said.

Laura's teeth shone, stained slightly by the dark red of the wine, and she tipped her glass toward Ellie and then toward Maya. Maya reached across the table and tried to take hold of her daughter's shoulder, but Ellie leaned out of her reach, fisted her wine glass with a tip toward Laura's, and drank.

Maya had felt almost smug walking back to Brooklyn with her daughter, over the bridge, and through Brooklyn Heights and Boerum Hill. It was awful, sure. But they'd made it to the other side. She'd gotten her a prescription for birth control and they'd talked about how irresponsible Ellie had been. But it hadn't felt like the time for scolding. She wanted to be sure Ellie still felt Maya was someone she could trust.

She'd thought then that they were coming out of something, that that moment had represented a sort of end. Crisis had come and Ellie had gone to her. She felt shaken by it, terrified. But also, she felt relief. This was the great awful thing she'd been afraid of happening to her daughter: It had happened. She had come to Maya. It could all start to get better after this.

"You're going to be okay," Maya said to Ellie.

And Ellie smiled, a wool hat pulled down over her hair, her great big eyes peeking out from underneath. "I know, Ma," she said.

"So," says Laura.

"So," Maya says.

"Ben still home?"

Maya nods.

"Holding up?"

Maya shrugs. She looks past Laura toward the door.

"He'll go back soon."

"Right," Laura says.

Both of them are quiet. Maya's mind goes immediately to Jack, to Annie. It's clear, based on the face her friend makes, that's where her mind's gone too. "Any word?" Laura asks.

Maya shakes her head. "She hasn't brought any charges." She shuffles the papers on her desk, then grabs her wedding band with her thumb and two fingers and pushes it up and down over her knuckle as they talk.

"That's good?" Laura says. Maya's not sure her friend meant this as a question.

"I'm not sure what any of it is." That they might release Ellie from the lockup that they themselves have inflicted, that Annie might not hold her accountable for her son's death beyond that, that the state seems not to have enough evidence to bring charges, all of this is both impossible to ponder and terrifying to consider too often or too clearly—it's terrifying in both directions, because of course Maya wants to have her daughter back, of course she always wants her daughter close, but then she's not sure who that is, her daughter, she's not sure what any of them would do if Ellie were to suddenly, after all this time, after all she's done, appear.

Maya stares at the bare branches out her window. Some days, she worries Stephen will have her committed also. There are days she thinks this might not be the worst idea. When she thinks of this, she thinks Laura would be the one to save her. She'd free her and they'd run off to somewhere warm with water where Ellie would be and everything that's happened could be taken back somehow and done again.

"Maybe you should go home, sweetie," Laura says.

"What would I do there?" She keeps her eyes on the papers on her desk. The words blur.

"Honey," Laura says again.

Someone knocks and Maya jumps and faces Laura, who turns toward the door, flattening her hair down against her head.

"Professor?"

Charles wears a sweater zipped up to his neck. It's gray over a dark green T-shirt; both look impossibly soft. He's awkward, bumbling, tall, and very quiet. He's her teaching assistant, a graduate student, twenty-eight or -nine she figures, younger, possibly.

He studies Tennyson: *Someone had blundered!* Maya always thinks when she sees him. *Someone had blundered!* And she hopes it isn't her or him.

"Come in," Maya says.

Laura pulls her face back to the shape it always is when facing almost anyone but Maya: warm, a little hard at the edges, ready to laugh or attack in equal measure, sharp and tight around the lips.

"Charles," says Maya. "Please."

She nods toward the seat next to Laura, but Charles shakes his head and remains standing.

"I'm good." He smiles at Laura. "Hi."

Laura grins, crosses her legs, and turns to face him.

"Hi," she says.

Charles bites down on his lower lip, which is full and pops out still from underneath his teeth. He has a broad flat nose that scrunches up when he sits with Maya and talks about his thesis. Sometimes she keeps an eye turned toward his nose when she's teaching, knowing if it's scrunching she's said something that has made him think.

She sits up on the edge of her chair and holds the corners of her desk. "How are you?" she asks.

"Fine." He nods. "Good. I've been thinking . . . I wanted to tell you." She watches him reel in whatever it is he means to say as Laura watches him.

Laura leans forward and wraps her hand around her ankle as Charles starts to speak again.

"I think I have some ideas for the fall."

His dissertation is due next month. Only now does Maya realize how much she'll miss him when he leaves here. He's been sitting in the front row of her classroom, at office hours, department meetings, for the past six years.

"Tomorrow?" Maya says. "You ready?" She's asked him to teach the class of hers for which he's an assistant. It's a year-long course, required for all the undergrads in the major, and he's spent the last semester observing her and grading the papers she assigns.

He nods and repositions his squared-off thick-rimmed glasses on the bridge of his nose and seems to stand up straight. "Yes," he says. "I think."

She smiles at him. "We'll talk about fall after?"

He looks down at her desk. His hair has grown long in the past couple years and falls down now in his face. Sometimes Maya wonders if he simply hasn't thought to get it cut, if she might offer to cut it for him, as she's done for Ben most of his life.

"You'll be great," she says.

"Wonderful," Laura says.

Maya watches Laura's purple fingernails tap methodically against her shin.

"I'll email you my plans?"

"If you want," Maya says. "I trust you'll do fine."

He reddens. He's taller than she's realized. As he leaves, Maya smiles at the paperback folded and shoved into the back pocket of his pants.

"He's in love with you!" Laura has uncrossed her legs and almost stands up with the force of her assertion. The door has hardly shut before she speaks.

"Christ, Laura. Of course he isn't," says Maya. There have been moments in the past year when she's worried Charles looks a bit too long at her, listens too intently. In those moments, she wants to run his hands over the wrinkles of her face, to lift her shirt and let him roam the curves of stretch marks on her belly, to finger the thin line of her cesarean scar.

"Oh, sugar. He is."

"He's twenty-something," says Maya.

Laura grabs hold of her left earring, the leaf glints and faintly rustles as she lets go of it. "It's exactly what you need."

Summer 2011

Her mom's waiting on the stoop when Ellie gets home from walking. She left Joseph's before it got dark out. It feels possible she's been walking days or years. She's been up and down Broadway, around the bottom of the island. She sat on a bench in Battery Park and stared out long at the water and the wind. She's come to no conclusions beside the need to keep on moving. Until she felt so tired she could hardly breathe.

Yet somehow she's managed to get back here. And here's her mother sitting on the stoop.

"Where were you?" Her mom is wearing running clothes, as if she meant to sprint around all of Brooklyn and Manhattan till she found her, till she could scoop her up and bring her home. Ellie wants to ask her to just please let her sleep and they'll talk later. That she's sorry and could they just forget this. Could they please forget every person Ellie's ever been before.

"Walking," she says. It's so strange, being honest. It somehow comes out sounding less like the truth than all the lies she used to tell.

"It's four in the morning."

Ellie folds her arms over her chest.

"You don't have your phone on?"

"It died," says Ellie, which is also true. Though it was on for long enough for her to see the word *mom* over and over as it vibrated on Joseph's desk and then in her shorts pocket. She held it the last few times before the phone died; she liked looking at her mom's picture as it rang—smiling halfway, sitting alone in her office, averting her eyes from Ellie as she snapped her picture with her phone.

"You understand you've broken the agreement?" her mom says. She's measured, careful.

Ellie sits and digs her hands into her boots.

"I can't live like this, okay?" her mom says. "If you live here, you can't do this anymore."

There's something sad about the way her mother says this.

"I'm sorry, Mommy," Ellie says. *Mommy*, like if she's nice enough, acts young enough, the past five years might disappear and they'll all be better again soon. They stare at one another. Her mom's exactly the same height as Ellie, but Ellie looks down at her, since she's seated one step farther up. She wraps her hands around her ankles, still stuffed inside her boots, and sidles herself closer to her mom.

"Were you with him?"

She has an image first of Joseph, his thin, almost hairless body, pale and careful, apologetically descending upon her.

Dylan, she thinks right after that.

Ellie shakes her head.

"All right," her mom says. They've told her they won't question what she tells them. It's something she's pretty sure her mom read in a book. They'll assume she's telling the truth and will act accordingly, but if she's caught in a lie, that's yet another rule they've said will result in her having to go.

"El, I don't think you can stay here anymore."

Ellie has shoved almost all of both her arms into her boots. She looks across the street, away from her mother. She's not sure she'll survive if they really make her go.

"I called Annie." This is her mom's student, from years ago, when her mom taught high school. She lives in Florida, where her mom grew up. "She says you can come down there awhile." Her mom looks like she might cry. If her mom cries, Ellie can convince her that she has to stay.

"I think we have to do it," her mom says. "She has a son . . ." She doesn't want to warn Ellie to be careful with him. They are not supposed to *Overparent* the twenty-year-old fuckup Ellie is.

"They need help with him. You'll be near the water." She isn't crying. Her mom's hand comes toward her wrist, but stops before grabbing hold of her.

"El, why don't you come with me?"

Ellie looks up from her sketchpad. She's been trying to draw the water stain from Dylan's basement in pencil and charcoal; she used to lie on the floor and stare at it for hours, all blacks and browns and purples, thinking it beautiful, thinking it the most perfect thing on earth. She drew a lot when she was little and still does now sometimes in private, still thinks sometimes in terms of what something would look like if she could hold it still.

"Where?" She's been up in her room since she got home hours earlier. She has three missed calls from Joseph and two from Dylan. She's shoved her phone into a drawer inside a drawer in her dresser so she's not tempted to call either of them back. She's heard her mom leave for her run.

"We need milk and I need a walk," her father says.

She has no excuse to offer. She slips on sandals, places a pair of sunglasses on top of her head. They leave the apartment and walk up toward the park. Her dad flips his keys around his finger. Ellie situates the glasses on her nose.

"So," her dad says dragging out the *o*, and she watches his keys almost slide from his finger. They clank quietly as they roll back into his palm.

"So," she says.

"How's life?" He slips the keys into his pocket and they enter the park.

"Fine," she says. "Same." The world is muted behind her glasses, her dad's face farther away.

They walk through the farmers' market. Her dad eyes the flowers, then the muffins, cakes, and cookies. "Wanna split one?" Ellie asks.

Her mom seldom allows sugar in the house.

"Sure," he says.

This used to happen often on weekend mornings—especially when her mom escaped into her office for hours at a time, or when she went for runs that seemed to go on for half the day—Ellie and her dad would walk up the street to the farmers' market, get something sweet, juice or coffee, flowers for his garden that they would plant together. He would plant, and Ellie would sit cross-legged in the dirt.

They buy milk and a chocolate chip muffin and walk over to a bench facing Long Meadow.

"Listen," says her dad. He breaks off a piece of muffin. "I know you're still figuring things out."

When she didn't go to college, he reacted more aggressively than he had in years. He'd assumed somehow, amid everything, that she'd be together enough by then to get a sweatshirt from some place in New England or the Midwest that they could ship her off to in September. They'd assumed maybe that their own success would somehow finally seep through to her. He'd yelled, over a period of a month. Ellie had sat or stood and let him, staying still and quiet. She'd gotten stoned alone up in her room and didn't mind much when they said she couldn't leave the house until she figured out a Plan For Her Life. Most of her friends had gone to college. She seldom had anywhere to go. She refused to attend her high school graduation and only her mother took much issue with this. She could tell, by that point, her dad would rather not have to answer questions about his daughter's plans for the next year. They'd briefly pushed the idea of her moving out, making her way of things, but her mother couldn't stomach it, wanted her to *steady* herself first. And her dad, as much as he presented himself as the stronger parent, was nothing in the face of her mom when she was sure.

He sits with enough space between them to fit the muffin and the half gallon of milk. "I know you've experimented," he says. A girl is being dragged, both hands clutching the leash, by a small, panting pit bull mix in front of them. The dog is yellow with a white stripe down his back and his legs clench as he tries hard to go after a squirrel ten feet ahead. Ellie holds the muffin and picks off two small pieces. The chocolate melts a little in her hands.

She thinks of telling him that once she was so high that Dylan had to carry her up the steps of the subway, that she took her shirt off in a cab so she could look at the contours of her shoulders in the rearview mirror while they drove, that Dylan liked it when she was high enough to want to sleep with him, but not so high that she couldn't be on top. She wants to tell him yesterday she let Joseph fuck her, because it's the only thing she still knows how to do that is allowed. That Recovery, or whatever it is they've decided to call what they're forcing on her, is bullshit if you don't feel like you're getting any better, if you're not totally sure about what you're meant to recover from, that she's scared and now she can't even convince her mom to be with her any longer, that putting her in charge of someone else's kid is almost definitely a terrible idea.

Ellie's dad pulls his ankle onto his knee, sits back farther on the bench, and stretches his arm out along the backrest, careful not to graze Ellie as he does.

"There's this part," he says. "In *Beyond Good and Evil*." Her dad traveled a lot—to conferences, guest lectures—when she and Ben were little. They helped him in the garden. He helped with homework and cooked most of the meals. But it has always been their mom who *Parented*. Her mom *Parented* so much sometimes that Ellie couldn't breathe.

"Seriously, Dad?" She picks herself another piece and watches as the girl with the pit bull pulls a handful of dog treats from her bag and is able, only briefly, to distract the dog from the squirrel.

"Just bear with me, okay?"

She folds her legs up on the bench.

"There's this part where Nietzsche talks about being young and saying yes to everything." He looks over at her. She licks a piece of chocolate off her lip. "I spent a lot of time in that phase, I think, the yes phase. You know. I was an only child. I wanted to do well, to prove I was worthy of . . ." He stops. He breaks himself another piece of muffin. "Anyway, then Friedrich says that there's another phase." Her dad has always spoken of philosophers by their first names; Ellie's always liked this, as if he knows them, as if all of them are friends. "A phase in which he said no to everything. Exhausted maybe by all that yes. Maybe exhausted by what it has or hasn't brought. A lot of people do, they reach a certain age and they get angry; they start rejecting everything that came before them, as a way of asserting themselves more certainly on the world. I think about that now, when I watch you. I'm not sure I ever hit that stage, not like you." He stops a minute and she feels his eyes on her. She picks at a small splinter of wood on the corner of the bench. "I respect it, you know," he says. "I respect your saying no. I think it takes courage to be willing to make people mad or not do what they ask of you." She watches him try to get it just right. He doesn't want to make her angry. He wants her to listen. He wants to give her something that might make her better than she is. "I never had courage like that," her dad says. "But it's too destructive, I think, the way you're doing it." Ellie's lost sight of the pit bull. She watches a very pregnant woman walk slowly past. "So then," her dad says, "he says eventually he realized the saying no to everything was just as much youth as the yes, because neither of these things were thoughtful. Neither of them was actually choosing what to be."

Ellie nods, handing her dad the last bite of muffin. She wants to sidle closer to him and let him tell her exactly how she might make everything better. She's not sure she's willing to concede.

Winter 2013

"You want company?"

Maya turns around. It's four-thirty in the morning. Ben wears shorts and running shoes, a long-sleeved dark red shirt. He stands halfway up the steps. She's so grateful now that they were never the type of family to cover their walls in photos of each other, of their friends. Now, as she stares up toward her son, she catches sight of the massive Neil Welliver print Stephen got her years ago. *Cora's Sky*, it's called, and she's always been comforted by the broad swaths of oranges and blues.

Maya smiles. "Sure." She double-knots her second shoe.

Ben bounds down the steps.

"I'm going to be too slow for you," she says.

He shrugs. "I'm not in training for anything."

"Well, no pressure to stay close."

He shakes his head, pulls his arms up, fingers laced, and places his palms behind his head. They walk out of the apartment and Maya locks the door.

"Park or bridge?" says Ben.

"Your call," she says.

"Bridge." And Maya's so grateful for his choosing the longer, her preferred, route, she almost wraps her arms around her son.

They take her usual route down Bergen. The city smells like trash, exhaust, and bacon. She watches him hold his long legs in check.

"She used to come into my room sometimes," he says. His head keeps facing straight.

Maya's breath catches a few seconds. She sees Ben's feet clip in even closer as her pace has briefly slowed. She stretches her legs out once and then another couple times before he speaks again.

"I don't . . . I'm not sure when it started. Or if she even knew what she was doing. But she did it a bunch of times."

"I didn't . . ." She says it quietly. They pass a road under construction: dug up asphalt, crumbled concrete, and orange cones.

"One time, she got up and started yelling at me to get out of her bed. But it's not like I could explain to her that it was *my* bed." A small bodega on the corner, with rows of flowers outside, a school, a yoga studio. "She was too fucked up to know which room was hers." He shakes his head, rolls his shoulders. "I just went to her room."

"Do you miss her?" Maya asks him. She's not sure this is right, but she wants him to keep talking. When she first went down to Florida, Ben was the only one that Ellie spoke to on the phone.

"Yeah, I mean . . ." He's quiet awhile, and Maya eyes the park just north of the bridge and then the courthouse, columns, concrete, and a blockade setup in front. The traffic's heavier as they approach the bridge and someone honks and tires screech as they wait for the light to change.

"She's my sister, you know?" her son says.

Two years before: she'd taken him to dinner, picked him up from practice. He didn't need picking up anymore; she'd sat on the sidelines like she had all those years of his forming, watching the boys yell to one another, gesture, run, the thwack of foot to ball, their impossibly long limbs. They all wore shorts, though it was just beginning to get cold out. They wore the socks up to their knees and the shorts that almost fell as far. Patches of bright red skin, knees and sides of thighs, popped out as they ran after one another and the ball.

She was, mostly, a terrible watcher. She was the type to pull out a book in lines or on the subway, on trains or buses, when the kids or Stephen would keep their eyes on the world. Maya wasn't capable of that much stillness, that much sustained attention to the outside world. Soccer had seduced her over the years, though, its beautiful simplicity, the boys' doggedness, their strength. The crack of the whistle breaking through the low steady yells. The boys falling down the field in patches, the way they looked back at one another, could get free sometimes, just the ball and boy then, the steady, rushed control. She often felt winded when it was over, as if she'd held her breath through the whole thing.

After he had sat with his friends to take off his shoes and shin guards, pull on sweatpants, gulp down water, Ben had come over easily, happily, to her. They walked the fifteen minutes to the restaurant.

"I think I chose," he said, refilling his water with the jug the waiter had left on the table, then refilling hers. He'd been on official visits all up and down the coast and a handful out West. Stephen was obsessive, so Maya had backed off. Her son's face was still flushed as he spoke to her and ordered his dinner. He was still, daily, slipping between all the various men he might one day be and then back again to the boy she'd always known.

"Ohio," he said. They'd gone out there together, the three of them; Maya had needed to be convinced to leave Ellie home alone. She was nineteen then, but Maya had called her three, four times a day. The school had been small, bucolic, frighteningly quiet. She'd wondered the whole time how people stayed sane amid all that empty space. None of them thought he'd choose it. It was a smaller school, a smaller team, than any of the others. Even the coach had seemed sure Ben would play someplace else. Stephen had made light of the coach's desperation, had suggested the competition was not of sufficient rigor. Ben seemed to know this now, looking at her, chastened, his chin dipped to his chest as he began to eat his pasta.

"I guess," Maya said. She wanted to say the thing that would prove he was right to tell her, that she could be trusted. That she would help him no matter where or what he chose. "It's a great school," she said.

Her son nodded into his plate. This wasn't enough, maybe, he needed more, she thought. "That sort of change," she said. She thought again of all that quiet, all those trees. "It could be edifying, maybe," she said.

Her son smiled then, like he did sometimes when she drifted. "Sure, Ma," he said. "It could be."

She laughed, took a bite of her fish. "We'll miss you," she said, once she'd swallowed. "Benny," she said. She thought of El then, all that worry, the not knowing, the way it seemed to rush through every crevice of their lives that was not already solidly filled in. "We'll miss you desperately," she said.

Her son gulped more water. He held his napkin to his mouth and scraped his fork along the bottom of his plate. "I need it, though, you know?" he said. "I think . . ." He stopped again. He brought his hands up to the table, his shoulders rose, his head went down, then up, "I need to get away," he said.

The way he'd looked then, the way he'd held her there, signaling a different sort of man than all the ones she'd seen in him before that, she'd almost asked if she could come along.

The light changes and they cross. A large clock blinks atop a building: It's twenty-eight degrees, not quite five a.m.

As they cross the middle of the bridge, between the two arches, they pass a woman whom Maya sees often when she runs at this time, late sixties maybe. She wears the same long large mink every morning, a full face of makeup, and old Converse shoes. She swings her arms and walks, her feet crossing in front of one another, her gaze never straying from straight ahead.

"I don't want to go back," Ben says.

Maya keeps her eyes toward her toes.

"To school," he says. "I hate it. I hate everyone who's there."

It's as if he's been practicing these sentences for months.

"What would you do?" she asks her son.

They pass two women walking in unison, both wearing neon tights; matching headbands hold their hair.

"Dad's going to hate me."

The air burns Maya's throat, cold and sharp, then sluices through her lungs. She finally looks at him. His face looks round and small.

"He won't be able to handle two fucked-up kids."

"Fuck Dad, Benny," she finally says.

He smirks and turns to her. "Right," he says.

He picks up speed and she stays with him. Her whole body feels warmer now, firmer and more sure. They pass a skateboard park and a playground, a row of tennis courts. They can hear the whoosh of the first smattering of cars out on the West Side Highway. There's a thin layer of mist hovering over the whole city still.

"Do you want to take the semester?"

"I just feel like I'm wasting everyone's time," he says. "I don't know what I'm doing there."

"I think that's what college is for, though," Maya says. Her children are finally the age she'd always looked toward: the age of her students, whom she's always loved, whom she's nearly always known how to help.

"But I don't like anything," he says.

"Benny . . ." She tugs his arm and they turn off the path just as the signal turns green and they cross into the city. They're all the way west, just south of Times Square, but the streets are still quiet this early in the morning. They pass storage warehouses, then apartments, billboards for Broadway plays, then lines of theaters, finally the fluorescent flashing lights of the main square. The morning shows are getting started up in some of the glass-walled buildings. Cameras glint and anchors settle into chairs. Cars are no longer allowed here and the streets are filled with flimsy metal chairs and tables. Everything around them is too bright and too big.

"I miss . . ." he begins. "I miss it here," he says.

She wants to ask him to be more specific. Does he miss them? Does he miss the city? Was the quiet as awful as Maya had feared?

"Benny, I think it's fine, okay? I just don't want you to feel stuck here," she says. This isn't right exactly. "I don't . . ." She's not sure she's capable of staying functional for him.

"Dave says I can come help him this semester. He says he'll pay me to be his assistant coach."

"All right," says Maya. "That sounds . . ." They pass Grand Central, then go south a block to get off Forty-second Street. They pass beautiful apartments and hotels.

Her whole life, September's served as her beginning. May has meant the end. She likes the sound of the word *semester*, how it cuts the school year into halves and the whole year feels more surmountable somehow. She doesn't want him running back and forth, reacting and escaping. She's not sure what else there is to do.

"If it's what you think you need to do," she says, "you should."

"Can you tell him?"

Him is Stephen. *Him* is Dad.

Maya nods. "Sure, Benny," she says. "I can tell him."

She stays with her son all the way down the East Side of the island, up into Chinatown and along the bike path on the Manhattan Bridge. He slows down a bit once they get back into Brooklyn, and Maya's grateful. They take the most direct route, straight up Flatbush, then right just before the park. They've covered probably twelve or thirteen miles in a little over ninety minutes. It's only when they get to their stoop and stop running that Maya feels the weight of what they've run, the tightening of her muscles and the rush of lactic acid. She grabs the wrought-iron rail that runs along each side of the steps that lead to the apartment and tries to keep her breathing steady as she watches her son begin to stretch.

"I'm old," she says. She has hold of both her knees, but turns to face him.

Ben laughs and sets his right foot up on the highest step, leaning over it, then does the same with his left. He stops the timer on his watch. "Still pretty impressive," he says.

He rests his hand briefly on her back.

"Stretch," he says.

She shakes her head and positions her feet as he has. She leans forward, feeling that first satisfying pull of her muscles loosening.

"You'll be a wonderful coach," she says.

"How the fuck did we get this so wrong?" says Stephen. Ben's out with friends. She and Stephen sit with cartons of take-out Thai food. They have a daughter they've locked up in rehab, and a son who's dropping out of college. Maya has decided to bring Ben up first.

"Two kids who've fucked up so royally," Stephen says. His knuckles look sharp and white on top of his chopsticks. They hover over a large plastic container of greasy pork and vegetable pad thai.

"Stephen." She watches a noodle split between his teeth.

"Should I just accept this? One of us has to actually face all this. To *parent*, Maya. He's a child."

She picks up her chopsticks and flips them back and forth through her fingers. She's left-handed and they make a hollow knocking sound against her simple white gold wedding band. "He's nineteen."

"Exactly. He has no idea what he's doing. You can't get a job busing tables without a college degree."

"Please, just give him a little time. They were so close, you know? We should have realized how much all of this affected him. I think it's admirable, that he acknowledges he's not getting anything from school."

"Are you serious? We must have made them this way, you know. It can't have been easy, being so wonderful all the time, having everything given to you, having everything come so easily."

"Just give him a break. He'll come back on his own."

"From what? He needs a kick in the ass, is what he needs. You let them think they deserved things without having to work for them. You're so committed to your catering to them, giving everything you could think to give to them, but then you were the one who would disappear. I never got so scared or sad or whatever it was you got that I needed breaks from parenting."

Once, when Ben was two and El was four, she'd flown down to Florida for three weeks, just to be quiet for a while, just to be alone with the water and her books and not have to love quite as much as she did when her kids were there. She escaped sometimes, either to her study, or right there in front of them. She curled into herself for fear of how all that love—more than she could feel she had a hold of—might inflict itself in ways she hadn't meant.

"That's because you weren't around as much as I was."

"Because I was working, remember? You wanted them to feel loved the way you didn't. You wanted to right all that shit with your dad. You taught them this."

Maya's father. Ice clinking on the thick highball glass he always carried, filled with scotch when she was younger, then gin later, the brush of his hand cold and quick across her cheek, the meticulousness with which he dressed each morning, his thumb and forefinger—meaty, hardened from working closely with the contractors at the houses that he bought and sold—working carefully to button each side of his shirt collar, dark socks and the musty heavy leather smell of his newly polished shoes.

Her mother had left them, three months, nearly to the day, after Maya was born. She knew this through the one letter that her mother had written to her father. She'd dated it, in some odd attempt at propriety, in the moment that she'd absconded in the face of life's demands. The letter said that she was sorry. It said this was not the life she wanted. Maya wasn't. Maya had understood then that she was something people had to work to want. Her father had taken on the role of dad most earnestly. Though he was awkward, though he was uncomfortable often around his girl, he did adore his daughter; he adored her in the bumbling self-centered way that sad and callow men love their little girls.

He was in real estate, self-made and later self-destroyed. He'd bought in with a development company with offerings in the middle of the state, deeds handed over, for properties that could be used only for camping and hiking, some of it completely swampland, to buyers far away who thought they were getting land to build. And though the bulk of sales had happened in the sixties, it was nearly ten years later that he'd finally been bankrupt as a result.

She was fourteen and home from St. George's. Upstairs, trying to sleep in her room. It was a room that never felt like hers because her father had moved the year she'd left for boarding school. It felt like someone's approximation of a girl's room, which in fact it was: a designer that he'd hired. It was how it felt when her dad looked at her, like she was an approximation of a daughter, something he had conjured, less somehow than he'd hoped.

This night, like all nights, he'd been drinking. He padded barefoot through the house. She could still summon the smell of him. Aftershave from a dark green bottle, old, slightly watered gin. He'd taken a lime when she was younger but he didn't anymore. She'd noticed this because she watched him, she studied him for lack of knowing what to say. He read three papers every morning cover to cover. He ate his breakfast quickly, standing up, drank his coffee black. Instead of interacting with one another, on her trips home they each sat quietly across the table at dinner, next to one another in the car, and noted how the other smelled and moved. They took each other in with care and a safe distance and, both of them maybe, hoped that added up to love.

He seldom touched her. She made him nervous, especially as she'd grown slightly taller, begun to grow breasts and shave her legs. These were all things she'd learned to deal with on her own, reading magazines furtively at grocery stores and at the doctor's, listening to girls at school, to women on TV. When she'd first used a tampon, she hadn't realized she was supposed to remove the applicator and instead had left it in the entire time, tearing herself up, having to wear pads for the next month.

They said good night that night, all nights, in the kitchen, Maya leaning toward him, kissing his cheek. "Daddy," she still called him. "My girl," he still said. He'd never come into her bedroom, though sometimes she would check on him in his room, slipping off his shoes or pulling down the duvet and the sheets.

But this night, late, he came to her. And what he did had been so simple, could have been, had he been an altogether different father, a thing she remembered with a sort of loving, quiet angst. But instead it left her squirming, nauseous, nervous, each time after. And each time after, he did it again and then again.

He was slurring, his shoulders folded inward. He wore his undershirt and shorts. She hardly ever saw his legs and was shocked by their thinness, how pale and thick with dark coarse hair. She was supposed to be asleep but wasn't. The room was still so new and foreign. She was up reading, a small light she'd gotten at school to read by while her roommate slept. She was under the covers with Charlotte Brontë: Bertha was in the attic and Jane had just run away.

Her father said her name once in a whisper, then pulled the covers up and climbed in next to her. She felt the coarseness of the hairs along his legs against her, the warmth of his breath, and smelled the aftershave and gin. It was then she realized he was crying, shaking heavily, a bit of snot caught thickly in her hair. He pulled her close to him. And though she stiffened, though her stomach turned and her skin itched and ached to get away, she lay there and let him hold her, knowing finally, this was something she could give.

He'd lost all of his money. Somehow, brilliantly, with the same sweeping unexpectedness of its arrival, all of it was gone. He was sad and desperate and he clung to Maya. He whispered she was all that he had left. And she stayed completely still and tried to empty her brain of everything. She tried not to breathe or move or let him feel her flinch as he held her, because she knew he was her father and he loved her, because she knew she should be glad to give to him.

From then on this happened each time she came home. And each time, Maya stayed very still and waited for her dad to fall asleep. He didn't always cry, and sometimes she was able to slip out from beside him. But those few times he woke up late in the night or early in the morning, still drunk and blubbering, saying that she had slipped from him because she knew he wasn't worthy of her. He cried and said if even his daughter didn't love him, what was there left for him. And then Maya would have to beg him to please stop, to promise him she loved him, to calm him, hold him, until he fell asleep again.

She was terrified each time she went back to school that he wouldn't be there the next time she came home, that she was betraying him in leaving, in not staying there to keep him safe. Each time she came back, she was terrified that he would be there, that this time he wouldn't let her leave again.

It would have been easier, she thought, if he'd done something more explicitly detestable: hit her, fucked her. Then maybe she could have rid herself of him, then maybe she could have finally been free. Instead she carried with her all he needed, all she knew she couldn't give.

Back at school, she had trouble sleeping, reading like she always had but then still needing more. She piled books into her bed and hardly slept. She woke up with pages sticking to her, flitting from one world to the other, feeling jarred and confused when she had to leave her room and interact with a world not made up of words. She discovered Woolf during this period, crying under the covers upon her first encounter with Mrs. Ramsay's death. The paragraphs then, the way they caught inside her brain and stuck there. They ran back and forth over all her other thoughts and dulled, then sharpened them. She loved the vastness all wrapped up inside the minutiae: a house come to life, wind and dust sweeping through corners, suddenly enough to sustain a whole page. She knew she didn't completely understand it, but that was part of what was so attractive, the knowledge that she could return later for more.

What she can't do, though, is situate her past within her present. She can't apologize for the ways in which it's made her less capable than she might have been. Stephen knows this, but he's asked her for it anyway.

She turns from him, pulls her boots on, grabs her coat; she leaves.

Summer 2011

"Food?" says Ellie, peering through her brother's door, where he's still in bed and half asleep. Their mom's in her study with the door locked. Ben calls to her that they're going, and he and Ellie walk the ten blocks to his favorite diner on the other side of Flatbush. Their neighborhood is different than it was when they were little. Ellie remembers being scared often, when her mom pulled her close walking up the stairs from the subway. A few times she remembers walking right past their apartment when her mom thought someone might be following too close. Now there are fancy coffee shops, a Barnes & Noble, a Starbucks, strollers and tiny scooters everywhere, dogs and kids. This all makes Ellie a different kind of nervous, like maybe she's what's dangerous about the place where they live.

Her brother: he still looks like a little boy to Ellie. He was shorter than most of his classmates in middle school, and rounder. Ellie's mom would rub her hands over his cheeks and smile at him and Ellie'd want to grab her mom's hand and remind her she was hers. But then suddenly, sometime at the end of middle school, he'd shot straight up, all crooked aimless height and limbs, twisted and folded and hanging over couches, curled up in the backseat of the car.

"Mom's pissed," he says, walking to the left of her, separating Ellie from the street.

"I don't want to talk about it, Benny."

"El."

"What's it like?" she says. "Being the good one. Don't you get bored?"

"Please, El." He looks angry.

She doesn't want to hear his answer.

He says, "The only person who's allowed to think in terms of what they want in our family is you."

She wants to start again. Her brother is the only person in the world she always likes.

"I'm sorry, Benny," she says. "I'm trying this time, though, okay? Please?"

"Sure," he says, not looking at her.

"And you're free of me now anyway. She's shipping me off, and you're a college kid." She loops her arm through his elbow. He keeps his arm limp, but doesn't pull away. "Seems like you're having plenty of fun up at school."

He called her the second month of classes. He'd tried LSD. There had briefly been a girlfriend. He'd been crying. Her little brother. He sounded six years old. A friend of his had had the tabs and they'd slipped them on their tongues and let them melt while sitting on the dirty couch at some off-campus party. "Oh, Benny," she kept saying, as he blubbered at her, "it's not the seventies."

"My mind is *wild*," he said.

Ellie swallowed a laugh.

"I can't make it stop," her brother said.

He'd run out of the party. The music was too loud, he told her. It was too hot. There were too many people. Too, too, too. He'd run out onto the street and almost been run over by a Camry.

Even the cars that almost hit him were reasonable and good.

She'd talked to him until he fell asleep. He became more and more coherent and she ached to go to him. To curl up with him in his tiny dorm bed and tell stories like they had when they were little. He hated soccer. He'd met a girl. Ellie'd seen her Facebook pictures. She'd texted her brother immediately. "Stay away," she'd said. It took a girl like her to know another one. And then the week after that Benny called with the LSD scare, and once they'd hung up Ellie couldn't help but smile at herself. Her poor sweet brother: he'd called her.

"I thought I'd be so happy to be free of all your shit," he says now. He bumbles through, but talks more than he maybe ever has. Ellie eats slowly, mostly picking at her omelet, watching her brother form before her eyes.

"But you know the most fucked-up thing?" he says. "You're the only person I can talk to. You're awful and you continue to make everybody else's life impossible, but I still think about you all the time and worry whether you're okay."

It was the way she seemed to always be suggesting that there was something somewhere that she could be doing that was more exciting than the thing everyone else was doing around her, he said. The way she had a place she went sometimes when she was right in front of you that could make you feel like, no matter what you did or said, it wasn't as good as what she was refusing to do or say in front of you.

Before he left he'd felt it was his job, in the face of her, to act as some kind of corrective for their parents. He was Good and Safe and Dependable. Sometimes he went out with friends and sometimes girls stood too close to him at parties. And sometimes he let them corner him in the kitchen of whoever's parents' apartment they were at that time and he'd kiss them. But he never let them lead him to another room. Everything he knew about girls—his mom, his sister—told him they couldn't be trusted. There was nothing to be sure of when they got you alone.

Once he got to college there had finally been a girl with whom he'd wanted to escape no matter what happened, no matter how out of control she made him feel. But then she'd turned out to be just as batshit as he knew she would. She fucked him in the dirty bed of some frat dude who had sheets with race cars on them and a hard white stain in the middle and then cried herself to sleep. She was almost too skinny, just like his sister. Just like his mom. He'd tried to hold her as she slept, all those bones jutting up against him, but she'd slipped from him and then asked him to please not talk to her as they dressed later and left.

He was exhausted by and avoided the soccer guys. They were all such bros, a term he hadn't understood until leaving New York. They grunted at one another. They took off their shirts. They said "screw" when they talked about sleeping with girls and called each other "fag" and "homo." He found himself missing his sister more and more. He wasn't as impressive when he wasn't being constantly compared to her.

He'd taken a philosophy class and macroeconomics. Though he loved it, he'd almost failed philosophy. He got so excited about the assignments he usually ended up not answering the questions that were asked, but going on for pages about some tangential idea that interested him more than the specific prompt. He got an A in econ only because it was so mind-numbingly boring that he had taken vigorous notes in order to stay awake.

"I started saying I was an econ major at parties, just to see if people thought that might seem like a thing a person like me might do."

He's managed to consume completely his stack of pancakes. Now, as he talks, Ellie dips her finger in the syrup.

She wants to tell him that she's sorry. It was supposed to be her job to take care of him. When they were very small, when their mom disappeared, before he didn't seem to need her any-more, Ellie would spend hours concocting games to distract him from their mom having locked herself inside her office again. Ellie could always tell when their mom had decided she couldn't be their mom for a little while. (When she disappeared, her voice changed, the look of her was firmer in the jaw, tight around the eyes and mouth. Her gestures were all slow and heavy and she flinched sometimes if either Ben or Ellie came too close.) They had adventures among their dad's flowers, dressed in hats with nets and magnifying glasses, with picks and shovels, in search of unknown treasures, sometimes digging up some of their dad's plants accidentally, frantically replanting them, laughing, before he came home (he never noticed, was fastidious in his work even in the time he spent out in the garden, but Ellie figured he didn't think quite enough about his children, when he wasn't with them, to imagine that it might have been his kids, and not the weather or a bird, who had dug up or overturned his plants), building forts in the bunk beds in Ben's room, piling up blanket after blanket until they might as well have not been in their house anymore, until their whole world was just color after color all around them, and they could lie back and Ellie'd read aloud to her brother, or they'd tell each other secrets, about nothing, really, about people that they knew or neighbors that they'd never spoken to, that, often, they just made up on the spot. Ben would wind his limbs over the top of her on the couch as they watched the same movies over and over, or they danced together to their mom's records.

Sometimes, after their mom had come out again, unlocking her office door and coming toward them slowly, seeming better somehow, seeming just barely willing to be their mom again, Ellie would put something fast and fun on the turntable and turn the music up loud. And she'd grab hold of Ben and her mom would sit and watch them until finally, sometimes, she'd dance with them. Her hair would fall from its bun, reaching down the middle of her back. They would all three swing their limbs and sing and dance. And those times, that fun, their mom free and careless, laughing with them after not even wanting them too close, all would have been because of Ellie. She'd known how to save all of them then.

Her brother cups his coffee in one long-fingered hand and watches Ellie. She dips her finger, one more time, into his syrup, and keeps her eyes turned toward his plate.

"I love you, you know?" she says.

Her brother fingers the rim of the coffee with his free hand and looks down too into his empty plate.

She passes him the rest of her omelet and sips her coffee. "I'm sorry, Benny," she says.

"I know, El," her brother says. "Me too."

Winter 2013

When the phone rings, it's the middle of the night, and every time, before she remembers, Maya thinks: *Ellie*. But then right after that she holds her breath, picks up the phone, and waits.

Maya thinks later that she knew it was her even before she started speaking, the way she paused, the way she breathed in once, long, then spoke in one big rush.

Annie gives no preamble. "I don't sleep, right?" she says.

This is the first that Maya's heard from her since the day before it happened. She almost doesn't know her voice.

"I mean, I guess I must, because I'm still, vaguely, somehow functional. Restaurant to run. Responsibilities. I'm grateful for it, actually. Because then, at home, there's Jack. And Jack. And Jack. And I can't look away from it. I'm still such a mess and all to myself, it's no good. But I don't ever remember sleeping. I don't remember waking up. I always have noise going, in the bedroom, in the living room. I keep the radio on all day. The other day there was this story of this man who made a speech at a wedding about a friend of his from childhood who died. A kid, you know?"

Maya digs her fingernails into her palms.

"They didn't give much backstory, but he seemed like your average sort of best-man type, friend from college, lawyer or something at the time of the speech. The program was about people getting things wrong in some accidental, public way. I missed the first part. He gives this awful speech about his friend dying. About him being shot accidentally with a left-out hunting rifle when he was ten years old. Well, it was incredibly articulate and *felt*, you know? How he never really knew how to process it, how he thought about it still. But the groom was interviewed briefly and said the whole tent of people just went quiet. And when the guy was done, he was smiling through the tears he'd managed to evoke both in himself and nearly half the room. It was clear he either had no idea what he'd just said or somehow thought it'd done the job. Someone came on after that, an expert. He said sometimes people confuse the quality of their feelings. They're too caught up in their weight. So this guy, he was just giving his friend and his new wife the thing so far in his life that felt as weighty as the thing that they'd just done."

Maya tries to keep her breathing quiet. She keeps the comforter close to her face and sits up with three pillows propped behind her. She is, luckily, in Ellie's room, so she doesn't have to worry about Stephen hearing, asking questions, hanging up the phone. She listens to her friend talk and wishes she could go to her and help make her better. She grabs hold of the blanket. She can feel her fingernails, still digging in her palms, through the thick duvet.

"I called you because I don't want the weight of this sadness any longer," says Annie. "Because I know you have to take it if I can just figure out how to pass it off to you."

Maya was twenty-one. She'd just graduated from Harvard. Moving out of her dorm room months before, she'd felt weightless, lost, like the last four years had been meant to give her something beyond the grades she'd always gotten, a few professors who seemed interested in the papers that she wrote. She'd gone to the best school. She'd made what she guessed might pass for friends. But she knew mostly they'd drift from her. At graduation, she'd accidentally sat alone. She'd assumed they'd sit the graduates alphabetically, that she didn't need to worry about finding a group to spend the hours of speeches and name-calling with. She lived in a house with three other girls who would happily have brought her with them, but it would have been her coming along, not being a part. And she'd preferred spending the hour and a half running along the Charles beforehand instead, watching the sculls glide along the water, the faint echo of the coxswains in the large boats calling, *Pull.*

Her dad had been there. He'd stayed at a hotel near Central Square and come the night before to take her to a steak dinner on Beacon Street. She'd worn a dress; he'd gotten drunk. She'd taken him back to his hotel and pulled off his shoes and socks and put him to bed, kissing his cheek brusquely, escaping quickly. She slept up in the attic of the house she shared. Sometimes she'd go days or weeks without talking to the girls at all. It was the night before graduation, and everyone was still out. There were parties to which she could have gone. The window next to her bed opened out onto the roof and she sat out there in a sweater with a blanket wrapped around her. It was May, but New England May, and the air still bit. She waited for some feeling to come over her, some sense of what might come next. She'd won a prize for her thesis. Her advisor had suggested a PhD. But she thought then there might be some other thing, some thing that wasn't so predictable, that might take her outside herself. She thought life would come and tell her what to do. The plan was to move to New York. She sat alone the next day. She had a worn copy of *To the Lighthouse* on her lap. After, she'd gone to brunch with her dad, but neither of them seemed sure of what to do. Both of them seemed disappointed by all that the day wasn't giving them. There was just the silly cap and gown, runny eggs, Macallan neat (celebratory, he said; a change) for Maya's dad, black coffee for her. "My girl," he said, grabbing her hand across the table. And Maya flinched a moment, then let him hold it until the waiter brought his refreshed drink. He should have remarried. He should have found someone else in whom to channel all that need. But he seemed to prefer disappointment. She told him about her paper, the award. She said she might apply next year for doctoral programs. He brightened briefly, seemed to like the idea of more time to find a way to properly appreciate whatever it was she was becoming then. She had no job in New York but had found an apartment in Alphabet City and told her dad about a few leads she had, friends of friends in publishing and doing admin work. It had felt important, to declare herself as only herself. To try, for a while, to not be wrapped up inside her books.

She was only in New York a month and a half before she got the phone call. It was two days before the Fourth. She was working sixty-hour weeks and hated every minute of it. Everyone she worked with was an actress or performer and spoke more loudly and gestured more aggressively than felt appropriate to Maya if one was not onstage. They were nice enough to her, the same as everyone who came before. They would let her come along to whichever bar they planned to stay at until closing and buy drinks until all the cash they'd accumulated the past seven or eight hours was depleted down to just enough to take a cab back to their shitty apartment shares. It was her one day off and she'd slept till two in the afternoon, then got up and ran two hours along the water, coming home feeling cleaner, straighter, more capable of being in the world. She'd bought a quarter of a watermelon at the better bodega a few blocks farther from her place and had ripped open the cellophane, cutting large chunks of it without bothering to put it in a bowl, holding it on her lap and letting the sticky juices fall onto her bare sweaty legs. She'd let the phone ring and then the sound of the machine, the click and then the beep. "At your earliest convenience," said the voice she didn't know but that mentioned her father's name in full. Just like that. They didn't tell her on the message, but she knew. For a moment, she thought, maybe she'd never call back.

An errant cousin from Indiana sent a bouquet of irises. Maya had him cremated and took an old surfboard from the garage and paddled him out past the break in the Atlantic and said goodbye to her dad. He was fifty-one. Aneurysm. She'd talked to him on the phone the day before and he'd said his head ached. That was as much advance warning as she got. And then there she was in that house again with no one and nowhere to go, besides the early morning runs barefoot in the sand, followed by long swims. Every morning she thought about not ever coming up out of the water, but then she would, crawling up out of the shore break and over the layer of shells back to her clothes and keys, back to the house that now belonged to her, walking from room to room, waiting for someone to come tell her how to live.

She drove to the public library just to have a place to go. She sat at one of the tables with people in their sixties and seventies on either side, also reading, sometimes talking to one another, just to be close to other people for some portion of the day.

It was there she got the job. She ran into her former middle school English teacher, who had since become high school vice principal. Mrs. Skinner had always been generous with Maya, had even gone on a date or two with her dad before coming to her senses and marrying someone much more practical and child-less the next year. She was doughy, bleached-blond hair, flouncy shirts, and too-tight pants. They were in a pickle, she'd said to Maya. She said things like that. Two weeks before the start of the school year the AP English teacher had decided to extend her maternity leave. Maya had been an English major. She'd tutored in the drop-in center at school. She'd helped TA her senior year. She had nothing else to do. And just like that she was a long-term sub. Mrs. Skinner fast-tracked a temporary certification that would last her through the year. She did two weeks of teacher training at the community center a few miles from the school. They took personality tests and stood in circles talking about the sorts of learners they were, how that might be translated to communicating their goals to students. She was given a "mentor" in the form of a seventy-year-old freshman English teacher who showed Maya her laminated lesson plans that she'd been using since before Maya was born—*The Odyssey*, then *To Kill a Mockingbird*, multiple choice tests every Friday, and grammar diagramming every other week.

The first day Maya taught, she wore a blazer, regretting it immediately. She kept bumping her chin on the shoulder pads. She was terrified. But something happened once she was in front of that room. It was different than bars or parties, even class-rooms, where she was in the back instead of up front in charge.

She believed in what she was giving: books, communication, it was the world that saved her once.

Annie was in her second-to-last class of the day. Eighteen juniors. AP language and composition. Annie stayed separate in the back left corner of the room. Maya had to give vocabulary tests as decreed by the school board. To make them interesting, she did away with multiple choice. Instead, she said the words out loud and the students had to write them, then write the definitions, followed by a sentence in which they used the word in proper context. *Agnostic* was one of the words. *An atheist without a spine*, wrote Annie. She wasn't even right, but Maya didn't care. It was clever. It made Maya laugh. Annie answered the questions quickly and then drew little cartoons of her classmates next to certain of the words. *Lugubrious. Capricious. Mercurial. Diffident.* Her cartoons were always coupled perfectly with her peers.

It was a two-thousand-person high school and mostly Maya was left alone. She couldn't bear to call any of the teachers by their first names and therefore referred to everyone as Mr. and Mrs., which only made them like her less. She ate lunch alone in her classroom instead of in the teacher's lounge, where the women (the entire English department was made up of women) microwaved their Lean Cuisines and Hot Pockets and complained about the same cycle of students again and again. Maya felt both older and younger than she ever had. She hadn't been living in this place, in that house, since she was thirteen. She was in charge of six classes of twenty-plus students each day. Exposing them to literature was a delicious and exciting task and one she felt she'd somehow tricked her way into. Some days the kids were restless and they whined and she hated them and wanted to just get in her car and drive out to the beach and run until her legs ached and then dive into the ocean till her skin was wrinkled and her limbs began to noodle and go limp, to lie out on the sand and go to sleep. But every morning, she got up before the sun and either ran or showered and brewed coffee. Sometimes she made up her lesson plans on the twenty-minute drive to work. And it was the best thing she'd ever done. She saw them see. Not all the time, not even most of it. But she was giving to them, and it didn't even matter that much whether they took it. It was the giving that felt good.

At first Annie was a good, if not stellar, student. She always seemed to be halfway somewhere else. But sometime in the end of September, she began to drift more. Twice, Maya had to wake her as she'd fallen asleep in the middle of class. The second time, the same week she'd left all the words blank on a vocab test, Maya called in Annie's mom and dad.

"She's lazy." Annie's mother wore a bright pink dress with lines of yellow giraffes. Maya'd never met people like this, couldn't believe they'd made this girl she liked so much. Rumor was that they'd owned half of South Florida at one point. They still owned a good portion of the Keys.

"Where did you go to school?" The dad was all business. He'd just opened the restaurant, pure vanity. The mom was a lawyer.

Maya looked down at her feet. "Harvard?"

"Right," he said. "Well, then, you know the standards she should be holding herself to."

"Oh, please, Tom, she's too fucked up for Harvard."

"She's extremely bright," said Maya, defensive suddenly.

"Exactly," said the dad. He nodded at his wife, but she just shook her head, then fiddled through her purse.

"She's also very young," said Maya as the mom applied a thick layer of lipstick.

"And how old are you?" she asked.

"I don't . . ." Maya held on to the edge of her desk. She'd just turned twenty-two.

"Emily, please." He looked at Maya apologetically, leaned forward, pushed the sleeves of his shirt up to his elbows, and placed them on his knees.

His voice lowered. "We've taken her to someone."

"Total bullshit," muttered the mother.

"Emily." He stopped. He shook his head, as if clearing it from his wife. "He said maybe she's sick somehow, maybe . . ."

"She's sick with her head up her ass."

"He suggested lithium."

Maya grabbed the *Norton Reader* off her desk and held it in her lap.

"He said bipolar, maybe. Maybe to settle her moods."

"Lithium?" Maya only knew it sounded strong.

"She refuses to take it. But she seems like she responds to you."

On the board were the objectives for the day: a summary of the first three acts of *Antigone*, constructing a firm thesis statement, how to guide your reader carefully.

"I don't think I could tell her to take lithium."

There were probably rules about this. They maybe talked about some of this at the staff development meetings, except Maya skipped most of them.

And then right after that, for a week, Annie wasn't in class. Because she didn't have any friends, there was no one Maya could ask. She still couldn't call any of her colleagues by their first names, much less reach out about where Annie might have gone. She did say something one day to the class, casually, while taking roll. "Has anyone heard from Annie?" she said, just after she'd reached her name on the roster, trying to seem nonchalant.

"Crazy girl?" This was a boy up front, Paul: Annie'd doodled his face next to the word "malapropos" before she'd stopped taking the tests.

"Someone said she went to Lawnwood," he said.

This was the inpatient center two towns away. When Maya was in middle school one of her classmates was found hung from the ceiling fan in the basement of Lawnwood.

"Right," she said.

The next Monday though Annie was back. Maya was so relieved she almost cried. She almost cried right up to the point when she looked more closely at Annie, and then, immediately, her eyes did begin to pool and she had to turn away. Annie's face was flat and puffy. Her skin was wan. She wore sweatpants and a large sweater, even though this October was still hot like August or July.

Maya split the kids into groups and told them to close-read a passage from *An American Childhood*. She read it out loud before she let them begin to rearrange their desks. She wanted to be sure that Annie heard. *The hard water pelts your skull, bangs in bits on your shoulders and arms. The strong water dashes down beside you and you feel it along your calves and thighs rising roughly back up, up to the roiling surface, full of bubbles that slide up your skin or break at you at full speed. Can you breathe here? Here where the force is the greatest and only the strength of your neck holds the river out of your face?*

She stopped herself before finishing the passage. Annie's shoulders shook. Maya walked over to her while the others got up, moved chairs and bags and notebooks, set to work. "You okay?" she said. Annie's hair was spread across her desk; the only sign of life was her foot shaking, tapping the heel of her sandal against one of the desk's metal legs. Maya reached down and grabbed hold of Annie's upper arm. It was freezing in the classroom. It was so hot outside, but they pumped the AC through, and the fluorescent lights shone down on the pallor of Annie's skin. Maya'd been to just enough staff meetings to know that touching was not all right—one of the few contributions her mentor had given her was a flyer about sexual harassment her second day—but she grabbed hold of Annie's arm again and pushed, trying to get her to raise her head.

"Annie?" she said again. "You okay?"

Instead of lifting her head, Annie groaned. She made her body heavy enough that Maya would have had to use both hands to raise her arm. The whole class looked up from their groups. Paul and a girl next to him began to laugh.

Maya left Annie and walked over to their group. They both stopped laughing. "Back to work," she said and turned back to Annie, whose head had fallen again on the desk.

She didn't want the others gawking, so she left her. She went from group to group, keeping them on task. Annie was out the door before the bell rang. Maya meant to grab her, talk to her, but she'd chickened out. The next period she had free and often left early to go running, but she stayed put awhile, reorganizing her plans for the next day, staring at the desk where Annie had been. And then there Annie was again, walking back through the door. She didn't have her stuff; just one of the laminated yellow slips of paper the whole school used as passes to walk through the halls during class. Maya started to say her name, but Annie spoke first. "I couldn't," she said. "I didn't want to be there anymore."

Maya wondered briefly about the protocol. They weren't supposed to be alone in any rooms with students when the doors were closed. She pulled a chair up close to her desk and nodded to Annie to sit.

"Where are you supposed to be?"

Annie looked at her. This was the wrong question, what every other teacher knew to ask.

"Pre-calc," Annie said. "But I can't."

"Okay." Maya nodded. "What, then? What do you need?"

"Can I just stay here?" Annie asked.

Maya nodded. She handed her the bag of chips she'd brought with her sandwich and sat back in her chair. Annie held her hand up to her mouth. "I just . . ." She crumpled the paper. "I started to feel really sick."

Maya figured eventually someone would come to look for her, although someone might have, they just might not have thought to look in Maya's room.

"They made me take these drugs," said Annie. "They said if I didn't I had to go to the hospital." She took a napkin off of Maya's desk and began ripping it into pieces, rolling each into tiny balls with her thumb and index finger as she talked. "But there's nothing wrong with me. I mean, everything is wrong, but mostly it's just I'm not who they want."

Maya leaned in then and hugged her. She held her tight and let her cry.

For two weeks after that, Annie came and sat in Maya's classroom every day. It took the administration that long to realize where she'd been. Finally, Maya was called in for a meeting. She knew very well from the outset the trouble she might be getting herself into. She just hadn't thought to care.

"This is serious," said Mrs. Skinner. Her face was pleading. She'd gotten her this job, fast-tracked Maya's temporary teaching certificate. She'd been telling everyone what a talent Maya had with the kids. "There are rules," she said.

She'd convinced Annie's parents to let her speak to Maya alone first.

Maya could feel the fluorescence of Annie's mother's dress straight through the door.

"The mother's threatening to sue." Mrs. Skinner was wearing a dark blue suit and her hair was slicked back tightly into a bun. She reached up and brushed back a nonexistent errant hair. "These aren't people you want to mess with, Maya," she said.

A file was created. Annie was pulled from her class. At the end of the semester, the teacher Maya had been filling in for decided to come back.

Maya applied to grad school. Within two months, she was making plans to head back to New York in the fall. She'd never meant to be in Florida and now she had a reason to leave again. In the meantime, it felt fine to let Annie come over to her father's house. She figured Annie was lying to her parents, but Maya didn't ask. She was too hungry for Annie's company, too happy to have her there. They sat out on the dock watching the sun go down and the alligators sunning themselves on the shore on the opposite side of the creek and talked about life and books and whatever it was they hoped to be someday.

Annie was still skipping school often, just barely getting through. She'd been in a car accident out by the beach in the middle of the afternoon and totaled her brand-new car. Her parents sent her to a new therapist every couple weeks, each time expressing frustration, firing the therapist violently, angry that after that small span of time their daughter still didn't seem to be fixed.

"The last one just let me talk for a really long time, then told me I was probably born to the wrong family."

Annie laughed, so did Maya.

"What the fuck am I supposed to do with that?" Annie asked.

"Did you ask her?"

Annie shrugged, raising her eyebrows, her eyes rolling up in her head. "We ran out of time."

"Did you tell your parents that one?"

"They prefer the ones who recommend the meds."

Maya looked down at the bottle of Riesling she'd opened, which they were sharing. It didn't feel wrong, though later, looking back, she'd worry for both her and Annie then.

There were times when Maya felt infinitely older. The five years that separated them were major, transformative years. They were supposed to be. Except Maya had spent most of them all wrapped up in books. So, now, with Annie challenging her, engaging with her outside the classroom, she didn't always feel like she was the one who might know what to do.

"I think they figure the sicker I am, the better, you know? If whatever's wrong with me is really bad, then when I'm finally fixed, I'll be that much closer to the person they wish I was."

Across the creek, something slithered in and under. They heard what might have been the slap of a heavy scaly tail.

"For a while, I had headaches," Maya said. "I don't remember how I did it. I think one day I mentioned my head hurt. You know, in the way thirteen-year-old girls mention things." Of course, it hadn't been so long ago for either of them that they'd been thirteen. "And my dad got worried, I guess. He wanted me to see specialists. He loved projects; he could find the newest, the best, the farthest away. He took me to a friend of a friend's doctor who'd been recommended and they'd ask how much does it hurt, when, where. They would ask me to describe in detail the extent of the pain. And I started to get confused if I'd ever felt anything, you know? They would show me that pain scale, with the ten faces that represent different gradations of pain. I almost always picked the middle one." She looked over at Annie, who had grabbed the wine and refilled her glass. She handed the bottle to Maya, who then did the same. "We went to acupuncturists and therapists. He got me this bed with magnets in it that was supposed to help. And every time, I would search for some vaguely appropriate approximation of the pain. It never felt like lying, really, but it was all basically made up. No one ever found anything. It was just the thing we did for a while: we went to doctors and they took pictures of and asked questions about my brain. He'd ask me sometimes, years later. But I don't know, you know? I've always had a hard time figuring out what's real and what's just in my head."

"You think I'm making it up?"

Maya stared at Annie. She'd somehow gone off track. "Of course not," she said. She reached toward her, held her shoulder. "I'm sorry. I was just—I was trying to tell you, it's weird, you know? The way people love and try to understand all our different versions of not-rightness. I don't think it makes much sense most of the time."

When Maya finally left a few months later, it was summer, before classes started. She was antsy in Florida, ready for the city—the water only worked on her for finite bits of time. Annie came to the house and cried and helped her pack. They would talk always after that. Sometimes months would pass. Sometimes they wouldn't see one another for years. But they were constants for one another, when neither of them had had much constant before that.

"I reconciled myself to not having a mother a long time ago," says Annie. Maya's hardly moved since she picked up the phone. It's snowing outside Ellie's window, tiny blustery flakes. "Long before my actual mom died," Annie says. "I figured most people had it a lot worse than me. She just wasn't the type to nurture. And when I thought of a person that I could count on for those sorts of phone calls, I always thought of you. I liked that we'd chosen one another, that we could be peers as well as whatever we'd started as. But I don't know. I guess there are things that connect us to the people who gave birth to us, to the people that we gave birth to." She stops a minute. Maya chokes back a sob.

"I'm not going to pursue charges, Maya. I don't want her to be locked up her whole life." Maya's knuckles ache, they hold so tightly to her phone. "She didn't . . ." Annie says. "We're all culpable, Maya, you and me much more than her."

Summer 2011

Ellie's last day in New York, she comes home to the sound of her mom in her office, rifling through papers, doing whatever it is she does with all her books. She thinks of listening to the lock turn when she and Ben were small. It's an old door. There was no mistaking the sound of the large bolt creaking. And they all had to pretend their mom hadn't done it on purpose, that she wasn't terrified suddenly of her own kids. Sometimes, when their dad was home, when Ben and Ellie were upstairs and he didn't think that they could hear him, he would yell straight through the door. He'd hiss awful things at her. "You pathetic child," he'd say. "What the fuck is wrong with you?" They never heard the things their mom said back to him. Though Ellie guessed that she was silent. Whatever her mom felt or thought, she pulled it in, like Ellie, rather than throw it back out into the world.

"El."

She jumps. They've hardly spoken since the trip was scheduled. Ellie has a plane ticket for the next morning. She still can't believe how quickly her mom has managed to do away with her.

"Come in here?" her mother says.

Ellie stays still at the threshold of her mom's office. She looks at all the shelves, full to overflowing, the papers a mess over her desk.

Her mom turns her chair so that she's facing Ellie. Ellie looks along the shelves, then briefly at her mom. She is only accidentally pretty, Ellie's mother. She wears her hair pulled back most of the time and hardly any makeup. A lot of the time, she sort of looks just like a mom. She looks tired and her skin is worn from all that sun she got growing up in Florida, the hours she spends running almost every day all year. But then Ellie will catch her from a certain angle, she'll be smiling just a little, or her nose will scrunch in approval, usually over something Benny says, and Ellie will think she has a very lovely mother, she'll wish they were the sort of mom and daughter that she could tell her this.

"When you were really little," her mom says. She crosses her arms over her chest.

Ellie wants to stop her. She doesn't want some lesson or consolation. But when she turns to see her mom's face, looking straight ahead and tight from jaw to temple, she stays quiet and lets her talk. "When you were just born," her mom says. "You slept every night on my chest for months." Her mom smiles, looking down into her shirt. "Just your skin and my skin and that tiny diaper. I thought everything good in the whole world had something to do with what it felt like to hold you like that." Ellie's not sure she wants to hear this. She's not sure where to fit it in with all her other thoughts about her mom. "But then, you know, you got bigger and your dad was going a little crazy with you in the bed every night. I wasn't really sleeping. And someone told us." She feels her mom smile again. "It's amazing how easily we took advice from almost anyone. It felt like the whole world must know more about how to parent than we did. But someone told us wherever you were at five to six months, wherever you were sleeping, was where you'd be your whole childhood, so I agreed to move you to the crib." Her mom has a rounder nose and her eyes are smaller than Ellie's. But they're the exact same color, dark with tiny flecks of green around the edge. She shakes her head again, looks down. "The idea of being away from you, of not feeling you breathing every night, it scared me," her mom says. Ellie doesn't mean to, but she laughs and looks at her. Both of them smile shyly. Ellie looks back down at her boots. "I got up at night six or seven times. Sometimes I never slept. I must have, but I don't remember any sleep. I'd just sit in your room on this little stool I brought from the kitchen and watch your chest move. You were so tiny still. Sometimes I'd place my hand on your chest just to be sure." Her mom shakes her head. "Anyway." She grabs a book off of her desk, then sets it down. "Your dad was worried that I wasn't sleeping. You know, I wasn't being *productive at work*, I'm sure." She stops. Ellie watches as she turns from this thought of her dad back to her. "So, the next appointment with the doctor, he comes and tells him what I'm doing." Her mom's shoulders tense and she takes hold of both sides of her chair, leaning forward. She looks at her daughter. "I was so angry, you know? Like he'd betrayed me somehow. Like no one on earth could understand this need I felt to be sure every second that you stayed alive. And I'd been unsure of the doctor to begin with. I wanted a woman. I wanted only to be surrounded by women after you were born. But he was a good guy. He'd been dealing with new mothers for many, many years. I remember he touched me. It was somehow exactly as he should. He held my arm in this extremely paternal way. I was so young then." Her mom's shoulders curve so that her chin comes toward her chest, but she raises her eyes, still looking at her. "I was twenty-eight. Which must have felt old then. But with him holding my arm and me close to tears with fear, he said, very firmly, but very simply, 'They want to live.'"

Ellie's mom stands up and walks toward her. Ellie holds tight to each of her elbows, her arms still crossed over her chest. Her mom stands close to her and grabs hold of her arm.

"I want to trust you, Ellie," she says. She smells like this room, dark and shut in. "I want to not feel like an idiot for trusting you."

Ellie leans closer to her mother. "I . . ." She feels like she might vomit. "I want that too," she says.

Winter 2013

Maya gets to class early. She sits on the desk in the small old whitewashed room with the radiator clanking beside her, the barely used blackboard hanging anachronistically behind. She's grateful for its sameness, how certainly it asserts itself as just like every other room in which she's taught. She's assigned "Cathedral" for this class. She's been craving Carver as a sort of antidote to all the blur and complication of her life.

She watches all the girls carefully: the hopeful ponytails, the defiant extra bits of weight spread through their bellies and their hips. She wants to take them each aside and place her hand up on their arms and tell them to cherish this time, their freedom. They will squander it, she knows, mostly. They will be silly, worry too much, sleep with the wrong boys. At least they're trying, though. At least they're not locked up already, trapped inside a consequence from which there might not be escape.

She opens her book and reads the first few pages. She has made a class packet, all the stories, poems, and essays bound together in a red construction-paper-covered book, but she brings her own copies when she teaches. She likes looking at all the different notes and comments she's made to herself over the years.

Charles comes in just after her. He carries a big coffee and a handful of books, a WNYC tote bag. He wears his thick round glasses, a long unbuttoned wool black coat. His beige shirt is covered in lines of pink and blue paisley. He does this often, shirts like this that make no sense.

"Morning," says Charles. She brightens at the sight of him, at the idea of being the one who knows what to do.

She wants to be able to just listen to him, to sit back and maybe learn. She has sent along her own notes on Carver, notes she put together mostly straight from the text she now holds in her hand. He emailed a long outline of plans for every minute of the seventy-minute period, some of which was scripted. Maya'd skimmed it, smiling, sure he'd end up using very little of what he'd written down.

"Good morning," Maya says. She straightens her legs and hops slowly from the desk. "You ready?"

He nods. "I think I am."

"The plans look great." She has them printed out and holds them now to show him. Five pages single-spaced. He's broken the time up into painstaking ten-minute increments.

His nose scrunches and his ears redden. "I thought I'd go off-script a bit," he says. "Maybe just discuss the story and then I'd assign a sort of reader's response."

"Sounds good," says Maya. Her book's still open and she runs her thumbs along the pages, dropping his script back onto her desk.

"I love this story," he says, taking off his glasses. He lifts his shirt to rub his lenses. He always wears the glasses and she likes the look of him without them. His abdomen—the bottom part, just above his jeans—appears from underneath his shirt as he wipes carefully. His skin is taut along his hip, darker than she'd figured, firm.

Maya fixes her eyes on the snow that comes down in tiny flakes outside and holds her hands firmly on either side of the open book.

Two girls come tittering through the hallway, peacoats, soft black stretch pants. They come into the classroom; Jackie is the chubbier, the more self-conscious, and the smarter, and Chloe— the smaller girl, the one who wears a bright splash of sometimes pink and sometimes red lipstick, even with her T-shirt and sweatpants and artfully messed-up hair, who raises her hand before thinking of what she'll say—Maya has ignored her hand a few times, looking out the window as she lectures, waiting for the other, more insightful kids to speak.

More kids shuffle in over the next few minutes. There are the few who are two and then five minutes late and they avert their eyes from Maya, who makes a big speech at the beginning of each semester about her strict lateness policy and then is terrible about docking or scolding them as the semester proceeds. Their coats and hair and shoes all have tiny snow splotches. Their faces are all flushed and damp.

Charles is patient. He looks down at his notes, then over at Maya once they're seated, still shuffling, murmuring to one another, zipping and unzipping bags.

He welcomes them, stumbling a little, mumbling. His book is open on the desk and he lifts it as he dives into discussion. He looks up at them, makes eye contact with Chloe, then a couple of kids near the back. His is the same copy, *Where I'm Calling From*, that Maya has. Maya sits at one of the desks in the front of the classroom. She pulls her feet up on the chair, then places them back on the floor. She watches Charles carefully, feels the students' attentions wander at first, then grow steady on him. He's careful, speaks slowly, makes a point to look up from the text and around the room as he speaks. He brings his palms together and holds his index fingers firm against his chin.

He's delicate with the final pieces of the story, the nuances of the main character's ambivalence, that moment Maya's always loved or hated depending on the men in her life—the point at which the man's wife falls asleep and then her robe falls open. And he goes to close it, before realizing the other man is blind, and just leaves the robe as it is.

"Charl—" Jackie says, and then stops herself. "Professor Megalos." He's red, a little on the tops of his cheeks and ears, and Maya wonders if they've had a dalliance, if maybe they've been together, if maybe things unbecoming to their student-teacher interaction have taken place. Briefly, she feels something she doesn't recognize at first, but then sees and is amused and then uncertain: jealousy.

"Do you think we're supposed to like the narrator?" Jackie asks him.

Charles smirks and his shoulders square. He's prepared for this. Perhaps he will not blunder; perhaps one day he'll find and do all that he meant. She hopes this for him as he bounds through the answer. She hopes this in a way that's overwhelming and complete.

"I'm not sure it matters," finishes Charles, "though, especially with Carver, I've thought a lot about this." He turns toward the class, addressing all of them, bringing them in. "Do you guys like him?" He'll be a good teacher, she thinks. He will find his way.

A couple of the girls shake their heads; one nods. Jackie watches, interested but not willing to decide. A couple boys in back, who have hardly spoken all semester, shrug and look back into their books.

"Do you think you'd be more engaged with the story if you liked him? Would you be more likely to return to it?"

"I think it's more interesting," says Jackie, "him being kind of an ass."

Charles is silent when Maya would have already jumped in to flesh the point out, but in this silence, she watches Jackie gaining strength.

"And in the end, it's more, I think. I think it's better. And that line, you know? At the end?" She flips the pages of the story. Charles, Maya, and the other kids join in. There are few things Maya enjoys more than pages shuffling. Jackie reads, "'I was in my house. I knew that. But I didn't feel like I was inside anything.'"

Jackie glances briefly at Maya, then back at Charles. "I don't know what it means," she says. "It doesn't even make any real kind of sense, you know? But it's exactly right, I think."

Maya sighs. Charles nods and sits up on the desk. "Yeah," he says. He's smiling. "It is, isn't it?"

Maya breathes out long and grins.

"You did wonderfully," she says when the room has emptied. She feels happy, maybe. Strong.

She takes hold of his arm and finds herself standing too close to him. She can smell his soap, a little sweat; she thinks that she can feel the churning of his excitement.

"Thanks," he says. He curls his neck down and curves his shoulders. She wants to hold his chin, to lift it up and make his shoulders square again. *Stand up straight!* she wants to say.

And he does look up and then down at her face.

They are very close. She leans toward him. There is a single, closed-mouth kiss.

Summer 2011

"You're so grown up!" Annie says, then laughs at herself. She's waiting at the bottom of the escalator near the baggage claim, off to the right of where the drivers stand in suits with signs. She bounds toward Ellie when Ellie is still five steps from the floor. Annie wears yellow Bermuda shorts and a white tunic, flip-flops—her hair is pulled back off her face—sunglasses perched atop her head. She's thin the way lots of yoga in your forties makes you thin. No part of her looks like an accident.

"Of course you are," she says. She has a wide mouth, a great big smile. She reaches for one of Ellie's bags and slings it over her shoulder. "I'm not sure when I got so old!"

And she is old, older than Ellie expected. Her face is tan and lines form around her eyes when she smiles. There are two creases on her forehead that remain even when she's looking straight ahead.

It's been years since Ellie's seen her. They used to come down at least twice a year when she and Ben were small. But for a while after that Annie was traveling. She sent Ellie's mom emails from different places Ellie had never heard of, the names of which Ellie liked to repeat quietly to herself for days—Luang Prabang, Phnom Penh, Vientiane—the way the syllables slipped into one another, the way their endings slid along her tongue. Then she was in San Francisco, then New Orleans. She'd moved around a bunch and then suddenly she'd come back here when Ellie was ten. She'd met her husband and took over the restaurant that had previously been owned by her parents. She'd had a kid. But in Ellie's head she was still young and gorgeous in a silk backless wedding dress that had clung to her as if there were nothing about her that was not worth showing. She'd had her hair down and all crimped and artfully messy, blowing in her face; she'd been barefoot on the beach. El's mom had made a speech during the reception; Annie had clasped her hands in front of her chest and grinned, her husband, younger by a couple of years, handsome with long thick sun-streaked floppy hair, in flip-flops and beige linen, had leaned over and kissed her cheek, his hand big and firm on her bare back.

"You're your mom," Annie says.

Ellie bristles for a minute, pulling out from the embrace Annie has so readily given her; she shakes her head. "No one says that," Ellie says.

"Oh, no, you are," Annie says. "She was about your age when I met her. You had to know her then. She's always that age in my head. Time passes and all that. But, this, you." Annie swings her hand in front of Ellie, her fingers long and thin.

Ellie angles her pinkie finger into her mouth and bites down on the little that remains of her nail. "Maybe." She repositions her backpack on her shoulder and glances at the conveyer belt that has just begun rotating, searching for, then grabbing her bag.

"The flight was okay?" Annie moves to help, but Ellie pulls free of her. They walk toward the automatic doors.

"Sure," Ellie says. Her immediate reaction is to firm and harden. Annie's tone, her trying, it's too much like Ellie's mom.

"The car's just out here," Annie says as the doors swish open and they enter the thick humid air. Ellie's forgotten the feel of summer in Florida, like the air's so wet and thick it's lapping at you, dulling your senses and weighing down your limbs. Annie's car is a convertible. It's a small black VW Bug, and as Ellie settles into the beige leather seat Annie starts the car and unlatches each side of the top, reaching over Ellie briefly, her shoulder almost brushing Ellie's nose; she presses a button, quiet, as the top folds back into the trunk.

"Nice," says Ellie.

Annie nods. "Jeff hates it." They start driving, through the parking lot and out onto the highway. Ellie hasn't been down here in a couple of years; there wasn't time or space enough for such things with everyone so busy trying to *Save Ellie From Herself*. But it's all exactly like it's always been, the heat and the moisture, over-grown grass, short stretches of trees, the rolling too-bright green of golf courses, concrete walls in front of rows of cookie-cutter— beige, brown, green, repeat—houses of the same concrete.

It's forty minutes to Annie's, but they have to stop halfway there to put the top up as a cloud comes out of nowhere—a big loud Florida storm that rains torrentially for fifteen minutes before they're clear of it. Annie reaches past Ellie to relatch the car's top and Ellie presses herself hard against the seat to be sure their skin doesn't brush.

"He doesn't hate it," Annie says. It takes Ellie a minute to real-ize to whom Annie's referring. It's been half an hour since the comment about Jeff hating the car. "He just gets worried about me and Jack. He thinks I drive too fast." Ellie's eyes wander to the speedometer. Annie's been going ninety the whole trip. Annie laughs, watching Ellie's eyes. "I'm better with Jack." She reaches up to the thick expanse of plastic that stretches across the middle of the car. "We have the roll bar. I always make him wear his seat belt and sit in his booster. It's not much different from any other car." Annie keeps one hand on the roll bar, arching her back and rolling her head down to her chest and then right and left, ears against shoulders. She turns and winks at Ellie. "The fresh air's good for us."

She looks a little younger than forty now, though when Ellie does the math she realizes she must be closer to forty-three or -four. Ellie's mom was twenty-two when she was Annie's teacher. They're only six years apart.

"How's everyone?" Annie asks her. "Your mom?"

"Fine," says Ellie. It's her father's least favorite word. He says it doesn't mean anything. But Ellie's not sure what or how much she wants to give Annie yet.

Annie nods.

"And you? How are you?"

Ellie wants to ask her what she knows, how much her mom has told her, how much she's left out. She thinks, briefly, of telling her the whole thing start to finish, just to see if she's still willing to let her near her kid.

"I'm fine," El says.

"Right," Annie says.

Ellie holds her right arm out the window. She straightens her elbow and moves her hand in waves up and down as they hit the exit and head toward Annie's house. It's the same exit that takes them to her mom's.

"You know, just trying to be Good this time," Ellie says. She

smiles straight ahead. "I'm the Great Struggle of all their lives."
She keeps her voice low as she says the last part and her eyes roll
up higher in her head.

"Hmmm," says Annie. "I used to be one of those."

At Annie's wedding: Ellie'd worn a yellow dress that she'd
loved when she'd found it with her mom in a little store near
their house in Brooklyn. It was a simple sheath but flared at the
waist with lines of slightly brighter yellows folded in. Her mom
had told her she looked beautiful and she'd believed her. She'd
been grinning, proud, as the saleslady stood behind her watching
when she'd tried it on. They'd done her hair up in a simple twist.
She'd worn drop pearl earrings that were her mom's, and she'd felt
grown-up the whole ride to the wedding. Benny wore a blue bow
tie and El had held his hand. She'd liked the feel of her mom so
close to her and proud to be there, other people smiling down at
her and then up at her mom. But then everyone had gotten quiet
and Annie had come up over the dunes all by herself and perfect,
not looking like a bride at all. Her dress was nothing like the ones
Ellie had seen in pictures or at the handful of other weddings
they'd been to. She didn't wear a veil. The dress had thick twisted
straps and the neckline bunched down into her chest. It was a perfect cream, falling down her body with no ornamentation until
below her waist. Then, just above her knees, layers of thin lace fell
one atop the other, blowing in the ocean's breeze. And every face,
hands reaching up to shade against the setting sun, smiled, eyes
focused on Annie. And Ellie felt herself begin to disappear.

"You tired?" Annie asks. "Hungry?"

Ellie shakes her head. She'd stayed up all night staring out her
upstairs window, wishing she were free enough to roam around
instead of being trapped inside. She hadn't wanted to worry her
mother. It was her last night with them and she had resolved

no matter what to try her very best to be Good. They'd eaten a quiet, simple dinner, pasta with spinach and sausage, her dad had cooked, and afterward she'd sat on the couch with her feet in her mom's lap.

"I wasn't with him," she'd said. Her mom held a book and was looking down at it. Ben was flipping channels on the TV. Their dad was outside working in the garden in the twilight. Ellie's mom shook her head.

"All right, El."

She'd wanted to hold her face up close to her mom and beg to be believed, to have Joseph call her to confirm she hadn't been with Dylan. But there was no point in proving just this once that she had been better than her mom thought. She had years of proving still to do no matter what.

She'd curled in with Benny after everyone had gone to bed. He didn't say anything to her. They were too old to touch; she just liked being close to him. She'd left his room before the sun rose, slipped on shorts and boots and one of her mom's old sweaters, and left before anyone woke up. She'd walked out down Seventh Avenue and smelled the city wake up one last time.

It's still early afternoon when they get to Annie's house, which is smaller than Ellie's mom's house, simple with mounds of overly lush landscaping obscuring it almost completely from the street. The exterior is a mustard-yellow and the roof an orange-red. There's a screened-in room right off the driveway. The door has a latch but no lock and there's a large couch and two chairs covering one full side of the room, a brown ceiling fan whirring on high overhead. Behind that room is a frosted glass door with slats in it. You can make out only shadows on the other side.

Annie nods toward the slatted door. "That'll be your room," she says.

Ellie looks over at Annie, who nods again, and Ellie lets herself in. It's a single room, but separate from the main house. There's a small bathroom off the back. The bed is built into the wall, with two levels of bookshelves built-in around the edge. There's a window AC unit in the side window and the other window looks out over the lush backyard. There's a desk across from the bed and drawers underneath.

"It's a little tight," says Annie. "But it'll give you some privacy."

The bed's been made up in a simple white comforter with large green and yellow flowers; the walls are yellow too. A sort of bright but unobtrusive yellow that has Ellie smiling despite herself. "It's fine," she says. "Thanks."

She finally turns to Annie, looking full at her for the first time since the airport. And, before Ellie can think of how to stop her, Annie leans in and hugs Ellie tight against her, and Ellie rests her fingers on two separate nubs of spine and stretches her neck up, not willing to let her head settle too close to Annie's face.

"Oh, El," she says. "I'm really so happy you're here."

Ellie keeps her back hard and straight till Annie finally lets her go. They hear a car pull up behind them, and then a man's voice, with laughter coursing through it: "You were suffocating the poor girl." Both Ellie and Annie turn toward the driveway. Jeffrey looks much the same as he did ten years ago. He wears swimming shorts and flip-flops. His hair is long and floppy and he's not wearing a shirt. His whole body's firm. He walks over to the passenger's side and opens the back door, then pulls a blond, wiry boy from the backseat. He's a near-replica of Jeffrey, and Ellie wonders how Annie could have had so little to do with what this boy's turned out to be.

"Hi, boys," says Annie. She grins at Ellie, the lines around her eyes all bunched up and lovely, then turns her smile to her son. The boy jumps from his father's arms and walks shyly toward them. Annie scoops him up and kisses his cheek.

"Jack"—she nods toward the boy—"this is Elinor. Ellie, Jack."

"Hey," Ellie says to the little boy, offering her hand to him. She used to babysit, when she was fourteen and fifteen, before people in the neighborhood knew enough to call other, less troubled kids. But Ellie had always been a hit with this age group, mostly because she treated them like peers. Jack's eyes are small and blue and set wide on his face. His skin is nut-brown and he has a full head of white-blond hair.

Jack looks at his mom, then over at Ellie. "Nor," he says, then smiles big.

"That works," says Ellie. "Hi," she says again.

"I like it," says Jeffrey. He's close to her suddenly. He kisses Annie on the cheek and offers his hand to Ellie. "Wonderful to see you again, Nor." His eyes wander up the length of her and he leans in to kiss her too. "You've aged much better than we have, it seems."

Jack fingers the thin white linen of his mother's shirt, glancing at Ellie. "You want to go swimming?"

Annie repositions Jack on her hip and chirps a bit too loudly, "What do you say Ellie, no better way to welcome you back down here than a swim?"

Ellie smiles at Jack, then glances briefly at his father. "Sure," she says. And she's not tired suddenly. "I guess."

Jeffrey walks past her into the room Annie has said is Ellie's and turns on the air conditioner. "All right, then," he says. "You two get changed before it gets too late." He turns toward Ellie and she feels small beside him. He's only a couple of inches taller than

Annie, but he's so much broader. He has a little stubble spread across his chin and cheeks.

The air conditioner chokes, then coughs, getting started, then blows cold and hard with a low chug against her back.

Jeffrey rests his hand just below her shoulder. "Leave this on while we're out so it cools down for you," he says. "It'll take you a while to get used to this heat."

Ellie nods and waits for them to filter into the main part of the house. She goes into her room and breathes in deep. She unpacks her toiletries in the bathroom, where Annie has laid out clean towels and washcloths. There's shampoo and conditioner in the shower, face wash, lotion, Tylenol, two kinds of sunscreen (one for face and one for body), and aloe all lined up in the cabinet over the sink.

Ellie washes her face, then applies the sunscreen. She stands naked in front of the full-length mirror that hangs on the bathroom door. Her hip bones jut out below her abdomen and she runs one hand over her pale stomach, then up to her chest. She thinks briefly again of Annie long ago, tan and perfect in that dress. She walks out into the main room and begins rifling through her suitcase. Of course the bathing suit has managed to fall to the bottom.

She hears the door to the main house open. She's cold from the window unit that continues to blow hard across her skin. She hears the smack of flip-flops and then nothing but the chugging of the air conditioner. Through the clear slats of the door she sees a wide expanse of shoulders. She stands still a minute, freezing without her clothes on, then pulls a shirt over her head and dumps her bag over the bed to find her bathing suit.

Winter 2013

"I didn't . . . I'm so sorry," Charles says.

Maya looks around. The hall outside the room is empty. The paisley on his shirt makes Maya want to cry.

"No," she says. "*I'm* sorry. I just . . ."

He grabs his book from the desk and holds it. It's like a shield against his chest.

She smiles at him, slowly. She wants to sit somewhere and let him put his head across her lap.

"I've been wanting—"

She stops him. "Oh, honey," she says. "Don't."

She's been too hard. The "honey." He steps back from her and his face closes off.

She walks quickly back to her office. She's hot. It's twenty-three degrees, but she holds her coat over her arm. She's left him there, Charles. She feels twelve years old.

She brushes past a colleague, then another, nods, cannot broach a smile. She thought she'd remembered the lock, but her office door is open; she goes in.

He's sitting in her desk chair. She stops and thinks he knows, then realizes that he can't.

She breathes out long.

He holds up his key ring. "I forgot I had a key." He looks more closely at her.

"You okay?"

She's fine. She's been silly. Nothing even happened. Everything is fine.

Her husband's legs cross at the ankles, stretched out beneath her desk. His shoes have tassels that hang above his toes. "Maya?"

"Fine." She attempts a smile. "What do you need?"

He looks at her. Careful. He cocks his head, his eyes rolling down her length.

"I was in class." Her vowels are all wrong. She watches Stephen swallow hard a wince. He sits up straight in her desk chair. He wears a dark blue blazer, a yellow shirt, no tie. He's hung his coat up on the rack near the door to Maya's office. She still holds hers over her arm.

"I know Maya. You sure you're okay?"

"Just cold out."

He leans forward, motioning toward her. "You forgot to put on your coat."

She sits down across from him. She's not sure she's ever been on this side of her desk.

"Maya, listen." He's trying to be careful with her. His voice is like balancing an egg out on a spoon. "Her doctor called."

There are options here that she feels she might be privy to. Crawling underneath the desk, for example, holding tight to Stephen's tassels as he talks to her about these things she'd rather try not to look directly at.

"You have to stop with the letters, Maya." He's acting as if there has not been a fight. As if, if he works very hard to help direct her toward actions that are good and reasonable, he should be forgiven for not loving his wife or his children as he should.

"It's the only way we're allowed to communicate with her."

She's only written two. She has both of them memorized, runs over and over them now to see if maybe she'd gotten at least some of what she means and needs to tell her daughter right.

"Maya." He's gaining strength now, the words are leveling. Her name's a word he's said confidently and just like this so many million times. "He thinks you should be seeing someone."

"How does he know to be worried about me?"

"You know they read the letters. They screen everything."

She must have been told this. But Stephen would have been the one to tell her. She was still refusing to speak to the doctors those first few months.

"You didn't even tell me you were writing her."

"I have to tell her everything I can," Maya says. "I'm trying to give her something, Stephen, to help her. I keep thinking, maybe if I shape things properly . . ." She tries not to think when she writes to her. Her hope is that something greater than what she's tried to give all these years will slip through these almost unconscious utterances, that something whole is passing through and into Ellie, helping fill her up again.

"He says you're enabling."

"What kind of asshole doctor tells on me to my husband, instead of calling me?"

"You can't give him the impression we're negligent," he says. He's trying so hard to be steady. He rubs the curve of the left side of his collar with his thumb. "He's concerned that you're not fully competent to make decisions without me."

"This is serious? Like I'm some hysteric? We need to find her someone else to see."

"I'm worried about you, Maya."

She looks past him through her one small window. The snow has started up again. "We have to get her another doctor. A woman."

"This man is supposed to be one of the best, Maya. He's why we sent her there..."

"Well, he's not, obviously. Obviously..." She stops. She picks a few stray flakes of snow off her coat. "I'm trying to figure out how to love her again." She almost whispers this.

Her husband's voice gets firmer, quieter. He crosses his arms and wheels the chair in closer to the desk and shakes his head. "You think you can make it better? What she did?"

She sees the curve of Charles's waist below his shirt.

He looks across the desk at her, then around at all her books. He opens the copy of *Mrs. Dalloway* and starts flipping through it. It's the copy that he gave her, years ago, her birthday, twenty-fifth or twenty-sixth—she can't believe she can't remember—it was one of the first birthdays she had after they'd met. He'd forgotten. She'd been hurt, though she'd never thought herself a woman who cared much about birthdays. And then, late at night, he'd shown up at her apartment with this book, a book of which, he knew, she had probably five copies already, because, he'd said, he was certain she'd love it.

"You know what, Maya? The thing you hate about me? Whatever it is about me that's so reprehensible to you. It's something you created. We created it together. I had no choice but to become the stolid, cold one. There wasn't any room for me to be anything else."

That day: "Mommy"—Maya hadn't heard Ellie's voice in months. They'd communicated through short missive emails. Text messages, the punctuation of which hurt Maya's eyes. For less than a second Maya'd thought, *She's coming back to me. My girl.*

But then, quickly, violently, this thought dissolved. Ellie was in the car, Jeffrey's, the Jeep they'd given her to use. She was pulled over on the side of the road. She was afraid to go back to their house. But no one was there and she had to get her things. She had no wallet. No clothes, besides the underwear she'd been wearing when it happened, the wet shirt and T-shirt lost somewhere. Underwear, thought Maya. Why underwear? And she knew, of course. She understood what she, herself, had done, sending her daughter there. Inflicting her daughter on that boy. Telling Annie bits, but not enough, not warning her properly of what Ellie might be capable of. They'd given her scrubs at the hospital, Ellie said. Maya had an image of her. The flat hot roads of Florida, scrub grass, lines of houses that all looked the same. Ellie small and crying, shoulders bare, dark hair matted to her head, going under, maybe not coming back up.

"El," she said. But she couldn't help her, wasn't sure she could stand to hear what her daughter had done.

But she listened to the first part of the story. The whole of it unfurled over her like a cold wet stretch of cotton wool, and she thought briefly she was about to vomit in the sink. She looked out onto Stephen's garden. It was fall and the leaves on the maple tree were just turning, half green still, with reds and yellows creeping in. She felt Stephen come up behind her, and Maya handed the phone to him without saying anything to either him or Ellie. She walked slowly to her office. She closed the door, and turned the old heavy bolt into its place. She sat up on the couch with her legs pulled in until she was as small as she thought she could be. She rocked slowly back and forth and tried not to breathe or think.

The lawyer Stephen called said to get her into rehab. They needed to show that she was sorry. That she was ill and working to be cured. She wasn't reckless: she was sick. But Maya didn't know, she wasn't sure, what was the difference, and what was sick and what wasn't, and what did calling her daughter sick do but make her something that needed to be fixed? And even if there was a sort of comfort in imagining that fixing her was an option, it also felt as if it was all too fundamentally a part of her to not have consequences beyond getting well. But they would *do things*; they would listen to the lawyers and they wouldn't go to her. Maya wasn't sure she could. Every time she thought of her daughter those first few weeks, she thought just after that of Annie. She thought of the little girl, sitting at her desk and looking small and sad. She thought of the woman who'd done her this great favor. The woman to whom she'd not told the whole truth about her girl.

The snow melts between Maya's fingers. She lays her coat on her lap, places her palms on her thighs. She looks past him at the lines of books along each wall, the spines solid, darkly colored, mostly hardbacks. "I talked to Annie," she says to him.

Stephen stiffens, sits up straight. "You can't talk to her, Maya. The lawyer was very clear," he says.

"I will absolutely talk to her if she'll talk to me."

Stephen shakes his head. "Maya, this isn't negotiable."

"She's not contesting the release, Stephen. She's not going to press charges . . ."

Stephen's silent a long time and Maya stands, not sure where she's going. She walks over to the window, fixes her eyes on a single snowflake, and watches as it falls.

She feels his body tense, then slowly loosen.

"We can request another doctor," he says. "If she's released we'll have to find her someone new up here." He sets the book down on her desk and stands and walks toward the coat rack. "If she's released." He comes closer to her. He looks past her shoulder, his chin almost at the middle of her head. "If she's released, we'll find a way to help her here."

He's not terrible, her husband, Maya thinks. She burrows each of her hands beneath her thighs. "Okay," she says. "Okay."

Outside, a couple walks by under an umbrella. It's too small to share, but they try valiantly. Maya watches as one of the spokes gets caught in the boy's hair. Maya thinks of all the different ways they've failed to help their daughter until now.

"You think you'll always hate me?" asks her husband.

This is the last thing she expected. She keeps her eyes fixed on the snow. "Oh, Stephen. I don't. You know I don't."

"But you're angry."

She thinks how to answer this honestly. She is angry, but it's no longer so specific an anger as to be directed just at him.

"I'm angry at everything, maybe," she says. "Mostly myself."

She reaches over the desk and closes the books, shuffles the papers into a pile. He hates disorder. She's never sure what she might uncover when she clears her desk.

"Maya." He stands and steps closer to her. He holds her wrist, halts her rearranging. He stays hovered over her, and she can almost taste his breath.

She stiffens underneath his grasp, those nerves, the shoulders, then the clavicle. She can't remember the last time that they touched. They've brushed past one another. They've accidentally fallen close to one another when Maya's managed to sleep the night through in their bed, but this is only the second time she can recall, since before they sent Ellie down to Florida, when her husband's purposefully reached for her.

"You're so thin," he says. His voice is soft now, quiet; the taste of him so close to her is the same as it was twenty years before.

She could have been better for him. She has, also, not reached for him in all these months. She's thought of it. Sometimes the impulse almost blinds her, the need to touch him, grab hold of his face, but she is a master of tempering these impulses. The more she's felt the need to touch some part of him, the farther she has stayed away.

"Why don't we get something to eat?" he says. He lets go of her, steps back. Maya almost asks him to stay put.

She's still holding her coat and slips it on and buttons it. Stephen takes his from the rack and does the same. The snow's still falling on the cobbled concrete, then through the gates and, cars speeding past, honking, wipers running, on Broadway, so close to one another as they walk that Maya's shoulder almost touches Stephen's upper arm.

"So, Ben," her husband says. "You think he'll be okay?" It seems they're done with Ellie for the day.

Twice, she almost takes his hand—Maya crosses her arms over her chest.

"It must be so much for him," she says. "I think he needs a break."

"I guess it won't . . ." He grabs her elbow to stop her from stepping into the crosswalk. An SUV speeds past.

"It's nothing that he can't undo," she says. They wait for the walk signal, Stephen's hand still on her arm. "He can try out other things . . ."

They go into a diner, some self-conscious attempt at a Manhattan college hangout. Maya orders a plate of french fries and a glass of wine. They're silent till the food comes. Maya tries a single fry, then pushes her plate toward her husband, sips her wine. Stephen takes large bites of a chicken sandwich and picks at Maya's fries.

"I've been rereading *Zarathustra*," he says.

Of course, she thinks, *we're returning to these things*.

"You know the part with the dwarf?"

Maya nods, though she barely remembers. She read it years ago, lugging around the portable Nietzsche just after she met Stephen. She'd slogged her way through the lot of it, *Beyond Good and Evil*, *The Anti-Christ*, even some of the letters to Wagner. She and Stephen had had some interesting, what felt then like life-changing, conversations and she'd thought, *Yes. This*. But, really, she had hardly made sense of most of *Zarathustra*. She remembers something jarring about the part with the dwarf. He jumped on Zarathustra's shoulder and poured lead in his ear.

"I've always hated that part," Stephen says. "I always thought it couldn't be as straightforward as it felt. Even with the aphorisms, maybe because I've built my life on asking questions." He shakes his head. "We have this need to make everything mean five or six different things."

He passes her plate back toward her and nods toward the french fries. He pours ketchup on the side of the plate and hands her a freshly dipped fry as he speaks.

She eats, chewing slowly, her husband watching, the salt and grease mixed with the ketchup almost pleasurable along her tongue.

"I think part of the reason I focused on the Germans is because it all seemed so endless, every word they said had been driven all these different ways.

"Martin," he says. He smiles at her.

She shakes her head to make clear she doesn't know which Martin.

"Heidegger," he says. "God bless him, I don't think *he* knew what he meant half the time. Sometimes I think that's his whole point."

He hasn't even meant to, but she watches him turning back into the man she knew. The man with whom she chose to build a life.

"But I've decided to fall in love with the dwarf now. I want it to be that simple. I need something that just means what it says. I think it was the moment, maybe Friedrich was tired, but he was just playing straight for once. Things jump on our backs and overwhelm us, they pour into us and drown everything else out. For him it was this idea of the eternal recurrence, which, though you mustn't ever tell anyone, I really never understood. I mean, yes, things repeat, time is crooked, I think that makes sense, but the idea that it's a circle seems to me not quite accurate, and part of me wishes it was, because . . ."

He stops. She stares at him. He holds his sandwich in midair but doesn't move to put it down. Because then maybe they could do it all again.

She loves him, she thinks. She was right to marry him.

Maya—twenty-three—she sat outside Avery Library with her book. The weather had fallen into biting early winter cold, but she was desperate for the air and bundled up.

"He'd be proud," said Stephen, nodding toward her.

Maya jumped at the sound of him. He seemed grown-up, confident. He wore glasses with thick rims, a thin dark blue wool coat that looked smooth and costly. He wore a bag slung across his chest and had dark hair cut close to his head.

"Fyodor," said Stephen. "Dostoyevsky. He'd love you out here, *suffering* for your work." He said the last bit in a deeper voice than he'd said the first, scowling, then raising the corners of his lips.

Maya laughed at him, and shrugged. "I love him," she said. She hadn't meant to sound as emphatic as she did.

"Well, he'd love you too, on sight," said Stephen. "The *bluster* of you."

"Bluster?" said Maya. "Are you British?"

Stephen laughed. "Just stuck up."

He was a scholar of Nietzsche, all the Germans, political philosophy. He stood up very straight and once he smiled he looked much younger than he was. She felt her body leaning toward him. She smiled back at him, and when he asked her out for drinks she said yes and it felt good.

They had drinks and dinner. They had breakfast. Two weeks passed and then a month. He read the final draft of her dissertation over a single weekend. She made him stay at his apartment and she at hers while he read. "So serious," he said when she decreed this. And she could tell, and she was grateful: he appreciated gravity.

They met for breakfast that Monday morning. He hadn't slept, she thought. It was the first time she'd seen him with stubble and wanted to touch it, to ask him to run it slowly, a little forcefully, down her length. They were at a diner on Waverly near his apartment. They both lived downtown, separate from school. She was half an hour early, but Stephen was already there. He had his hands, one on top of the other, set atop the stack of now-worn white paper. His back was tall against the booth. The whole time he spoke she was incapable of holding still. She'd ordered water, orange juice, and coffee and kept fingering one glass and then the mug and then the other glass, sipping, cupping, lining rims.

It was better than him loving it. He had notes for her and more in the margins. They sat for hours with their half-filled plates and endless cups of coffee. He talked and talked and she thought yes.

"I love you," she said when they were done and back at her apartment. When they had discussed it all and she'd called her advisor and asked for one more month. After she'd led him to the shower, both of them drained and greasy from the diner—he'd had her up against the grimy black-and-white tiles, his hand cupping her left thigh, her right leg held up by the tips of her toes, almost slipping, grabbing tight to the shower rod.

There were water spots on Maya's pillows from their still-wet hair. She ran her hands along the dry and then the wet. It was the first time she'd said "I love you" to him, to anyone besides her dad. He laughed.

"I wonder if you don't just love my notes," he said.

They read out loud to one another things that they were working on, passages they hadn't quite made sense of yet. He liked to garden, would spend hours outside in ratty shorts and moccasins, looking exactly like the privileged boy from Collegiate that he'd always been. And sometimes he would yell things, stinging low-slung vitriol that he would later say he didn't mean, but that hung over them and threatened, long after the hurt had been repaired.

He traveled often and missed birthdays, holidays, trips to Florida that he would lament afterward, but when he left again he often seemed relieved. He took her out to the Cape to spend weekends with his parents—they'd relocated permanently once Stephen started grad school. His mother spent her days walking along the water every morning no matter the weather, cultivating a modest art collection that she didn't seem to have much interest in once the work had been acquired. His father spent his days reading, the newspaper in the morning, large nonfiction in the afternoons, then quizzing Stephen, Maya, and his wife over dinner about topics so obscure that he was almost certain to be the only one of the four of them to have the answers to.

They doted on her, loved her. She was smarter, they said, than Stephen's usual choices. They were wealthy liberal intellectuals, she was the exact sort of uncertain background, innate brilliance, acceptable attractive that they would have chosen for their son. Maya walked the water with his mother in the mornings and discussed de Kooning, Balthus, Rothko, Dubuffet, the colors of the Dutch. She knew hardly anything about visual art, but she was a quick study and paid close attention. She spent some of the afternoons she wasn't teaching at the MoMA, Met, Frick or Guggenheim, cultivating enough of an opinion to have more of her own ideas to offer on these walks.

As much as Maya loved and admired them, there was something constantly off-putting about the ease with which her in-laws existed in the world. They'd both come from a long line of money, perfectly educated, consistently loved. They, like Stephen, seemed to feel as if they had a right to all the pleasures they'd been given, while Maya sat most days waiting to be punished for all that she had somehow managed to acquire. Sometimes it scared her how much Stephen trusted the world. But mostly, especially early, she found it astonishing, lovely, in the way that one can see something from far away and appreciate its beauty, but never quite make sense of what it is.

"Why do you think you picked me?" he says to her. He's finished his sandwich. His plate sits bare in front of him and he reaches again for one of Maya's fries.

"You make it sound like you had no say," she says.

"Please," he says. "I was old already. I was a curmudgeon."

She eats two french fries dry, swallowing slowly. She hasn't eaten in days, it seems, weeks. "You were thirty-four," she says.

A smear of ketchup lingers on the left side of his lip.

"I loved you," Maya says.

"But why?"

"Jesus, Stephen."

She picks a napkin up to wipe his lip for him, then hands it off for him to wipe instead.

"I loved your brain," she says.

This is the answer he expected. She wonders how to make it something else. How to maybe give him something more.

"Your humor?" she says.

He laughs. "But I'm not funny."

She laughs too. "You made me laugh," she says.

"Everybody says that."

She smiles at him. "No one says that about you."

And he laughs then in the exact way that is maybe more than any other reason why she loves him: like he's ten years old and doesn't care who's watching, loudly. His large body unfurls. His head tilts back.

It's the sheer dissonance between this and every other aspect of the man she married that is the most charming. It still surprises her when he laughs, when he is dry, quiet, and biting, usually at his own expense. And she's so very grateful to him for this; she's more than grateful—these moments have always made her think there could be more surprise to come. Surprise for both of them, in what they might give to one another, in all, together, they might be capable of.

He waits for more.

"I thought . . . I think I thought the way you trusted the world. I wanted to be as certain as you were."

He laughs again. "Now you know better," he says.

Ten years before: "Christ, Maya!"

"If you use the word *reputation* I'll jump out of the car." There had been a party for the faculty in Stephen's department. He was angling for department chair.

He stared at her. He had only one hand on the wheel.

"Look at the road," she said.

He fiddled with his glasses, loosened up his tie. "It was two hours. Two hours when you could have just smiled and nodded and played the game a little bit."

"*The game*, Stephen? Seriously?" She had her foot up on her knee and was slowly peeling off her shoes.

"This is not a vocabulary thing."

"It is exactly. Since when do you care about a game?"

He waited, and she knew the answer before she'd even asked the question. He always had. She rolled her window down and rested her hand along the outside of the car.

She'd done nothing. She'd drunk more gin than she'd intended. She'd been asked about her specialty and had gone on a bit too long about Virginia Woolf and death.

She kept her eyes fixed on the trees along the West Side Highway, the stretch of cobbled concrete, and then the water just beyond. She wished that she were running. That she were all alone, feet pounding, and Stephen were safe and quiet in their bed. Her voice got quieter as she spoke. "I was explaining what I do," she said.

He'd called it proselytizing. "You were freaking people out."

"They're academics Stephen. They don't freak out that easily."

"You were too drunk to see."

"I wasn't drunk." She hardly ever drank and could not hold her liquor. Probably she had been a little drunk. "Would you rather I just talk about the children?" El was ten, Ben was eight.

He turned to her again. "Would that have been so hard?"

It would have been. Even when she wanted to just sit and gush about her children, take out pictures, tell stories of all the ways in which they astounded her each day, she was too terrified of losing hold of all she was outside of them. She was adamant in her need to be someone separate from their mom.

The car turned down into the tunnel. The smell of exhaust hit Maya, then the bright lights on either side. She rolled her window up.

It had been awkward. She'd tried at first. A man she'd never met had asked her what she did. He was condescending, the way he kept looking past her for some other, better conversation, feeling stuck, perhaps, sitting next to this small woman whom she did not know or care to get to know. She always felt slightly, in some specific but noticeable way, as if she were awkwardly dressed. This night it had been the shoes she was wearing, high-heeled and open-toed, shoes she aspired to wear with confidence and then was not quite able to walk in comfortably. They were garish, she saw as soon as they'd made it uptown, not quite right, and she was forced to spend the night seated, her feet tucked beneath her chair, leaning forward with her elbows resting on the table, wishing she were—like every other woman in the room—wearing flats.

"Woolf," she'd said in response to the man's question. Clipped and inappropriate. But she was gauging him, testing—Stephen hated when she did this; why, he asked her, could she not just be pleasant and smile and nod—she was interested in how he would respond. Would he think Thomas or Tom or Tobias, would he know immediately, because of her demeanor or the way she pulled tight on her shawl, that she meant the tragic female character, the one who'd chosen water over life? He was the husband of one of Stephen's colleagues, a mathematical philosopher, empiricism. If pushed, Stephen would have had to admit he didn't like the wife any more than Maya liked this man. He traded futures. Maya'd loved the sound of this, the idea of such a phrase. But it had been much less interesting than it sounded as he'd explained. And there was, then, the third glass of gin and lime.

"Virginia," she said when he stayed silent. "The presence of the absence." He looked at her as if she were speaking some language unknown to anyone but her. "Death," she said. "I look at how she has used it in her work to explore both the experience and effects of death, the particular way in which it's always present, entering the room, overtaking life, dissipating, *sliced like a knife through everything.*" She stopped to sip her drink again. "Death as communication when all other forms have failed." He squirmed and cupped the base of his drink with meaty fingers. He shook his glass and tipped it, then sucked slowly on a piece of ice.

"I also teach," she said.

"And the kids get that? They can make sense of all of that?" He had a fleshy face, and a burst blood vessel had left a splotch of red below his eye.

"Some of it," she said. "They're very bright, the kids I get. They're wonderful." She believed this as she said it, smiled thinking of them. "I teach intro classes also. It's a pretty universal concern, though, right?"

He nodded. "It's not really practical, though, huh? It certainly won't help them get jobs."

Maya sat up straighter and pulled her shawl more tightly to her chest. "Practical," she said. "It's literature."

She'd meant this as corrective. But he stared at her smugly, as if she'd just proven him right.

"This is the problem with liberal education," he said. "These kids are paying hundreds of thousands of dollars to leave school without a single marketable skill."

"Do you consider knowing how to think impractical?" she asked him. Her voice had risen. She was somehow, inexplicably, standing up. The shoes and then the gin: she was unsteady on her feet.

"I happen to think quite well," he said.

"You're a fucking idiot," Maya'd said.

She might have raised her voice.

People were watching. She could feel Stephen's eyes.

He pulled her away.

"You were about three seconds from throwing your drink."

"He was an ass, Stephen."

"Did you think you might convert him if you yelled more?"

"I wasn't yelling." Maya placed her now-bare feet back on the floor. Stephen glared at her. They'd just come through the tunnel. She looked ahead to avoid facing him. She watched the light turn to yellow and then red.

"Stephen!" she said. But they were halfway through the intersection by the time the brakes caught. Horns honked. Maya fell forward and her head hit hard on the dash.

Summer 2011

"I did in vitro," says Annie. She talks freely, ambling from topic to topic, not seeming to mind when or if Ellie or Jeffrey joins.

They've been swimming—after fifteen minutes in the car, Ellie staring down at her hands, nervous, Annie chatting, Jeffrey smiling, trekking over the boardwalk, Ellie barefoot on tiptoes forgetting how very hot the sand could get, finally then forgetting Jack and Jeff and Annie all behind her, diving in and thinking, *perfect*—those few minutes she was underwater like there might be no one in the world but her.

"It took us two years before it worked," Annie says.

All three of them have showered. Ellie put her clothes away while Jeffrey and Annie fed Jack and put him to bed. She tried on a dress and two pairs of shorts, before she chose a loose-fitting pair of jeans and one of Ben's old soccer shirts. They usually all eat together, Annie told her, but all the hours in the water have worn Jack's tiny body out.

"I never thought I wanted a family, you know?" She moves from the pantry to the stove and pours a cup of rice into boiling water; she grabs the cutting board from Ellie and scrapes the garlic and the onions into a pan. "I always felt so independent," she says. "But then, I was almost forty and desperate for someone to love like that." Ellie's still a minute, trying to figure out what "like that" means, but Annie doesn't explain and Ellie doesn't ask her. Annie takes the strips of peppers Ellie's cut and drops them in the pan. "Jeffrey." She nods toward him. He wears shorts and a short-sleeved white button-up. He holds his hair behind one ear and smiles at his wife. "I thought he would be ambivalent. We'd talked about it, you know? But it seemed like we'd decided by virtue of waiting as long as we did. He has his kids, you know, his patients. He gives so much to his work. But once we started trying, he was more attached to the idea than me."

She stops then and looks at Ellie. She puts the top on the pot with the rice and pulls a chair out so Ellie can sit. The kitchen's large, with bright yellow cabinets above burnt-red counters covering two full walls. They have an island in the middle with a stovetop and lines of spices. The kitchen opens straight onto the living room, where two long couches sit catty-corner to one another and look out lines of windows onto the overly lush yard and then the river beyond that. "You think you're not that caught up in your idea of yourself as woman, you know? But it turned out I wasn't above that sort of empty ache." For a minute she's quiet, turning down the rice, looking at Jeff. "It was the third time we tried that it finally stuck." Jeffrey sits at the table close to Ellie. He has a magazine in front of him, an old *New Yorker*. He flips pages as Annie talks.

"I guess I'll always be most grateful for that push," Annie continues, and Ellie watches as she smiles at her husband, his eyes still angled toward the pages of the magazine. "And I have him now." There's a way that the "him" sounds that makes clear to all of them that she means Jack. "It's hard to imagine there was a time when I might not have. I never thought I'd be living here either or running that restaurant." She says the last word like it tastes sour, raises an eyebrow, firms her lips. "But it suits me. And I like the water."

"Me too," says Jeffrey. He stands up now and grabs a green pepper from the pan where Annie's mixing them together with the garlic and large strips of onion. He kisses Annie once, brusquely, on the cheek. "All of it." He winks at Ellie. "Me too."

Annie goes to check on Jack as they sit down to dinner. Jeffrey offers Ellie wine as she settles in her chair. She almost says no, but he's already reaching up into the cupboard for another wine glass as he asks. Ellie doesn't want to be the sort of girl who can't handle a glass of wine when it's offered her. She likes the face that Jeffrey makes when she says sure and smiles. He's tall and tan and only looks his age when his skin crinkles on his forehead and around his eyes as he smiles, which he does, his head tilted toward Ellie, as he fills her glass. When Annie comes back she looks at Ellie's glass, then over at Jeffrey, but whatever thought she has she keeps to herself.

She must not know, Ellie thinks. Or what she does know isn't all there is.

Ellie loves the feel of the glass's stem between her fingers, the way the weight of the wine shifts subtly as she tips it to her lips. She drinks slowly so as not to have to pour herself another glass.

Annie tells her a bit about the restaurant. Things are slow now because it's summer. Like so much else in Florida, Jeffrey says, the tourist seasons are backward too. The whole place empties out from May to September. It gets too hot and the snowbirds head up north. So she'll have time to get to know Jack gradually. Jeffrey's schedule is also slower, since he works with kids and many of them have also gone for the too-hot months.

They eat quickly and move to the couches in the living room. The couches are a dark blue and the cushions are hard when Ellie sits. She pulls her legs underneath her in the corner. She wonders briefly if she should have asked first, if she should put her feet back on the floor. But, quickly, Annie does the same as Ellie; she rests her feet up underneath her, then stretches them out on Jeffrey's lap; Ellie settles in as Annie talks.

"You know, he was the prom king."

Jeffrey has one arm around the back of the couch and the fingers of his other hand move slowly up and down Annie's bare shin.

"And she was Daria," Jeffrey says. He'd spoken hardly at all during dinner and Ellie's startled a minute by the sound of him.

She looks at them blankly. She doesn't know who Daria is.

"Oh, god," says Jeffrey. He holds tight to Annie's ankle, face formed to pretend-terror. He hasn't looked directly at Ellie since he poured her wine. "We're really old."

Annie shakes her head at him and swats his hand away. "It was this show," she says. "On MTV."

"You know MTV, right?" asks Jeffrey.

Ellie nods. She takes one small sip of wine and doesn't swallow right away.

"She hated everyone," he says.

Annie hits him again, pulls her legs off of his lap, and pulls them underneath her. "I wasn't that bad."

"She was one of those girls who wore a lot of black and scowled at people." Jeffrey furrows his brow, first at Annie, then just shy of Ellie's ear.

"You make me sound awful," Annie says.

They both laugh, and Ellie envies this: the playful closeness, the story that's been told so many times.

"Your mom was her only friend."

Ellie stiffens at the mention of her mother. She reaches for her wine and takes too big a sip.

"Also true," Annie says.

"Did you guys know each other then?" Ellie asks. She wants to keep the story just on them.

"Definitely no," Annie says.

"She's much older," says Jeffrey.

"Screw you," Annie says to Jeffrey, then turns to Ellie. "Two years."

"But she's also a genius," he says. "So she was four years ahead of me in school."

"Geniuses don't run fried fish restaurants."

Jeffrey shrugs.

"I would have hated him," Annie says.

Jeffrey laughs, swatting Annie's ankle. "Right back at you, kid," he says.

Ellie pulls the blanket folded over the couch back and spreads it across herself. She stares out the window, rustling trees, takes two small sips of wine.

"Your mom saved me, though," says Annie. "I was this sad and angry little ball of nerves."

"Feral," inserts Jeffrey.

Annie ignores him, eyes on Ellie. "She took me in," she says.

"You know. She's not so good with boundaries, your mom." Annie smiles toward her feet. "She was so young then. At first you forgot how young she was because she was so smart. And she could talk, you know? Even then. She had no training and she was pretty clearly just making it up. But she talked and talked and at some point you realized what she was saying might be worth something. She wore flip-flops to class and she'd sneak out to run on the beach during her off periods. I had her in the afternoon and there were usually specks of sand on her feet by the time she taught our class."

Ellie can almost imagine all of this, but still, it's impossible for her to see it fully in her head. Her mom is so completely the person she's been Ellie's whole life.

"I was reckless. You know? I was sixteen. I had no idea what all of it was for. I went to school because I was supposed to. My parents' line was always, we go to work, so you go to school. That's an awful way to sell it. I skipped a ton of class. I drove around a lot and listened to the same awful music over and over. I'd drive six hours down to Key West, go swimming, and drive back."

"She had a convertible then too," says Jeffrey. "It's always more fun to be the tortured depressed teenager when your parents are rich."

Annie doesn't look at him. He gets up and pours himself a glass of wine. He brings the bottle from the kitchen into the living room and is already refilling Ellie's glass, not looking at Annie, before either of them can tell him no.

Annie eyes her husband. Then fixes her gaze on Ellie. "Your mom listened to me. All I really wanted was to *talk*, you know? To cry to someone without them telling me I was sick." She reaches behind the couch and pulls a throw out of the basket filled with blankets. It's still over eighty late at night, but Jeffrey keeps the air conditioner at sixty-two. Annie wraps the throw around herself and burrows back into the corner of the couch, not touching Jeffrey. She could be Ellie's mom in that moment, folding in on herself.

Winter 2013

Maya rides the subway just after rush hour, standing, holding the pole, and brushing up against a man in a suit who types furiously on his phone. There are empty seats, but she can't sit. She's going to a dinner party by herself. She and Stephen rarely socialize together anymore. She explained briefly where she was going. He's agreed to try to have a nice conciliatory dinner with their son.

Maya'd dressed carefully, showering, dabbing lipstick, swiping mascara, making herself stare back at herself longer than usual in the mirror over the sink in the bathroom in their room. She wears a dress, even though she hardly ever makes this effort in winter, the tights, the sweater, the slightly more than sensibly heeled boots. It's the third thing she tried on. She wanted to feel a little less like the person that she always is. The dress hits just above the knee, in big patches of blue and purple. She bought it with Laura. With Laura is the only time she shops and the only time she buys clothes in colors other than black or gray. She has brushed her hair back and fastened it loosely at her neck with a small wooden clip. She feels, if not pretty, necessarily, then foreign enough to feel capable of interacting in the unstructured setting of this gathering.

There are few people who could get Maya to leave the house after dark these days, but she hasn't seen Caitlin in almost two years. She is one of Maya's former students, applied to the program four years ago, explicitly to work with Maya. And Maya had lobbied hard to get Caitlin in. She'd gone to a not-well-thought-of state school, and while her grades were impeccable, her other achievements were unremarkable. Her writing sample had been messy, unedited, not academic really at all. It had read like a sort of literary love letter to Woolf, whom she'd meant to focus on. She'd written on the moment in *Mrs. Dalloway* when Septimus sits with his wife to make a hat. About how he had an eye for colors, could see things most people couldn't, but needed his wife to bring his ideas to fruition in the world, about the impossibility of communication, the need to turn the abstract into the tangible, how some people cannot achieve this without the help of someone else.

Maya'd been so moved by her writing. She'd finally managed to convince the committee that the potential evident in Caitlin's work was worth the risk of taking on a less-credentialed student. And Caitlin had, immediately, delivered on the potential Maya had seen. Caitlin had always seemed older than most of the other grad students; she lacked that smugness so many people her age possessed, that certainty that though they've made so few major life decisions up until this point, when they did they would somehow prove better and less compromising and complex than all those that came before. And then, after two years of being exactly what Maya hoped she'd be, Caitlin abruptly left. She'd been effusively apologetic. She wanted to write: novels, fiction, her own art—she'd said all of it in a whisper, in Maya's office, a sweater wrapped around her and her arms crossed as she spoke, afraid, maybe, to throw the full weight of such aspirations out into the world.

Caitlin had met Ellie once as well. Ellie loved it at first, Maya bringing students home for dinner. When she was small these students all doted on her. She was precocious then and perfect-looking, the big dark eyes, the long sharp nose. When Maya brought students home—twenty-somethings, quiet, awkward, with their broken-in leather bags and their furrowed brows—she promised them a home-cooked meal that Stephen then cooked. She was proud of this as well, being a woman for whom the man made the meals—she took pleasure in showing them off, her gorgeous happy family, the warm quiet world in Brooklyn that they'd built for themselves.

But soon after Ellie turned twelve there was a marked shift in how she received these young people. She sulked when they came over. She picked at her food and then snuck up to her room.

They'd been talking about the novel Caitlin was working on. It was still nascent then. She'd ridden the 2 train back with Maya from campus, the two of them sitting next to one another, knees touching, awkward suddenly outside their usual context.

"I've been charting out *To the Lighthouse*," she said to Maya at dinner, "trying to figure out how it's formed."

"How great!" Maya said. She hadn't touched her food and was staring at Caitlin. She felt her daughter's eyes on her.

Caitlin began to speak again. She was explaining the shift that happens in the "Time Passes" section, how she was trying to understand how to make large swaths of time speed up, then slow down.

"Have you ever had long hair?" asked Ellie, interrupting. She had turned toward Caitlin and her mouth pursed a bit as she appraised her face; Caitlin took another bite of the orzo with spinach and chicken Stephen had cooked.

"I'm sorry?" said Caitlin. She smiled at Ellie, looking briefly back at Maya, who sat slightly confused, then scared.

Caitlin was round around the edges. She was short, with thick thighs and a belly, her face a perfectly full moon.

"Your hair," said Ellie again. "Has it ever been long?" There was something in Ellie's voice, the flatness of it, like she was trying at something. Maya held tight to the edge of the table and begged her daughter silently to reel herself back in.

"Of course." Caitlin laughed, and reached up to the dark blond nubs that sat atop her head. "When I was at LSU. It got so hot in summers. I had a friend who was a physicist and she convinced me she understood angles, so she cut off all my hair." She looked at Maya, who smiled back. "We'd had some wine." Then back to Ellie, "I liked how easy it was, so I only went shorter after that."

"Ha," said Ellie, clearly not amused.

Caitlin reddened. She wore a purple T-shirt and jeans that pulled at the pockets. Her eyes and mouth were small. Maya thought it might be worse to scold her daughter. She wasn't sure what to do or say to make it all stop there.

"El . . ."

Her daughter interrupted her, still looking right at Caitlin. "It's slimming, you know, long hair."

Caitlin looked down at her plate. Maya stood, then stopped a second, not knowing which way to turn.

Caitlin had recovered valiantly. She'd initiated a conversation with Stephen about his Germans, talked soccer—she'd been a defender in high school—with Ben. Maya waited until she'd left and both Stephen and Ben had gone upstairs to confront Ellie. But when she found her, in her room with her charcoals and a large piece of thick white paper, Ellie was already crying, saying she was sorry, saying she didn't know why she'd been that way. Maya had no choice but to pull her in and comfort her, worrying only for a moment that she might still need to scold her for a thing she still wasn't completely sure her daughter knew she'd done.

The apartment is a twenty-minute walk east from the subway. Maya's just about at the water by the time she finds the address. She walks up four flights of stairs and hears the sound of bongo drums coming from the floor above, a sloppily strummed banjo, and smells the sweet smoky scent of weed. There are shoes outside each apartment, a stroller folded up in the corner across the hall.

She used to live in an apartment almost exactly like this, those few months before her dad died and then again before she married Stephen. The first summer after school she'd hardly left the apartment. She spent nearly all her time locked up in the tiny space where she knew she could be sure that she'd be left alone. She had no air conditioner and no TV, just an old stereo, a fan, and loads of books. In summer she would point the fan right on herself and lie naked on the floor most of the day. She took cold showers every few hours, walking around with the windows open, tying her hair up in a knot to keep the water in. She'd read and nap; she'd sit very still and listen to the cadence of the footsteps of her neighbors and try to imagine whatever it was they did every day. The family below her had three kids, shoved into the same tiny crooked studio as hers. She peeked whenever she could, when their door was open, as she was coming up or down the stairs. They were all stacked in there: beds on top of beds, shelves on top of shelves, with pots and pans and clothes and shoes all mixed in. They had twin girls and an older boy; the girls would clod along in their brother's hand-me-downs, those thick-soled athletic shoes that look oversized even when they fit. She always knew when they were coming up the stairs, the clop-clop of their feet, and then, almost every time, one of the kids would either laugh or scream. A lot of nights, she'd hear them coming in from wherever it was they'd been, late for children, ten, eleven, sometimes later, and then the smells would waft up through the open windows, all sorts of spices she'd never even thought to dream of, curries and onions so thick her eyes would run. And Maya would lie on the floor of her apartment, which felt huge with the image of all those stacks inside her head. And she'd wonder how she could shape her face or hold herself in just the way that would get them to knock on her door and ask her to come fold in with them.

Even before the door opens, Maya is accosted by the smell of garlic, onions, and grilling meat. Caitlin grabs hold of Maya before she's fully through the door. She's lambent, *of fire*, Maya thinks, as Caitlin leans toward her, so fresh and full of life. She's begun to grow her hair out and has it pulled back with a neon scarf; large chunks fall around the scarf and stick to Caitlin's neck and ears, curling at the ends. Her full round cheeks are flushed and there's a film of sweat above her upper lip. She's always had a defiant sort of doughiness that has, while maintaining nearly all its substance, gotten somehow firmer in the months since Maya saw her last. Her breasts heave freely beneath a smocked beige linen dress with intricate dark green embroidery and her feet are bare, with matching green toenails.

The door opens into the kitchen. There are three pans working on the stove. Everywhere, the remnants of Caitlin's cooking sit: clear glass bowls coated with the last bits of spices and finely chopped cilantro, colorful plastic measuring spoons, onion and garlic skins, cutting boards, and knives still wet from work.

It's freezing outside, but warm in the apartment. The smallness of the space and with the oven and three burners going, Maya's quickly peeling off her coat. The bed's pushed against the wall between two tall windows. Maya can see the staggered lines of projects across the street along the river and a large covered-for-the-winter community pool. Caitlin has set up a card table beside the bed and surrounded it with a hodgepodge of chairs—one yellow and thinly stuffed, one folding, one simple straight-backed wood—and a wooden bench along one side. The bench's seat is covered with pillows from the bed that Caitlin's tied down with some silk ribbons that look as if they might also serve as belts. An old red sheet serves as the tablecloth. The walls are all the same thick beige paint of nearly every New York apartment that has seen too many occupants, layer after layer of not quite white that seems to come out from the walls and hang just over the moldings, threatening, at any moment, to come down in dusty, spackled chunks. There are crooked plywood built-in bookshelves and the books are doubled up, balancing precariously close to the edges; Maya stands near to one of the shelves and runs her hand along the spines. The apartment is hastily ordered, but the remnants of prolific mess remain. Maya can make out piles of clothes underneath the bedframe, maybe a bowl and at least one plastic water bottle, balls of dust still lurking in the corners of the room. Books are piled on the small table by the bed and on each windowsill, and on the desk piles of paper sit slightly askew.

"It's my first dinner party," says Caitlin, watching Maya's eyes scan the room and settle on the table, set for five: wine glasses and simple white flatware, a sweating-in-the-warm-air water pitcher, filled with a bottom layer of mint and fruit.

"I had to improvise," Caitlin says, motioning toward the table. She has a wooden spoon in her left hand and is sautéing kale with onions and garlic. A pile of steaks, left to rest and slathered in what looks like some kind of cilantro pesto, sits on the last bit of counter space.

Maya hands her the bottle of Sangiovese she's brought. Caitlin holds it a minute, then grabs a wine key and passes the bottle back to Maya. "Perfect," she says. "You want a glass?"

Maya tears the foil slowly. She turns the screw into the cork and pops it out. Caitlin passes her a glass and Maya's careful with her wrist, twirling the bottle up in order that no drops fall.

"Thanks," says Caitlin. She looks expectant, her eyes staying on Maya as she sips her first glass.

"How are you?" Maya asks.

Caitlin shrugs. "Okay," she says. She stops, as if the room, or something just outside the window, will tell her how she really is. "Good, I think," she says.

Maya smiles at her, watching her hands deftly work the spoon, then cover the steaks with a white dish towel while they rest. "How's the writing?" Maya asks.

Caitlin shakes her head, but there's a smile forming on her lips. "Okay," she says. "You know."

"I don't," says Maya. She can't imagine the courage it must take, stories all her own. "Tell me."

"Well, there've been some big life things happening," says Caitlin. Her palm rests on her stomach briefly as she says this. Maya wonders. There's no sign of a partner in the apartment. She's noticed that Caitlin has so far left her wine untouched.

"Of course," Maya says, excited suddenly. She lets herself imagine it a moment, a child forming inside Caitlin. A whole new life from scratch.

"I started tutoring a few months ago." She moves back and forth between the pans with her wooden spoon and stirs and flips. She turns back to Maya. "It's better, you know? I'm so happy to be teaching again."

Maya nods. "Of course." She sips her wine again and tries to make out Caitlin's shape beneath her dress.

"Even if it's mostly standardized tests."

"Can I do something?" Maya asks as Caitlin pours herself a glass of water. It would be too forward to tell her to sit down.

"No. No, tell me about you. How's school? How're Ben and Ellie?" Maya stops breathing a minute. She watches Caitlin's face to see if she knows.

"Well," she says, "Ben's in his second year, but he might . . ." She wonders where the rest of the guests are. If maybe it could just be the two of them. Maybe she could just sit here quietly and Caitlin could help her to make sense of everything. "He might take a semester to figure some things out."

Caitlin nods. "I wish I'd been smart enough to do that at that age."

Maya smiles. She's so glad to be with Caitlin now.

"And Ellie?" Maya's been quiet too long, she realizes. She looks out at the pool across the street, wants to ask Caitlin to promise to have her over to go swimming in the spring.

Another time: Caitlin had come crying to Maya's office after class, distraught. It was her second year. Maya thought school, at first, that she was overwhelmed suddenly by too much coursework. It was what she was meant to advise students on, but then they ended up dissolving over so much worse once she had them all alone. It turned out, with Caitlin, to be much messier than her middle-ages obligations. There was a boy, apparently, a man, as Caitlin said, but when Maya looked at any of them, mostly all she saw were boys. Caitlin said he was a friend in the department. She'd made advances. He'd snubbed her. "Never in my life," she said, "have I actually tried to act on something like this." She was twenty-four then, Maya knew. The idea that she'd never pursued a boy until then, it both shocked Maya and made perfect sense. And now this.

"He's my only friend here," Caitlin said. "He's allowing me to blame the alcohol, though I'd hardly had a beer. He's trying very hard to act as if we're all just fine being friends." She gave no names. There was another girl involved, a friend of Caitlin's, with whom she thought the boy might be in love. "Of course, she has no use for him," said Caitlin. "She has no idea."

She was one of the strongest students Maya had ever taught, the brightest. Maya wanted so much to scrape all of the hurt out of her life and tell her just to focus, to show her somehow that the only certain satisfaction would come from her own mind. She wanted her not to be felled by so predictable a situation, to be a little less just like every other girl. "I don't have anyone but the two of them," said Caitlin. *You have me*, thought Maya, but that was different. She was too far away, too old. She reached across her desk to grab hold of Caitlin's hand. "Honey," she said.

Maya could not remember now how she'd gotten to talking that day about Ellie, the drugs, the boys, the Trouble. It had felt like all that she could offer. She'd meant to make herself vulnerable somehow and maybe more available for Caitlin. She wanted Caitlin to see how lucky she was to know so clearly who she was. She hadn't meant for it to all feel so exploitative. This was her daughter, after all. But nothing that she seemed capable of giving Ellie then was helping; she thought at least she could help Caitlin. She'd gone into greater depth than she ever had about her daughter to anyone. She knew Caitlin would listen. She told herself she was showing Caitlin what a gift it was to be herself and know so much.

When she was done, though, she was no longer able to look directly at the girl in front of her. When she got home she didn't look Ellie in the face either. She'd used one to help the other. She was pretty sure that neither would turn out better as a result.

"She's . . ." Maya says to Caitlin, not sure, still, how to say what Ellie is. She can lie or she can tell her everything. She wonders how Caitlin will react, if she won't be surprised. She watches her, cooking, maybe starting to fill up with a child of her own, asking earnestly about this girl who was so rude to her. Maya takes the last sip of her wine and tells Caitlin everything.

Summer 2011

"The atmospheric conditions have to be conducive to formation, in this case, summer and warm water." This is not how five-year-olds should talk, but Jack's reading from Weather.com as rain comes down in torrents and bangs loudly on the tin roof of the house. He has his laptop on his lap and refuses to look up at her. "Instead of the visible compactness of the hurricane, the satellite view of the tropical depression can often just resemble a large group of thunderstorms. But rotation can usually be perceived when looking at a group of pictures from satellites." He has unlimited access to the Internet, and this is what he spends his time on. It's been raining the past three days, since two days after Ellie's arrival. It's a tropical depression. Annie has promised the end is close. "Wind speed up to thirty-nine miles an hour." She's also explained this is one of Jack's "things." He looks everything up and recites the facts he finds. It is, Annie says, "his way of trying to feel more in control of life."

"Any higher than thirty-nine the depression is upgraded to a tropical storm." He wears a hooded sweatshirt and purple shorts. He sits and scrolls, his feet up on the couch. He articulates his words very slowly and carefully. "Organized circulation and lower pressure are the first signs it has formed."

For the hundred millionth time since she got here, Ellie watches Jack and thinks about her mom. She's all over this place and worse than ever, because here is where Ellie's always loved her mother most.

Magic happened to her mom in Florida. She was this other, happier, steadier person, so different from the person she was in New York. She woke them early in the morning to go sailing or watch the waves break. She didn't mind that their dad often didn't come with them. She cooked big elaborate breakfasts. Breakfast was the only meal that she could cook. She let Ben and Ellie stay up late watching movies, though she hardly ever let them watch TV at home. After a long day at the beach and everyone freshly showered, they'd all sit together, ordering a pizza and dozing through the sun-drenched afternoon.

One summer: Ben was six and El was eight; storms threatened often, hurricanes, tornadoes, big whirling masses of green and gray and orange coming at them on the TV screen. They seldom actually hit. Ellie learned then about low- and high-pressure systems, the eyes and tails of storms. Each time Ellie worried, and her mom stocked them up on water and canned foods and filled the bathtubs. Each time, she had some guy from down the road come and help her put up shutters. Usually their dad wasn't there. This time they'd already heard the storm was missing them. Ellie sat close to her mom, and Ben was out back somewhere kicking around a ball, though it was dark and the ground was still soaking wet from that afternoon's rain. The guy on the TV said the storm had turned within hours of the eye hitting, and Ellie's mom explained to her again how the eye was the still and quiet that sat right in the center of the worst part of the storm. They sat and Ellie watched her mom's breathing, slow again, as she wrapped a sweater around her chest and legs.

And then the switch that happened sometimes in her mother. She was strong again, and looked over at El and smiled. "You want to see something amazing?" her mom asked. Ellie could never in her life say no to the face her mom made then. She called to Ben out in the back and he came running. He was flushed and asked if they knew if the storm was going to come.

"Missed us," said their mom. And she shook her head at Ben for asking with so much excitement. She found it wonderful, El knew, nearly everything her brother was. "Let's go out," her mother said.

Ben looked at Ellie, then back at their mother. Ellie smiled at him. If Mom wanted to go out, they would. They packed into the rental—their mom always splurged on a convertible on the trips when their dad didn't come. She rolled down the top even though the clouds were out and the wind was blowing, even though it was already very dark. Almost immediately Ellie worried her mom would be too cold with the top down. But she was smiling. Her hair was long then, and though she mostly wore it up, that night it was down and twisted in the wind.

El sat up front and Ben got in back without anyone asking. When it was the two of them with their dad, it was the other way around. Their mom turned on her music, Jackson Browne this time, whom Ellie knew by the way her mom's neck curved and softened as she sang along. They drove the six or seven minutes to the water. Ellie watched her mom, her hand over the side of the car and hanging, her sunglasses on her head to keep her hair from getting in her face. They crossed a bridge to get out to the ocean, and Ellie watched the chop of water underneath them, thick and frothy, rock the boats both moored and docked.

They parked and walked barefoot over the boardwalk and out onto the sand. The beach was empty of people, but it was a mess of stuff left over. The storm had come close enough that the tides had risen, dumping all sorts of debris out on the beach. Mounds of seaweed—it looked living—glistened in the dark. The sand was wet even far up by the boardwalk, and her mom pointed out the lines on the wooden poles where the water had reached. Ellie touched the line along one of the poles—it hit just above her head—the wood still wet and dark and slick. The ocean, though, was quiet now. It came in small rolls, trickles of black and gray, to shore.

Ellie's mom wore shorts and one of their dad's sweaters. She walked on tiptoes, long freckled legs. Her messy hair hung dark down her back. Her eyes were big and *searching*. Ellie loved them best when they found her. Her mom caught them both, Ellie and Ben, within her vision. She grinned. She walked closer to the water and stood a minute, letting the trickles splash over her feet. She nodded toward Ben and Ellie. They both followed, though Ben wandered quickly farther out. Her mom took Ellie's hand and leaned down a foot or two from the shore break. Carefully, her sweater open and her hair fallen forward, she knelt, her shin and then her knee covered in sand. She picked up a mound of seaweed and held it in her hand. Her eyes up again, she shook her head and blew her hair out of her face, holding Ellie close.

"Come here, Benny," she said. He stopped a minute, then came toward them. He'd gone in past his waist, his shorts and shirt now soaking wet.

Ellie smelled the seaweed that her mother held and wanted to ask if they could take it home.

"Watch," their mom said, once Ben was beside her. She whispered. And Ben and Ellie leaned in very close.

Ellie's mother shook the seaweed. It was dark brown and black, wet and shining. As it shook, Ellie got drops of salt water on her face and in her eyes. She watched Ben pinch his eyes shut and his lips puckered. It was there, though, when Ellie looked back down at the plant. Light, like a hundred tiny Christmas tree bulbs popping up out of it. *Alive*, thought El, and stopped breathing as she watched.

Ellie feels Annie somewhere close but doesn't turn to find her. Either Jeff or Annie is always there somewhere when she's with Jack. She wonders if they'll ever trust her to be with him without them. It's July and the sort of hot that Ellie had forgotten. She'd been so looking forward to the swimming; but all this time inside these past few days has begun to wear on her. She's getting itchy, anxious, crazy. They keep all the doors open and she can feel his parents listening as she plods through her first attempts with Jack. She asks awkward unsure questions. And Jack is on and on with this stuff he finds on the Internet.

As welcoming as he was the first day, he seems to be pulling away from her instead of opening up. Annie has mentioned something about separation issues. Ellie's not sure what this means. He always knows where his parents are, and the farther they are, the less likely he is to speak to Ellie. He likes bugs and she's never been squeamish. She felt him suppress a smile her first full day, when she asked to hold one of the scorpions. He has two iguanas, countless lizards, an ant farm, and an assortment of spiders and beetles he's caught himself and placed in jars. He has a small Jack-sized table set up in the corner where he dissects the ones that he finds already dead.

He leaves the computer now and goes back to his bugs, administering to each of them in some five-year-old version of efficiency, opening cages and jars, changing water pans and dropping food. Ellie flips through a book of stories that her mother sent down with her. Deborah Eisenberg. Her mom marked a story called "Rosie Gets a Soul." Rosie, of course, is an addict, but Ellie's read the whole thing since she got here. Against her will, certain bits of it—*she's had her hands full just standing upright. Just trying to work up some traction. Just dealing with the fact of herself, which pops up in front of her every day when she awakes, like some doltish puppet. So certain other worrisome items have slid off the agenda*—have lodged themselves inside her brain.

"We should go somewhere," she says to Jack.

He looks up at her, suspicious. She wonders if he can tell somehow what she's thinking. "Annie," she calls loudly, pretending that she doesn't know how close she is. Annie comes to the entrance to Jack's room.

"What's up?"

"I think we need to get out of here."

Annie holds the doorframe hard with her right hand and grabs hold of a wisp of hair come loose from her ponytail with her left.

"Sure," she says.

Ellie has briefly lost her confidence, but she keeps talking. Either she'll take Jack or she'll go alone, but she has to get out.

"What do you think, Jack?" Annie asks.

He seems nervous. He has a beetle crawling over his hand and up onto his forearm. He places it carefully back in its jar and walks toward his mom. "We all go?"

Annie looks down at her watch. "I have to go in to work soon, baby." She and Jeff usually pass the baton of watching Ellie watch Jack. Jeff comes home at three-fifteen and Annie leaves about twenty minutes after. She whispers something to Jack that Ellie strains to hear.

"Why don't the two of you go?" She nods down at the book that Ellie's been lugging around. "Why not Barnes & Noble? It's close and you can get another book."

"Me too?" Jack says. He has shelves across one wall of his room with the usual children's picture books as well as piles and piles of species catalogues for all the bugs.

"If you're very good," his mom says.

She turns to Ellie, fishes twenty dollars from her pocket. "Only one," she says to both of them. "And only if you're nice to Ellie the whole time."

The rain still comes down hard and Ellie can't remember the last time she's driven. She only got her license so she could drive when they're down here. The wipers swish one-two as the water rushes to fill the windshield, and there are a couple seconds each time when Ellie can't see the road at all. They have Jeffrey's old Bronco. Ellie thinks she might smell weed, something smoky and illicit settled deep in the canvas seats. She thinks maybe when they get back, once Annie and Jack and Jeffrey are all safely in bed, she could search underneath the seats for some remnants. She wouldn't smoke it. She just wants to know what's available in case.

"You okay?" Ellie says, catching Jack's eye in the rearview mirror. But Jack just looks down at the book he's brought and doesn't speak. He's strapped into his booster and looks taller than he is.

She lets him go in front of her when they get there. She's forgotten an umbrella and they run through the parking lot, Jack jumping through two massive puddles, water splashing up into Ellie's face and covering Jack's shorts, splattering the back of his shirt as they head toward the double doors. He seems so sure—

so much surer than she's ever been—she doesn't think twice about letting him off alone. She heads to the literature section and searches for more Deborah Eisenberg. The book she has is the only one they carry, and she wanders farther through the alphabet, coming to Woolf. She opens *To The Lighthouse*. Her mother never leaves the house without this book, a book Ellie's never read. She opens to a random page and begins reading. For a while, she sinks down deep:

They both smiled, standing there. They both felt a common hilarity, excited by the moving waves; and then by the swift cutting race of a sailing boat, which, having sliced a curve in the bay, stopped; shivered; let its sails drop down; and then, with a natural instinct to complete the picture, after this swift movement, both of them looked at the dunes far away, and instead of merriment felt come over them some sadness—because the thing was completed partly, and partly because distant views seem to outlast a million years (Lily thought) the gazer and to be communing already with a sky which beholds an earth entirely at rest.

She reaches for her cell phone in her pocket. She almost calls her mom. She wants to read this paragraph out loud to her. Her mom probably has it memorized, but she thinks maybe if Ellie calls to give it to her, it will be something both of them can keep.

She's forgotten Jack until she remembers. It's been half an hour. Briefly, on and off until she finds him, she feels a rush of tight hot panic through her shoulders, straight up to her teeth. But then he's there in front of her. He's cross-legged on the floor in the

Science section, immersed in a book on scorpions. "You know, there's a scorpion in Laos—my mom's been there—it's called the *Heterometrus laoticus*. It's black in the daylight, but it glows blue under UV light." Ellie nods. She's so relieved to see him, she's almost interested in whatever it is he's babbling about. "Scientists don't know if it's sun protection or if it's meant to alert them if the night's too bright for them to go out without being eaten by some predator."

"Sure," Ellie says. She's still thinking about the Woolf, her mom; her mind catches on the words *night* and *predator*.

"Come on." She's still holding the Woolf until she realizes she doesn't have the money to pay for it. She has a credit card her mom gave her for emergencies and she fingers it inside her wallet, deciding if this counts. "We have to go."

He seems surprised that she's still standing there. He piles four books into his arms and stands. "I need all of these."

Ellie still has the credit card between her fingers and thinks a minute that she should get them all for him, that maybe he'll like her if she does. "No," she says.

She puts down the Woolf. She'll come back and get it with the money she's meant to get from Jeff and Annie. She kneels close to Jack. "Pick one, okay?"

He clutches the stack to his chest and glares at her. His shoes don't match. They're those rubber clog things with little buttons stuck into them. One of them is green and one of them is blue.

"No," he says.

It's quiet at first, like he's trying it out. Ellie stands up and tries to take the books from Jack.

"No," he says again.

"Please, Jack," she says. This isn't right, she thinks. She shouldn't plead with him. She reaches for the books again and he runs from her, squeals. "Noooo!" he yells as he bolts for the front door. They're in a massive concrete shopping center and just outside is a broad expanse of parking lot, beyond which is a major road. Ellie's quick behind him and grabs him up into her arms right before he's out the door, but Jack is yelling now and she's not sure what to do. He's strong and heavier than he looked running in front of her; she's afraid suddenly she'll drop him on the tile floor. People stare from all sides of the store and Ellie almost starts to cry, she's so afraid of what might happen. "Please," she whispers now, as if the people will stop staring. Jack screams and she keeps hold of him so he doesn't make it out the door. "Please," she says again. He's lost a clog in their scuffle and all the books have fallen. "We'll get the books," says Ellie. "Please."

Winter 2013

The buzzer buzzes and Maya starts and almost drops her wine glass. She's been crying. Caitlin hands her a paper towel and holds Maya's arm up by her shoulder, briefly, before turning to buzz in whoever has arrived. Maya's heart beats too quickly. She clutches her glass, which she has refilled once while telling Caitlin what her daughter's done. "Sorry," she says. She shakes her head and fixes her eyes on Caitlin's green toenails.

Caitlin's been an intent, quiet listener. She shakes her head and grabs hold of Maya once more before she reaches for the door. "It's fine, Maya," she says. "You know that."

Maya hardly has time to mourn the loss of this closeness before the first of the other guests arrive. It's a man and woman. Bryant, Caitlin calls him. She hugs him big, then is very delicate with the woman, kissing her, her hand up on her shoulder, then helping her take off her coat. The man—Maya guesses very quickly that they're married, there are simple gold bands on both, he's slow to get even a few steps from the woman—watches, ready, it seems, to swoop in if Caitlin fails at retrieving her coat. And underneath the coat is what he also must be so diligently protecting; large stretches of brown cotton are wrapped tightly over the woman's shoulders and around her waist. Maya glimpses just a patch of newborn baby head peeking out from against the woman's chest.

Caitlin breathes in the minute that she catches sight of the tiny child. She holds her fingers to her lips, then reaches for the baby without touching her. She puts her arms around the woman, careful to stay clear of the tiny head. "Lana," she says to the woman. She leans in once more very close to the baby, then smiles back up toward her friend. She whispers, "You made this."

She leads her to Maya. "Alana." She nods toward Maya. "Maya." Alana smiles. "And Vivian," she says, nodding toward the newborn head. Alana's very tall and her eyes are round and large and dark and her nose has a bump up top, then curves in. She has a wide mouth and long hair, thick and wavy, that reaches below the child on either side.

"No one looks like this after having a baby," Caitlin says. She's back at the stove and transferring the kale to a serving plate, stirring the quinoa. She waves the spoon at Alana as if measuring her, then steps toward her once more and holds her face, kissing her once and then a second time on each cheek.

Alana's husband is close behind her and offers up his hand to Maya. "We've heard so much," he says and smiles. Up close Maya sees how much older he is than his wife: fifty, at least, to her maybe twenty-five. The girl seems suddenly impossibly young to have a person to take care of. The man rests the hand he has not offered to Maya on the small of his wife's back. "Bryant," he says.

Caitlin's back's to them. "He teaches too," she says.

Maya finds her wine again. She takes very small sips, feeling the first rush of warmth of excess spread through her as she does.

But she feels too unmoored by the prospect of having nothing to do with her hands to put the glass down. "What do you teach?" she says.

"Writing." He nods toward Alana. "Both of us."

"They're both novelists," Caitlin interjects, taking hold of Alana's arm and smiling up at her. The girl looks down and brushes her nose along her baby's head.

"How old?" says Maya, facing Alana. And then she's still a moment, hoping it's clear she meant the child.

"Seven and a half weeks," Alana says.

"My God," Maya says. "Just cooked." She tries to smile at the girl.

Maya eyes Caitlin again and wonders if this is all a party to prepare everyone for Caitlin's own revelation. She wonders what part Maya might be allowed to play. Perhaps, if there is no father, she could play the role of partner. She imagines the possibility of getting to make all those choices all over, to do it equipped with the knowledge she has now, twice over. She could scour the apartment, change the diapers. She could hold the baby very tight up on her chest and let it sleep.

The door opens behind them. "Someone let me in." The voice is familiar. Maya turns. She almost drops her wine glass: Charles. Caitlin seems to hesitate before deciding how to greet him. She reaches her hand up to his shoulder, but he loops his arm around her waist and hugs her close.

"Hi," Caitlin says, a little breathless, Charles's arms still around her waist.

Maya averts her eyes, her whole head turning toward the window, as Charles frees himself from Caitlin and catches sight of her.

"Hi." his voice is very close, and when she looks back he's right in front of her. Alana and Bryant have slipped past her to the bed.

Charles looks back at Caitlin. "You didn't tell me . . ."

Caitlin shrugs, blushing slightly. "It's not your party."

They're friends, Maya sees, of course. They're close. Perhaps what might be inside of Caitlin belongs to Charles. He stands a minute, quiet. He finally leans in close to her, his arms stick straight, and brushes her cheek with his.

"It's really wonderful to see you," he says. He smells exactly like he tasted when they kissed.

"You too," Maya says.

Charles's eyes stay on her a moment longer.

"Hey, you." It's Alana behind her. "Come meet her."

Charles looks at Maya one last time.

"Baby," whispers Charles, taking three big steps, then leaning in to see the child. He's awkward with Bryant. He shakes his hand brusquely, his eyes already stuck on the infant. He sidles up close to Alana on the bed and peers in at the baby. "She's wonderful," he says.

Alana grabs hold of his arm. "I know," she says.

Charles grins and leans in once more and nuzzles the top of the baby's head.

Maya wants to stand next to him and do the same. She can nearly conjure it standing here: that baby feel and smell, the weight of it against her. She wonders if later she could ask to hold her. She wants to settle her, feet curled up underneath, breathing quickly, onto her chest.

Maya has no idea why she's so sure. The proximity of this other just-formed baby, the sheen of Caitlin's skin. Her hair is thick like it gets in those months when the body's so slow to let go of things, keeping everything just in case. She wonders again who the father is, but only briefly. Perhaps Caitlin's gotten one of those procedures where the father is never a person. In many ways this would be easiest. Or he was a one-night stand. She looks around the room. She can't imagine Bryant has offered his sperm so freely. That leaves only Charles. She breathes in quickly, then thinks it couldn't possibly be. Charles catches her eye and she feels her face get warm.

They all settle in their chairs. Caitlin's just finished grilling the steaks and the air's still filled with the smell and smoke of it as she comes to pass around the salad. Pomegranates and large chunks of avocado, crumbled walnuts, a homemade vinaigrette. Maya cuts her lettuce into tiny pieces. She has a small mouth, a tendency to get food stuck around its edges. She's self-conscious like she hasn't been in years. She feels Caitlin's eyes on her and looks up, smiling. She drops her fork, picks up her wine glass, and nods at Caitlin, who grins, shoveling a large piece of avocado into her mouth.

Bryant holds the baby, who has begun to stir again but seems content once repositioned, and Alana sits back, weightless suddenly. Maya watches Alana watching Charles. She's very still and seems to be willing him to look at her again as her husband caters to their baby. She twists her hair around her hand and knots it on top of her head. It stays that way only a few seconds, then slowly, over the next few minutes, loosens and unfurls itself, finally falling down her back in heavy clumps.

Maya turns toward Bryant. He's settled into the chair next to her and he's still careful, a little awkward, cradling the girl.

"How is it so far?" Maya asks. She nods toward the child.

She realizes she's whispering. "You know," he says. The baby squirms and she watches Bryant try to keep her steady. Her eyes are open, big and blue, long lashes. For a moment Maya doesn't envy them the years ahead. "All the adjectives are shit in trying to describe it," he says. "My wife has become this other person. I sleep a little and she doesn't sleep at all." He's old, Maya thinks, older than Maya, and he's starting this. He looks as if he's lived as much life as his years suggest, if not more. But he has somehow just now discovered there's something to be made here. He's like a person who's been trapped inside a darkened room and not allowed to interact with others, now suddenly trying to live in the world, to help to teach someone else. "Every second," he says, "is consumed by this thing that really contributes nothing to the conversation. And yet, when I really look at her, I think, how did I live so long without her? And I mind much less how long the days feel."

Maya nods. She's not sure how to hold it, this rush of honesty. Slowly, having to look down at her plate a moment, she takes a bite of food and grabs hold of her glass. She'd expected him to say, *Wonderful, amazing.* She says: "That sounds about right."

Maya nods toward Alana. "She seems wonderful with her."

He's emphatic now, comes outside himself. "Unquestionably," he says.

"Have you two been married long?"

He shakes his head. "Four months," he says.

Maya watches the baby's eyes as cars pass by the window: her gaze follows the shadows they make along the wall.

"I was a mess before I met her," Bryant says. "I know I'm too old for such things, but I've always been a mess. It took me this long. Or maybe it took all of this happening." He looks, careful, down at the baby as he whispers this. "It's cleared me up, I guess," he says. "Lana." He's talking to himself now. Maya watches Charles in the corner, where he's followed Alana. They talk quietly. She's tying her hair up again; he's wiping his glasses with his shirt. Caitlin lays out the steaks on a fresh plate and sets them on the table. "All this," Bryant says.

She and Caitlin could be like these two: this new life, this new baby, it could clear her up. But then the baby would get older. She would resent them, hate them. She would have too many questions about what happened to her dad. There would be hell to pay for all the thousand million things that they did wrong as she grew and formed before them. But, Maya thinks, even with all of it coming out terribly, she'd be willing to do it over. Maybe so things would turn out differently. But also, only for the in-between time, the brilliant promise of incompleteness, that smell, that warmth, that soft, soft skin up close.

They pass around the steaks and the quinoa. Alana and Charles sit down again. Caitlin stands up. Charles tings his wine glass. Whatever is about to be announced, he already knows. Maya feels briefly nauseous. She might be losing him as well.

Maya only realizes it seconds before Caitlin starts speaking— Caitlin's had a glass of wine now, she's yet to place her hand on her abdomen again—how wrong she's been. And she feels her body fold in on itself as if she's been exposed. As if all of them see and know the fantasy she's been quietly entertaining as they've talked and eaten: Caitlin isn't pregnant. There will be no starting over here.

"Book," Maya hears, and she has to play back in her head what's just happened. She registers through the reactions of those around her: Charles is standing. Alana keeps her eyes toward her plate. Bryant offers his hand awkwardly to Caitlin, his back tall and firm, brushing past his wife as he stands. Maya realizes Caitlin's the only woman Bryant has failed all night to address. A book. Maya listens intently to the murmurings, the exclamations; Charles catches Maya's eye again and says, while still holding her,

"Caitlin, this is wonderful!" Caitlin demurs, then reaches toward Charles before seeming to forget what she meant to do once she had hold of him; she sits back down in her chair instead.

"It really isn't much money," Caitlin says. "And, you know, it could turn out to be nothing."

Alana has not stopped staring at her hands in too long. Bryant shakes his head, his shoulder turned toward his wife. "This is an accomplishment," he says steadily. His words are whole objects that he's handing carefully to Caitlin. He's not seemed such a sturdy presence all night. Caitlin flattens her napkin back across her lap.

"Thank you," she says. Just as sturdy, just as firm.

Maya feels small and impossibly matronly. She gets up to hug Caitlin. She's tearing up, though she can't tell why. "Oh, honey," she says. "Honey, this is wonderful." She buries her head a moment too long in the soft warmth and curve of Caitlin's shoulder, the embroidery of Caitlin's dress rough against Maya's skin. She thinks of the baby they have lost one more time, then pulls away, puts a knuckle to the corner of each of her eyes, and sits.

Summer 2011

"The kid hates me," she says. It was another twenty minutes getting him strapped into the car and back to Annie's. Ellie's not sure how she made it back without driving into another car. She'd tensed up, hunched over the steering wheel. He'd screamed the whole way until they were back in the house and he very quietly and smugly crawled into his mother's lap. The rest of the night she couldn't look at him. His eyes were red and swollen and each time she got too close to him she felt chastened, wrong.

"He's a kid, El." She wishes her brother were here instead of at his stupid college. Jack would love Ben. Jack might love anyone but her.

"He's not, though. He's smarter than me and he hates me. And all he wants is for me to take him back to his mom and dad."

"You just have to give him things they can't give him. Take him out. Have fun with him."

"Oh, please, Benny. He's not fun. He's a spoiled little brat."

"Does he like to swim?"

"It's been raining. We've been trapped inside."

"That's not his fault. He's a kid, El. He's probably going nuts."

"I'm going nuts."

She listens to her brother's drawn-out sigh. He sounds like her mom when he does this. "Just be good, El. You need to make this work, okay? Somehow. Okay. Just make this work."

"What did she say?"

"Nothing, El. She's just exhausted, I think."

"Just tired of me."

"Tired of worrying about you."

"Right."

Four years before: Ellie walked from the Lower East Side over the Brooklyn Bridge and to the park to watch her brother play soccer. Dylan was pissed. She'd taken both the pills he'd bought, when they'd agreed that they would share.

"Selfish bitch," he'd called her.

She'd flipped him off. Her arm felt heavy and she'd only lifted it halfway as her middle finger rose toward him. "Fuck you," she'd mumbled back. She left her backpack and her phone and walked the six miles, three hours, to her brother's game.

She saw Ben light up when he saw her. She thought he did, then wondered if it was the drugs mixed up with her joy in seeing him. "Benny," she said, suddenly breathless. Though he was across the field and only smiled and waved.

Her mom was there as well, right by the benches where the team sat. She'd supplied the snacks that week and was collecting granola wrappers as the boys tightened the laces of their cleats, their backs all rounded in a row. Ellie waved to her mom, but stayed far away. She lay down on the grass and felt the prickle of it and the dampness. A couple people turned from the game to watch. The high was drifting slowly from her, but she held tight to it and breathed in and out, marveling at the sweetness of the air.

She turned over on her stomach. She placed her elbows deep into the dirt and kicked up her feet. A whistle blew. It screeched between her ears and she buried her head more deeply in the grass. She got soil, rich, dark-smelling, on her lips and in her nose. And then her brother, running up closer, on the right side of the field. The whistle blew again. The ball was kicked from center field. There was a thwack. And then Ben ran toward it, feet pounding against dirt and grass, legs like long, sinewed sculptures, still-twiggy stretched-out graceful arms.

He came upon the ball, no one close to him, and made easy careful contact. Black white black white black white. She wished that she could hold tight to her brother's ankle and ride along with him as he ran.

"Benny," she said again.

She looked over at her mother, who was trying to focus on the game, but her eyes kept wandering to Ellie across the packs of boys in white and blue. Ellie waved to her, smiling. She turned over on her back again and listened to the cheering of the smattering of parents as her brother scored.

Her whole body felt heavy. The walk had been exhausting. She usually liked to lie and stare, walk slowly, watching lights, when she was stoned. And now she was paying for the extreme exertion of her walk. She thought she'd sleep forever, settle slowly into the damp grass.

There was a blank then. She heard pounding, feet against grass and ground, whistles blowing, boys yelling to one another,

her brother's name, she thought, more than once. She held the grass and smelled it. She slept and drifted in and out.

"El," she heard. The game was over; she saw feet walk past her, sandals, sneakers, a pair of large black steel toes with matching heels. She saw her brother's cleats and the socks that reached up high to cover his shin guards. They were royal blue with a bright white stripe around the top. She wanted to touch the hairs popping up over the socks with the bottom of her chin and then her cheeks and then her forehead. She wanted to burrow her head back in the grass and go to sleep.

She felt a little nauseous, bleary. "Yeah," she said.

"Elinor," said her mother. She leaned over and pulled Ellie up by her arm.

Ellie stared at her. She felt a blank space where the words to answer might have come from.

"Hey," she said.

"What's wrong with you?" her mother hissed, half worried, half angry, all not sure what to do.

"Nothing," Ellie said. She turned to Ben. "You win?"

"Yeah," he said. His voice was quiet.

Maybe she'd ask him to carry her home, to let her climb up onto his back and wrap her arms over his shoulders, to lay her whole self against him and rest. "Congrats," she said.

Her mother shook her head. She handed the cooler of snacks to Ben, who repositioned his soccer bag across his chest, over one shoulder, and took the cooler with both hands. The last bits of ice and water swished and clunked inside.

Her mom took hold of Ellie. She brought her face up close. "What's *wrong* with you?" she said.

Mommy. She wanted to sit her down and crawl into her lap and never leave her. She wanted to tell her she was sorry for everything, sorry that she'd turned out to be the girl that she'd turned out to be.

"Nothing," said Ellie. It came out slower than the first time. She dragged out the vowels. It might have been the only word she knew.

"El, listen," her brother says. "Call her, okay? Call her and tell her everything is wonderful. Tell her the kid's a brat, but you're making it work. You're so happy to be near the water. Annie's great. Whatever. Just let her think that you're okay. And then just be okay, all right? You're a mile from the beach and all you have to do is play with a five-year-old all day. Life's just really not that hard. Just don't fuck this up."

Ellie's quiet, tearing a piece of paper into tiny thumb-sized pieces, then rolling them into tight balls with her fingers on her desk.

Ellie knows nearly from the beginning the mistake she's made, not knowing enough, pretending, flirting with the boy behind the desk in the collared shirt and hat, the sunglasses resting on its brim, with the red face and small flakes of skin peeling off his nose, so that he would let her take one of the sailboats out without his help. She has to sign a waiver and pretends she's Jack's mom, another thing the boy allows himself to be convinced is true. His eyes wander down Ellie, from her forehead to her feet. She wears cutoff shorts and a beige tank top. She has on her black bikini underneath. He says he'll take her through a quick refresher, but she doesn't want him to come with them. She thinks if she can show Jack this he'll warm to her, maybe, finally. If he likes her, it will prove something sure.

Ellie hasn't cleared this trip with Annie. It's only her third day alone with Jack. Annie's starting to get ready for the fall rush and Jeffrey's patients have begun to come back from their summer camps. The seasonals and tourists have begun to filter in. The only other time besides the bookstore, Jack alternated between silent petulance in his room with his bugs and asking to call his mother. But they've spent this morning discussing different sailing tactics. Jack has made a list about lines and gibes, sheets, mainsails, jibs, and tacks.

He lit up at the mention of their maybe going sailing. Ellie was trying to convince him of her knowledge, telling him stories of sailing with her mom when she was small. It's been years now, but she remembers the water in her eyes and the burn of lines between her fingers.

Jack's small arms quiver in her grasp as she slips the life jacket over his shoulders and snaps him in. "Nor?" he says.

"We're good," she says. "Don't worry." Without thinking, she kisses him—the first time that she's done this—on the top of his head. He smiles and Ellie feels that she's accomplished something great.

The sail flops as she uncovers it and pulls the lines. Her arms reach up, one and then the other, full fists pulling down, old metal ratcheting up and up, as sweat trickles slowly between her shoulder blades. The sail jerks into place and fills a moment with a rush of wind; Jack sits quietly near the boat's front, hands holding both sides of his life jacket, his eyes steady on the sail. The red-faced boy comes out, hat off and sunglasses pulled down, and helps to push them from the dock. Ellie holds the tiller straight and then slowly turns it—the weight of it sluicing through the water is exactly as it was when she was small.

They drift slowly from the dock out toward the channel. They tack once, and though it's certainly imperfect, and Jack squeals in fear as the boat dips and lifts, they right themselves and his knuckles eventually hold less tightly to his side of the boat. For a second, Ellie feels full with her own competence. A gust hits them once and the boat dips, water splashing at them, and Jack's body lurches forward, his face almost falling on the metal wheel that controls the centerboard. But Ellie stays steady, loosening the sail until it luffs and the boat sits flat again. Her forearms and her hands burn with the weight of holding the tiller and the sail.

Usually, her mom would steer. Her mom would hold the mainsail too and El and Ben would split turns loosening and pulling in the jib. But she's settled into the feel of both the line that tightens the mainsail and the tiller working in her hands at the same time. It's almost less frightening, being in control. She smiles over at Jack, as he seems to settle in his seat, watching the thin red telltales fly back straight against the sail.

They hit a little enclave on the other side of the inlet; the wind is light and they practice turning, catching puffs of wind and moving swiftly for small stretches, then letting the sail luff again and trailing their hands in the water as they drift. Jack begins to shout instructions to her as she lets the wind catch in the sail again. They've been researching all morning, and he remembers all the proper terms. She calls out to warn him each time she tacks. He calls back in response. She lets him hold the tiller briefly, then they watch together as the sail fills and the boat heels hard with a strong puff that Ellie's seen headed toward them, picking up speed, Jack holding tight to her.

She's sitting lower in the boat to keep one hand on Jack but she can't see as well as if she were sitting on the rail. They slip into the channel. Ellie isn't practiced enough to keep an eye out for the powerboats. The wind fills the sail once more. The boat heels, dipping farther down than it has since they've been out together. A wave of water washes in the right side of the boat, and Jack's face transforms to shock as his lower half is drenched. Ellie stops, wanting to reach for him, wanting to pull the boat back flat, but not sure how. She grabs hold of the tiller, but she turns too quickly and another puff fills the sail before she's able to loosen it. The boat dips hard and suddenly, its edge nearly going underwater, and Ellie watches, too afraid to move, as Jack tips out of the boat.

Ellie dives in after him and the boat falls behind her, the sail slapping hard against the water, then filling slowly and dipping down. She keeps her eyes on Jack. She's only under for a minute. She opens her eyes wide—they sting—and there he is, the bright yellow of his life jacket bobbing a few feet from where she is; Ellie scoops Jack into her arms. He isn't frantic; he looks confused and scared, but too surprised to have reacted yet. They're in the channel and there are boats coming at them from both sides and Ellie waves, screaming loudly to be sure the people in the boats see them, and finally, bobbing up above the water, Ellie keeping hold of him, Jack begins to cry.

Winter 2013

Things devolve quickly after Caitlin's pronounce-
ment. Maya watches as her food seems to age years
over a period of minutes, wilting and congealing, looking suddenly inedible, when just an hour before it had seemed the most
nourishing assortment that she'd ever seen. No one's touched
their plate now for a while. Maya gets up and attempts to clear
the table before Caitlin tries to stop her. And though Caitlin
motions effusively and begs a couple times for Maya to stop, she
finally acquiesces and Maya has a brief respite, washing and drying dishes, putting away the pots and dishware for which she can
find the proper place.

The conversation has fragmented. Charles sits close to Caitlin, on the edge of his chair, leaning toward her, his legs crossed.
The color rises in Caitlin's cheeks and she looks impossibly
young, lovely, even. Her eyes look larger with her hair pulled
off her face and she smiles easily, not thinking about the shape
her face is making, not considering the things she says before

she speaks. Alana has moved to the bed again to feed the child. Maya, holding a rag and a large green pot, watches as Alana cups her breast with her right hand, and cradles the child in the crook of her left arm. Vivian has a dark shock of hair and wears a yellow purple-polka-dotted onesie. Her hand is wrapped around her mother's pinkie as she nuzzles into her and latches on.

Bryant sits back in his chair and sips the scotch he brought. A book, Maya thinks, a book. It's more than a child because it might outlive one, because it will stay still once it's out in the world. But then the book has no chance to ever be anything other than the thing it is right now.

"You didn't have to do this." Caitlin spreads both her arms, smiling. She's close to Maya, suddenly, and Maya starts, setting down the pot.

"I wanted to," Maya says.

"Well . . ." Caitlin looks down. She takes the pot and places it on top of the refrigerator. "Not much room," she says.

"I didn't know you and Charles were so close," Maya says. This is wrong. Not what she meant to talk about. Caitlin's hair has wilted and a sweat-wet chunk of it sticks to the right side of her face.

Caitlin stands very close to Maya. She's picked up the dishrag and starts drying as Maya washes the last dishes from the sink. Their fingers touch as Maya passes her a white ceramic plate.

"I was sort of in love with him awhile," Caitlin says.

Maya pulls a pan from the stove and lets the water scald her as she scrubs. She remembers the day in her office, Caitlin's unraveling, all the tears, the way that Maya'd talked and talked to calm her down.

"I was in love with an idea of him that's probably not real."

"You dated?" Maya wonders how this sounds. She thinks she feels Caitlin harden at the shape of Maya's words.

"No. No," Caitlin says.

The man she'd spoken of then had been tactful in his disinterest. Caitlin had felt worse, in fact, she'd told Maya, for the delicacy with which he'd declined. Maya watches the thickness of Caitlin's ankles underneath her smock dress, the awkward way her shoulders slump as she curves her toweled hand around a pan.

"I'm more of an admire-boys-from-afar, live-life-vicariously-through-books-and-other-people kind of girl anyway," Caitlin says.

Maya smiles. She wants to take care of her again, to hold her close, to straighten her shoulders and wipe the hair out of her face.

Caitlin shakes her head. "We're better as friends."

Maya's quiet, grabs another dirty dish. It's possible that Caitlin doesn't remember that day, could hardly recall all the things they've shared.

"I've been making people up my whole life," says Caitlin. She smiles this smile Maya thinks of as specifically hers. Caitlin's cheeks rise in gorgeous mounds as her lips turn up. She's put on mascara for the occasion—it's clumped into the corners of her eyes, and there's a faint smudge of black on her left cheek, her whole face damp from sweat. Maya wants to wet her thumb under the sink and brush her fingers over Caitlin's face. She runs her hands over her own face instead and loosens her hair from its clip. She pulls it back tight against her head and higher, and tries not to glance back at Charles, who, she knows, is watching them.

"Maya," says Caitlin. She grabs her arm, which surprises both of them.

Maya stays still, the sponge warm and wet in her hand.

"You should go to her," she says.

Maya's not sure whom she means at first. She backs away.

"You have to get her out," Caitlin says.

Maya turns briefly toward the sink and sets the sponge down. She's not used to this from anyone but Stephen. *Ellie*, she thinks, *Ellie*, like a shock straight through her brain. She looks down at Caitlin's toes; she nods.

"I'm sorry," Caitlin says. She crosses, then uncrosses her arms. "It's not my business," she says. "I'm sorry," she says again.

Maya still can't speak, grabs hold of the counter, finds her wine.

Caitlin shakes her head, maybe wanting to start over. "I wanted . . ." she says. "It was important to me."

"Honey," Maya interrupts her. She needs to take control again.

"It means a lot to me, you being here."

Caitlin grabs Maya again, this time with both hands, below the elbows, their faces very close. Maya squeezes back. They stand, not quite embracing, not quite willing to let go.

"I can't wait to read it, sweetie," Maya says. "I'm so very proud of you."

Summer 2011

It's a long time before Annie speaks to her. They've been home and both Jack and Ellie have showered. Ellie has stayed alone in her small room. She avoided looking at herself as she walked by the full-length mirror, put on long cotton pants and an oversized sweatshirt, though it's still a hundred degrees, thick and humid, just outside her room. She has sat quietly on her bed and tried to keep her mind from whirring. She's tried to read the book her mom sent, but then failed and stared up at the ceiling as she listened to Annie cook, Jeffrey come home. The hours pass in which they must eat, then put Jack to bed. No one comes to invite Ellie to join. She hears murmuring, loud for a minute, then quieter, then the whole world is silent for a long, long while.

Annie knocks on Ellie's door.

She looks like she's been crying. She's still wearing the crisp linen pants and silk shirt she wears when she goes into the restaurant, and Ellie feels useless and absurd, so small. She sits back in the corner of the bed. Annie sits across from her. She's brought her a plate of food, the fish and pasta Ellie'd listened to her cook. Ellie takes it and sets it down beside her on the bed. She says thank you and peels off a small piece of fish. Annie firms her lips.

"I lost him once," says Annie. Ellie looks down at her feet, where there are still grains of sand from when they sat out on the beach after they'd been brought to shore. She'd left her flip-flops on the boat. She and Jack drove home barefoot in bathing suits, with the towels wrapped around them that the boy with the hat and peeling nose had given them before he went out in a rubber-rimmed dinghy to try to save the boat. "I was at the grocery store and he was wandering behind me. You know how he gets distracted." She shakes her head. Ellie stays still. "I was alone with him all the time then." Her memory takes her far from Ellie now and Ellie doesn't mind it. "And it doesn't matter how much you love him, you know? He still drove me insane. It was one of those days, and I was counting the seconds till Jeff would be home to relieve me. I didn't even need anything at the grocery store, but I couldn't be alone with him anymore. And then all of a sudden he was gone, and I couldn't breathe, because it felt like I'd wished it, you know? I went to that kiosk thing and had them call for him. He was three and knew his name—he thought it was cool, being called over the loudspeaker—and we found him right away. But those seconds . . ." She looks up at Ellie then and Ellie leans away, startled to be sitting so close.

Ellie wraps her arms around her shoulders. She burrows her chin into her chest.

"I want us to be good for each other, Ellie," she says. She angles herself closer to Ellie and reaches toward her, her hand resting lightly on her knee. "I want this all to work."

Ellie wants to respond properly, to give her whatever it is she needs. She uncrosses her arms, then crosses them again.

"Listen," Annie says. She looks searchingly at Ellie, right in the eyes, and Ellie wonders if she's checking if she's stoned. "It's our fault." It takes Ellie a minute to realize the "our" isn't she and Annie. It isn't Ellie or her mom. "We kept him so isolated . . ." Ellie's slowly catching up with Annie, whose voice falls a little. Her hand stays on Ellie's knee. "I didn't think it mattered when he was really small. It might not have." She looks older, less sure. "There are probably plenty of kids who don't see other kids when they're little who acclimate fine to socializing later on. But he was brought up in the restaurant. It's the problem with having kids so late; it all feels so precious, you know? You've worked so hard for it. Even when I did just want a break, it felt ungrateful, spending any time away from him. I don't know how I expected preschool to go well. But you know." She stops a minute and takes her hand back. "You think just loving is enough no matter what. I thought my love had this sort of primacy over every other person's. But then all those kids I'd pitied when they were two in those carts they'd push around downtown with gaggles of little children, those kids just laughed that first morning I took him, and greeted one another happily, while Jack screamed and kicked and refused to let go of my shirt." As she says this she holds her shirt, which has come untucked near the bottom, rubbing her thumb along the edge. It's a thin, nearly translucent silk, light blue against the tan curve of her hand. "We thought that it'd get better. Lots of kids throw fits. But the kid has a will like nothing you've ever seen." She lets go of her shirt and grabs hold of her own knee, harder than she held Ellie's. "The first week we were back to get him every day before noon. And the worst part." Annie shakes her head. "It was only then I began to think of spending time with him as some kind of burden. Because I had made peace with him being away from me for a few hours every morning. And

then to not get that after all. I'd signed up for unlimited yoga."
She points her eyes to the floor. "I'd made plans to see friends I
hadn't spent more than an hour with in years. I didn't want to
give it up." She holds her hands, palms up, in front of her, then
sets them in her lap. "After two more weeks they recommended
we try to transition him more slowly. Jeff and I took turns shad-
owing him for a couple of weeks. But every time we tried to leave:
the same thing. And you know they tell you to let him just work
it out himself. That that's the best way." She looks up. She looks
past Ellie's right ear, at the wall behind the bed. "I could feel the
teacher's judgment from across the room every time I went to him
when he cried. But the idea that I could do something to stop it
and I didn't, I know it's not that simple but it felt that simple then.
Finally they told us either he would be placed in special ed until
they found a full-time aide or we'd have to find another place."
She stops a minute. She looks Ellie, briefly, in the face. "Jeff's a
therapist, you know? You think rational thought should get you
somewhere. We tried to talk to him about it, but my whole body
would tense up even thinking about the word *school*. We decided
to take another year and do homeschool. We had a woman come
three days a week, and one of us was always there. And he was a
dream as long as we didn't leave. I started to feel as if I would never
have a moment free again. The past four years began to fold in on
themselves and taunt me with all the things I hadn't been able to
do. We got him a therapist. Who gets a therapist for a four-year-
old? But the school recommended her. We stopped going when
she started trying to give us diagnoses. Spectrums, medications.
I wasn't ready yet to call him something other than himself. We
worked on smaller increments of separation. None of the help we
got ever lasted long. He'd throw the tantrums and they seemed
to be getting worse. By the end of the last school year, we couldn't

even do school at home anymore. I found someone on the Internet who said live-in help might be the best option. But the idea of a stranger in our house . . . I don't know. And your mom said you needed to get out of New York for a while. And I remembered you when you were little. You were such a perfect little kid, the way you always were with Benny. I thought maybe you and Jack could do each other good. He's wonderful, really. He just . . ." She holds her hands in front of her again, palms out, then holds them to her face. "We all have shit, right?" She speaks through the gaps between her fingers, then places them back on her lap. For the first time since she started speaking, she holds Ellie's gaze. "I know it doesn't feel like it, but he likes you," she says. "You understand him, I think. I think you might understand each other. This can be good for both of you."

Annie looks down at Ellie's half-eaten dinner. She nods toward the plate, looks up. "But Ellie," she says, "I am going to ask you to be careful."

Ellie picks up another piece of fish and slowly chews it. She wraps her arms around her shins and tries hard not to look away from Annie. If only she were someone else.

"I'm going to beg you to love my son as much as I do. I want you to know I trust you and I want you to be okay too."

Ellie wipes her nose with the sleeve of her sweatshirt. "I'm so sorry," she says. "I . . ." She wants to promise she'll be good.

Winter 2013

The new family has left them, the baby tucked back close to her mother, Bryant going dutifully behind. It's just Maya, Charles, and Caitlin, and no one seems sure of what to say next. Maya dumps her wine glass in the sink and grabs her coat. "I guess," she says.

Charles nods. "Yeah," he says, "me too."

Maya blanches, avoiding eye contact with Caitlin.

"Sure," Maya says. "Okay."

"Oh," Caitlin says. "You're sure?"

Charles holds her coat out for her. "I'll walk you," he says.

Maya grabs hold of Caitlin before her coat's back on. "Okay," she says, without looking at him, her head now safely nestled into Caitlin's neck.

"I didn't mean . . ." says Caitlin.

"I'm so proud of you," Maya says again.

Maya and Charles are just outside the apartment. It's dark out and music pulses from the buildings across the street.

"A book," Maya says. "It's wonderful."

She must clear her head of thoughts of Ellie. She walks quickly, snow crunching underneath her feet.

Charles nods, his hands dug into the pockets of his coat. "It is," he says.

"You knew already?"

"I had an idea."

"You two are close?" She watches the light in front of them change to green.

You have to go to her, she thinks.

She feels Charles nod next to her. "We're friends," he says.

They pass a small community garden; patches of snow spot the dirt on the other side of the chain-link fence. They're quiet awhile and Maya watches the packs of kids walking through Tompkins Square Park clutch their cigarettes with ungloved hands. She fixates on a small girl walking next to a thin boy, laughing, her fingertips are red and chapped, the nails bitten down.

"I used to live down here," she says.

"Really?" She thinks he looks skeptical, like maybe she's remembered wrong.

"Years ago," she says. She smiles briefly. The girl drops her cigarette and stamps it with the toe of her boot. "I wasn't always this old," Maya says.

He starts to correct her, but she holds up her hand.

"It wasn't this cool then."

"Right."

"It's like Disneyland." They're on Saint Marks and Third Avenue. Fluorescent lights and tattoo parlors, shops selling scarves and gloves and cheap jewelry jut out into the street, three designer yogurt shops within a single block. The smells are exhaust, falafel, and something curried, cigarettes every other breath. Beautiful young people, lithe limbs, firm everything, tourists clutching their maps and their bags. There are still the kids in ratty clothing, errant piercings, sitting with their backs against buildings, with their pit bulls and their dirty hair. But even they look like props now. Maya wouldn't be surprised to discover they take the subway home every night to Park Slope or Boerum Hill.

Maya rubs the nylon of her coat pocket between her thumb and forefinger as she burrows her hands in more deeply. A pack of laughing girls walks by; a couple leaning into one another almost bumps into Charles.

Ellie, Ellie, Ellie, Maya thinks.

"Auden," says Charles, nodding toward a brownstone to their left.

Maya turns to him.

"He lived there."

"Right," she says. She should be the one who knows.

"He had to walk to the liquor store across the street to pee."

He stands up straighter as he says this. He'll be a great teacher, she thinks again, the way his whole body changes as soon as he thinks he has something he might offer to someone else.

"The plumbing froze, and he had to walk across the street to use the toilet."

They pass the subway Maya would take to go back to Brooklyn. She has no idea where Charles lives. It seems they have agreed on something without agreeing to it. There's still the possibility to deny any agency in whatever they're about to do.

"He used to go to that church on Ninth Street," he says. "He gave the manuscript of *The Age of Anxiety* to a friend so he could sell it for an operation he couldn't afford."

"Nice guy," Maya says.

Charles smiles, turning toward her. "I've always thought."

They cross Broadway, still heading west, and Maya dips her chin to her chest as the wind picks up. Her shoulder brushes Charles's. The sidewalk gets more crowded, then thins out again; it's icy in places—she's drunker than she realized—and she almost grabs hold of Charles as her feet begin to slip.

Charles leads Maya into a bar off West Fourth. The streets no longer run in a grid, and West Fourth runs perpendicular to itself for a while.

"I forget how crooked everything gets down here," Maya says.

He settles a hand against her back.

"So that was . . ." She stops herself. "How do you all know each other?"

She doesn't want to talk about Caitlin. She wants even less to talk about herself.

"Caitlin, I guess," he says. "Though technically I met her through you." Maya stiffens, and Charles pulls his hand back as he pulls out a stool for her. They loosen limbs from coats and sidle onto their stools. Charles places his elbows on the bar. "Alana and Caitlin were in some writing group together when Caitlin first moved here. The three of us were inseparable for a while."

Maya thinks again about that day Caitlin cried to her. Alana: the other girl. "And then Bryant," she says.

He shakes his head. "I don't know." The bartender—thin, full beard, crooked posture, a blue T-shirt, and perfectly cut jeans—pours and delivers Charles's beer, then slides Maya her wine. "We were that sort of close that's not sustainable," he says, nodding thanks to the bartender. "And the strangeness of being three of any group of people; it was bound to get weird or messy if Bryant hadn't come along."

"Weird or messy how?" Maya says. She's asking too much.

"Oh, you know. Jealousy, maybe, or discomfort."

"But none of you dated?" She sees Alana again, those eyes, her height. Maya feels the heat rising to her cheeks.

"That's not the only kind of jealousy."

"Right," she says. "Of course."

"But Bryant."

Maya sips her wine, watches the bartender mix and pour a purple drink.

"He sort of swept Lana away."

"And you all didn't mind it."

"It wasn't our place to mind." Maya thinks she hears remorse.

"You and Caitlin are still close, then?"

He shrugs. "All relationships come in and out, right?"

"She loves you." She didn't mean to say this. She almost clamps her hand over her mouth.

He holds his beer glass at a diagonal and rubs the label with his thumb. "I'm not sure she knows what that means."

"She's pretty brilliant."

"She's not spent much of her life in the real world."

Maya shrugs. She didn't mean to stay on this as long as she has.

"She's not . . ." He stops himself.

She wants him to say something that proves Maya's not doing Caitlin wrong.

"Bryant's a douche," he says.

Maya almost laughs out loud. It's such an adolescent word. "A douche, huh?"

The bartender tops off her wine without her asking. She can't imagine how she'll make it home.

"Oh, you know what I mean. He's one of those guys who only feels comfortable with women. And only women who appreciate his genius." He says the last part in a lower voice, his glasses falling lower on his nose, and gulps his beer. "He always kind of hated Cait." He pushes up his glasses. "I worry about Lana now."

"He seems to really love her."

Charles gulps his beer. "Of course he loves her," he says. "She's twenty-eight and gorgeous and she worships him."

"And now she's had his kid."

He raises his hand, nods toward his beer as the bartender approaches. "Now that," he says.

"Do you think he'd leave her?"

"He wrote a story about her. Caitlin found it in some literary journal, right after they met. It wasn't about her, because they hadn't met yet when he wrote it, I guess he could have seen her before that, but it was about a girl that looked just like her. They're both from out West and the main character and the girl shared that too. It's this incredibly depressing twenty pages about him buying her lipstick at Barneys and popping Ativan in her mouth all day. I'm not sure he has any clue who she actually is."

"But we're all only just the people other people think we are."

"Maybe," he says. He shakes his head, hands the bartender his empty glass, and sips his new one. "Fuck," Charles says. "I hope not."

They both go quiet.

"What do you think I am?" he says.

Briefly, she hears Caitlin's words.

Maya drains her wine glass. She's quiet, just drunk enough, her eyes still angled toward the floor "Exactly what I need."

Summer 2011

The boards are old. A milky, sand-speckled gray across their fronts, they have chunks of wax solidified to them. They're heavy, big, and long—like standing on tables, Cooper tells them—instead of the slippery short boards being used by the kids already out offshore. He's a busboy at Annie's restaurant, a treat, Annie said, surf lessons for both Ellie and Jack

It's getting better, slowly. Jack talks to her sporadically. She's careful, listening. He does his searches, "research," that mostly involve Google and Wikipedia, and she listens carefully as he reads her the information he finds, about storms, more about sailing (though she's promised herself that she will never go again), tides and seasons, currents and storm patterns. He looks up bugs and New York, because Ellie told him that's where she's from and now he wants to go there. He asks her about Bloomberg and Cuomo, MoMA, Broadway, Central Park. His dream, he says, is to go to the Museum of Natural History. Not for the dinosaurs, that's the thing everyone wants to see, he says. He wants to see the space exhibit. He's interested in what still exists that has yet to be understood. Ellie has promised they'll go together someday soon.

The weather's been cooperating, at least until three or four in the afternoon each day, when the the sky seems so filled up with all the moisture that it crashes open in loud violent storms that Ellie loves, even if they trap them in the house for hours.

They spend an hour with Cooper in the sand before going into the water. Ellie and Jack giggle at first, failing to pop from belly to feet as seamlessly as Cooper's shown them. Instead, they each manage it in three steps, planted palms, then knees, then feet, and far too slowly. Cooper keeps pushing them to get it right.

"One. Two. Three!" he says over and over. He's tall, the color of an almond, with white-blond hair that's long and pulled back at the base of his neck. He's filled with confidence, demonstrating, more at ease on the board than he seems on land. He stands behind Ellie a moment. He holds her waist and lifts her. One. Two. Three. And finally she does it, one seamless motion, up onto her feet. And Jack claps, grinning, as Ellie stands.

Ellie reddens right up to her ears, Cooper's hands still on her, Jack happy, proud. Cooper lets go of Ellie and does the same with Jack, standing behind him, and he's up. Ellie claps and cheers.

"All right," says Cooper. He carries both their boards out to the water. He instructs them in paddling, positions Ellie far enough back that her board won't nose-dive, but close enough to the front that she has control. He sets Jack up closer to the front of his board, then Cooper pulls himself behind him. Jack holds on tight with both hands as Cooper paddles them out.

Ellie likes the weight of the floating board right from the start, the sound of the slap of water, the force with which she must push down to get beneath the waves. It's a struggle getting past the break, and she wonders at how easily Cooper gets Jack out. He places his hands on either side and tips the nose of the board beneath the waves before they break over him, Jack grinning, laughing the whole way. They come up farther out and hardly scathed, shaking their heads free of water as they do, Jack emulating Cooper, water pooling at their backs, hair slick against their heads. But each time Ellie tries this, she doesn't have the weight or strength to get the board under the whole wave. Each time it pushes her back and she falls off, twirling, fighting, forced to swim again after her twisting, flipping board. It takes her twice as long to get out to where the others sit, the noses of their boards flipped up over the water, their legs circling beneath them, ready to launch.

"Nor!" cries Jack, when she finally reaches them; the sun's thick on his face. He looks so strong and firm and certain, Ellie thinks of Ben, her mom, swimming, swimming, feeling strong.

She was eight and Ben was six. It was almost time to go, their last day in Florida, and Ellie had begged her mom for one more swim before they left. Her mom had already pulled on her pants and sweater, and Ellie told her she didn't need her to come in. She was old enough, a strong enough swimmer; she knew her mom was always cold. She'd swum out, on her own and happy. She'd looked back once and waved. She didn't plan it; she'd simply wanted to feel the wave crash on her. Her legs scissored, kicked, and she'd felt safe and strong. The wave wasn't huge and she thought it would be fun to fight against it. She watched, still, as it grew and curved. She breathed in once, kicked faster, and she kept her eyes open as the wave came down. She pushed the air hard from her nose and then the force of it took hold of her, like someone pushing, like Ben tackling her but softer, fuller, somehow both more completely and less real. The side of her thigh brushed quick against the sand floor and she felt each grain as it ran over her. She tried to grab hold of the current, to push up and over, like she did when the water was calm. But it had and held her. And she flailed a moment longer, then went limp. She let her body fall into the curves of water, let it shape her, turn her, twist her. She opened her eyes and saw her arms before her—blurry, pale, and crooked—and she felt safe and strong and warm. It must only have been seconds before her mom's hands were around her. Her mom's hands, which she knew just like her own hands. Her mom's sweater was all soaking wet and sandy and her mom was crying as she carried Ellie back to shore. She wrapped Ellie up, peeled off her sweater, and Ellie felt her mom's chest thump hard against her back. She covered them in all the extra towels, tiny grains of sand stuck to their arms and legs. Salt and sand bits rolled around in Ellie's mouth. And her mom kept holding tight to her and rubbing her hands up-down, up-down Ellie's arms. And Ellie started to get very hot, too hot, but she stayed still and let her mom hold her, because she thought if she was hot, maybe her mom was finally not cold.

"You..." says Annie, when Ellie comes into the living room before Cooper gets there. She's ecstatic, Annie, about Ellie going out with Cooper, like it's affirming something about Ellie's normalcy.

Ellie wears a sundress, no bra. It's the first time she's worn a dress since coming here.

"You look nice," Jeffrey finishes for his wife. His eyes are on her then, as he gets up from the couch, one leg folding to the floor and then the other, marking his place in a large hardcover book.

Cooper comes in shortly after. They all watch his headlights through Annie's vegetation, then hear the slap of his sandals as he comes to the door. Ellie's never been on a date that she can think of. She's been out with Dylan a thousand times. She's gotten stoned and accidentally slept with other boys. But Cooper's hair's still wet from his shower and he looks sweet and young as he hugs Annie, then stands awkwardly, shaking Jeffrey's hand.

"Where you guys going?" Jeffrey asks him. Annie glares at him. He's almost always the quieter of the two of them.

"I don't know," Cooper says. "I was going to leave that to her." He nods toward Ellie.

"Bad move, man," says Jeff.

Annie hits her husband on the shoulder.

"What?" he says. He laughs. "The guy should take the reins."

Ellie watches Cooper's face get red and wishes she could pity him. Instead, she's slightly grossed out by how young and small he looks.

She grabs his arm. "We'll figure it out," she says, not looking at Jeffrey, wishing they were closer to the water now, to make Cooper seem more sure again.

"You're close with Annie, huh?" says Ellie. They're at some chain restaurant in a strip mall. The lighting's an awkward too-dark orange and they sit across from one another in a booth against the wall.

"She likes to collect strays," Cooper says.

Ellie nods.

"The kid's been really hard for her, though. All his problems. She has less time for us."

"It was nice of you to take us out, though."

"She knows I need the money." Their food has come, and he drops his fork briefly after saying this. "I mean, I'm glad I did."

Ellie laughs. She wishes they could go outside again, go back to the ocean. She could swim out as far as she wanted and she wouldn't have to speak to anyone, to think of anyone, ever again.

"I went to New York once," says Cooper. The silence has gone on too long and Ellie's stopped making an effort. "It was awful," he says. "I don't know how anyone could live in that place."

"You're serious?" says Ellie. She can't imagine this, has never even heard it. She doesn't know it's true until she says it: "It's the only place I feel like it might one day be okay to be whatever I might be."

There were a few months, when she was twelve, when she went to an art teacher in DUMBO. She stopped showing up after always just going and began to wander around. She'd fallen deeply in love with the city then. It was winter when she started, cold, with mounds of dirty snow piled on the sidewalks. She'd burrow her hands into her pockets and dig her face into her scarf, a wool cap pulled down over her ears: she'd walk and walk. She'd discovered parts of New York she'd never known then. It was one of the great thrills of the city, how impossible it was to know. How there would always be another street or block she hadn't yet encountered. How there would always be large stretches of space where no one knew her.

Sometimes she went into the bookstores she knew her mother liked, the tiny one with dark wood paneling on West Tenth Street, where their mom used to drag her and Ben when they were kids. She fingered the spines of books she knew her mom liked, like she had when she was little. She sat in the back, on a wooden bench close to the end of the alphabet in the fiction section, sometimes taking out books and reading tiny snips of sentences, before placing them carefully back.

Ellie had refused to read for pleasure at a certain age, probably around the same time she began skipping her art lessons and walking around. She'd liked it, she remembered, liked it now that she'd returned to it, but there was something dangerous about letting her mom see her too often with a book. The way she looked so hopeful, the way she seemed to want to make something of Ellie's choices, to shape her, form her, show her, if only she could get hold of her long enough.

She'd thought, eventually, her mom would catch her in there wandering, skipping her hour sessions in DUMBO. Her art teacher, Catherine, would call and tell on her. But she was never caught and nothing ever came of it. She told her mom she wasn't into art any longer, and she still found time sometimes to wander around.

When she was older, sometimes, after Dylan got her stoned, she'd do the same thing, but this time she tended to interact with other people more. She'd go into bars and let men hit on her. She'd gone home twice with men who must have been twice, if not more, her age, one with a big apartment in the Financial District with shiny silver fixtures in the kitchen and the bathroom. Ellie'd let that guy have her on his sink. He'd wiped it with a Clorox wipe right after, Ellie standing in the too-bright light, cold, with all her clothes off, the guy rubbing, eyes intent on the silver till it shone. The other guy had lived in a tiny studio in Fort Greene with a roof deck. She'd snuck out after he fucked her—he'd come too quickly, she'd been relieved by this, his quick apology and then his passing out; she'd almost laughed at his awkward limbs and crooked nose, which had all looked so powerful and ominous when he'd been standing across the bar from her. She'd sat out on the deck for hours, finally climbing down the fire escape to avoid having to go back inside and see him standing up again.

She craved a sort of violence in all this time that she spent wandering. She wanted the city, someone deep inside it, something further underneath, to come up and shock her into a sort of certainty, to tear her open, break her, in order that she might have something she could work to fix.

"It's just loud and dirty," Cooper says. "And no real water."

"It's an island," Ellie says.

Cooper looks down into his food again. "Well, sure, but you can't surf a river."

Ellie laughs. "I guess you can't."

It's still light out when they pull back into Annie's. Ellie's relieved to get out of the car. She wants to be alone in her little room with her Deborah Eisenberg. She wants to get Jack out of bed early the next morning and spend the day in the water just the two of them.

She doesn't see Jeff at first when she comes in through the side door. Later, she'll tell herself he might not have been there at all. It could have been Annie, or a shadow from the trees, outside her door then, except she saw the same dark blue cover of the book he'd been reading when Cooper had come to pick her up.

She closes the door to her room but doesn't lock it.

Cooper had offered, without her saying anything, her body somehow signaling, on the drive home to get her high if she were ever in need while she was here. She'd demurred, her eyes fixed out the window, the quiet empty streets still disturbing to her; she'd wanted to ask him to drive her back to the East River instead.

Winter 2013

"Fucking Brooklyn," Laura says.

She's come to take Maya to dinner, to distract her from what's about to happen, to fortify her as only Laura can. Maya's called the doctors, bought the tickets. She'll be with her girl so soon.

"You're changing," Laura says, eyeing Maya's pants and baggy sweater. Stephen's convinced Ben to go with him to get the vegetables and meat for dinner. Maya lets Laura lead her back into her room. They stand before her full-length mirror. Maya unbuttons and takes off her jeans. "That thing too," says Laura, nodding toward Maya's big black sweater. She's located wine glasses, pours each of them a drink.

"We pretend," says Laura. Holding her glass toward Maya, then taking a big sip. "We women. We pretend we're okay by dressing up."

Maya holds her wine without drinking and stares at her now-bare pale goose-pimpled skin in the mirror, black underwear, a light pink, slightly padded bra. Her posture's slumped, always has been. Laura presses back her shoulders, places her hands on Maya's waist. Maya has freckles up both her arms, across her clavicle. Her stomach's flat, though the skin's still slightly stretched from her two kids. Her quadriceps extend out above her knees from all the running. Her arms hang long and limby, her hair pulled up high off her bare face.

She forces herself to let Laura keep hold of her hip bones. "You're an awful feminist," she says.

Laura pulls a dress from its bag and holds it in front of Maya. It's too big, too many colors, but Maya slips it over her head—it's sheer and soft against her. She stays still as Laura reaches in her bag for pins.

"I'm the sort of feminist who likes to take advantage of . . ." Laura narrows her eyes and grins, her lips full, her earrings— silver again, flat round plates with half-moon cutouts—angling themselves around her face. She pins the dress so it rests far below Maya's collarbone. She tightens it until it pulls at and hugs tight to Maya's waist. "All my feminine parts," she says.

They go into the city and are seated at a restaurant on West Tenth Street. It's small and dimly lit, rickety round tables stuck too close together, old straight-backed wooden chairs painted red. There's a single tea light set before them and Maya reaches her fingers out in front of her until their tips touch the burning glass.

"How's the stodge?" asks Laura.

She means Stephen. Each has only ever tolerated the other all this time.

Maya smiles, shakes her head. "He's not," she says.

They've had periods of deep affection, Laura and Stephen. She makes him laugh. He respects her brain. She quizzes him on obscure French philosophers to prove he's not as smart as he'd like to be, presumes he is. He often, apropos of nothing, mentions her Midwestern upbringing, wanting to remind whoever else is with them, maybe just to remind Laura, that she isn't as French or as mysterious as she might like to be.

"I'll take you if you leave him," Laura says. This is not the first time she's offered. "We'll go get El, just run away."

Laura's often spent whole weeks at Maya's house when Stephen's traveling. Holidays and birthdays, she's often come along with them. And Stephen let her, didn't question it. He smiled patiently when she gave him anal beads or brightly colored bow ties as gifts, for no other reason than to make him sit through their opening and say thanks.

"Don't," Maya says now. Not meaning the anger she feels. It feels imperative that she defend her husband. She wants to itemize for her friend all that he has done exactly right. "It's my fault much more than his," she says. Her voice is steadier and more certain.

Laura's bottom lip pulls in beneath her teeth.

"Of course."

The waiter comes. He's young, and Maya can't look up at him. Laura asks for waters, orders a bottle from the wine list, quickly scoots the boy away.

"I left my marriage because of my husband's sister's yellow dress," she says.

In all these years, her friend has hardly spoken of her marriage, and never has she said her husband's name.

"It must have been an awful yellow," Maya says; she fingers her napkin, reaches for her water with both hands.

The waiter sets down two wine glasses and pours a taste for Laura; she twirls the deep red, sips it, nods, and waits for him to fill each of their glasses, leave again.

"It was at our wedding," Laura says. She pushes Maya's wine glass toward her. Maya sips, sets down her glass.

"You left that day?" she asks.

"A year later," Laura says. "But it was over after that."

Candlelit downturned faces spot the restaurant; there's half a wall of mirrors lined with liquor bottles set behind the bar. Maya's fingers press again against the burning glass and then she grabs hold of her wine with both hands, cupping lightly with her right hand, holding tightly to the stem with her left.

They order quickly: a petite filet for Laura. Maya orders the same so that she won't have to read the menu while the waiter waits for her. Laura orders a burrata for them to share to start.

The waiter leaves, and the table next to them jostles as the couple gathers up their coats and scarves and mittens; the girl is young, the man much older, heavyset, both well dressed; the woman keeps mumbling, *Excuse me, sorry*, to Maya as she pushes out her chair, and Maya smiles at her, says, *I'm sorry*, back.

"It was lovely, actually, my husband's sister's dress," Laura says. The way that she says "husband": like the word might not be real.

Maya pulls herself closer to the table. She inches herself forward on her chair.

"Poor girl," Laura says. She laughs now, her face younger, barer. "I'd never seen her look so great," she says.

Bread's been set down in front of them without Maya noticing. Laura reaches for a piece and tears. "It wasn't," she says. "She wasn't beautiful." She pours oil onto the plate next to her wine glass, dips her bread. "There's a sort of carelessness that feels necessary for something to be beautiful." Laura chews and swallows. "She was the most desperate thing I'd ever seen."

She picks up a second piece of bread.

"She was *hungry*, you know?"

Their cheese comes and Laura cuts a large piece for Maya, serving her. She fails, though, to look at her straight-on.

"She must have been twenty-two or -three, just finished college, nursing school. She'd lost thirty pounds in the months leading up." She spoons the fig reduction onto Maya's plate. "I hadn't even noticed it," she says. "She'd always been a little chubby, the little sister. I'd known her her whole adolescent life."

Laura looks up then and smiles at Maya, who's cut the cheese into smaller pieces, chews a corner of it—smoke and milk—as her friend talks.

"She must have been starving herself," says Laura. "And there was this hunger on her, you know? And not just from not eating." She laughs again, cuts off a larger piece of cheese, then splits it between hers and Maya's plates. "She was out to be seen that night, to prove she could be, should be looked at; she was so desperate to be wanted, like that was all she needed to survive."

Maya pulls a piece of bread out of its basket just to hold it. She dips the edge of half into Laura's plate now filled with oil and slowly eats.

"And I was just so sad for her, so angry," Laura says. "That she could think something so seemingly simple was worth all that energy."

They each sip their wine and watch as tables fill and empty. Maya stares into her glass.

Their food comes and Maya watches Laura wink at their young waiter. He refills their glasses, gives each of them a sharper knife.

"The dress was strapless, old-fashioned," Laura says. "Her posture was perfect for the first time."

Laura gulps her wine. "It wasn't the dress." She shakes her head, cuts her first perfect slice of meat. "It was the idea that that was the best she had to hope for, those few hours, someone looking at her, feeling worth something, being, I don't know, a girl at whom people, men especially, but everybody—she wanted everyone to look."

Maya's not sure what to do with all the food in front of her, where to start, how she might ever finish it. She cuts off a small piece of asparagus and considers it, looking past her fork, the spear of green, back to her friend.

"I hated her for it," Laura says. "For showing me how small her world was, how small my life was about to be." She looks down into her glass again. "I was getting everything she wanted . . ."

"Except," Maya says.

"It was how desperate she was," Laura says. "How small and simple what she wanted seemed to me then."

Maya takes her first bite of steak, having sliced it slowly, lets the juice spread into her asparagus and under her potatoes; it sits awhile on her tongue, the salt and grease coating her mouth.

"I wanted something bigger," Laura says. "I wanted . . ." She cuts herself another piece of steak, considers it a moment before she chews and swallows. "Paris. Life. *Free Women*." Laura laughs. "I thought what I had then was something people got no matter what.

"I got it wrong, maybe," Laura says.

Maya sips her wine, sets down her glass, and picks up her fork again.

"I didn't see . . ." says Laura. She holds her glass a long time, considering its fullness; she dips it forward, holds it straight again, then tips it toward her lips.

"I left because I wanted to," says Laura.

Maya reaches for her napkin, wipes her mouth, her eyes searching for her friend again.

"But you should never listen to me; I know nothing about marriages," Laura says.

Summer 2011

"I'm so sorry," Jeffrey says, rushing through the door and breathless. He's promised to take Jack to dinner, but had an emergency with a patient and rushed out. Annie's at the restaurant, El and Jack still in their bathing suits. The day's storm has stopped and they're watching a movie. Outside, the whole world is very still.

Jack smells like salt and his skin sticks to Ellie's legs as he lies against her. She wears a T-shirt and no shorts. Jeffrey runs toward Jack and scoops him up, his arms brushing against Ellie's calf. "I'm so sorry," he says again.

His hair hangs heavy, mussed and limp in his face. He doesn't seem to have the energy to push it behind his ears. "One of my patients . . ." But he stops. He has stubble, Ellie notices. It's speckled through with streaks of gray.

She wants to ask him what happened. She waits to listen just in case.

"It was horrible," he says, shaking his head.

Jack takes hold of a tuft of his dad's hair. "I'm staaaaarving, Daddy," he says. They've had two bowls of popcorn, but Jack's been looking forward to this dinner with his dad. Jeffrey grins at him, burying his nose into his son's chest.

"Nor comes?" asks Jack, looking back at her. She's standing, holding her shirt down to cover the bottom of her bathing suit.

"Well, yes," says Jeffrey. "I think Nor should come."

He raises his eyebrows at her. He looks just like Jack.

She nods toward one and then the other of them. "Sure," she says. "Sounds great. I just . . ."

Jeffrey smiles down at her bare legs, then looks back at Jack.

"We'll wait," he says.

They walk twenty minutes to Jack's favorite Italian restaurant in the small stretch of busy peopled street a quarter mile from their house. "No one walks here," Jeffrey says, holding tight to his son's hand. "I like having a New Yorker around to remind us of all the ways we don't live right." The restaurant's nearly empty. Ellie can just make out the sound of the river lapping up against the seawall; she smells brackish water and the crab traps laid out to dry on the docks across the street from where they sit. They order spaghetti, meatballs on the side, all three of them.

"Is everything okay now?" Ellie asks Jeffrey.

"I hope so." He shakes his head. "Who knows?"

Ellie stays quiet, waiting. Their food comes; Jack slurps his noodles, leaving splotches of red on his white shirt. Ellie picks up her napkin and wipes the red sauce from Jack's mouth and nose, dips the napkin in her glass of water and dabs the spot out of his shirt. She cuts up the two massive meatballs on a separate plate, and drops the smaller pieces into his bowl.

"Thanks, Nor," he says, his mouth full. She feels Jeffrey watching her, but keeps her eyes on Jack, then on the food she's cutting for him. She takes a bite of her meatball and looks back at Jack before she speaks again.

"It must be hard," she says.

"It can be."

She feels competent and capable, taking care of Jack; she's never felt this before now. She sips her water, holds her hand up over her mouth as she chews.

Jeffrey pulls his napkin up off of his lap, places his palms on either side, and rips the napkin evenly in half.

"Tell me about painting," he says. She's started again. The days when Jack's with his parents, she sets up an easel in the yard or out at the beach.

He leans in close to her and Ellie eats small bites of pasta.

"I . . ." She wants to tell him; she doesn't know what she would say.

He's smiling. He sits back, his food only half eaten.

"It's not something I'm very good at explaining," she says.

The cuff of his shirt has a red spot just below his palm and she almost reaches over with her napkin. She stops herself, shakes her head, and shrugs.

"I went to this woman when I was little," Ellie says. She looks out toward the docks. "I thought she was the coolest person. She'd smoke cigarettes out on her balcony and walk around in old paint-stained jeans and clogs. She had this incredible wiry gray hair." Ellie reaches her hand up to her own hair. "One time, she asked me to draw her, you know? I'd only ever done still lifes, fruit and stuff. But then she said she was going to pose for me."

Both Jack and Jeff are listening, but Ellie looks at neither of them. She cuts her noodles into tiny unforkable pieces, then looks outside again.

"I got really into drawing her. The whole time I thought I was making this perfect *thing*, you know?" Ellie stares down at her plate. "She always told me I was good." She picks up another piece of bread and rolls it with her thumb. "I guess she probably told everyone that. But I was really deep in it, you know? All the lines and shades of her. She was all these incredibly thoughtful, layered lines. And now I had the chance to remake her, you know?" Jack angles his hand on her knee so he can lean closer in to his spaghetti. Ellie holds the back of his shorts so he doesn't slip off of the booth. "But then my mom came to get me, and I saw that I'd been . . ." She shakes her head. She doesn't know how she got here, why she's telling this to him. "I'd made her really ugly, you know? By accident?"

Jeffrey grabs a piece of bread and smiles at her. "She was very old?"

"Not really," Ellie says. "But her skin was wrinkled." She smiles at the floor, thinking of her mom scolding her when she caught her smoking in the park. "The cigarettes. I mean, I guess I got it right, you know; it was her. But I hadn't realized till I saw her that way. It felt like my fault."

Jeffrey takes a large gulp from his wine glass and nods toward Ellie; his chin and mouth are steady, firm.

"Anyway," says Ellie. She holds tight to Jack.

"Anyway," Jeffrey says.

"I never went back after that," she says.

She looks around the restaurant, which has emptied since they started talking. There are two waitresses leaning on the bar. Jeffrey, Jack, and Ellie are the only table left.

Ellie nods toward them. "I think they're waiting for us."

Jeffrey turns toward the girls and waves with two fingers. The girl who has waited on them—young, tall, with slick brown skin—walks over to them.

"I'm sorry, sweetie," says Jeffrey. He reaches up and holds her forearm. His other hand holds back his hair. "We're almost done. I promise." He shows almost his whole front row of teeth.

The waitress waves her hand at them, Jeffrey's hand still on her other arm. "Don't worry," she says. "Take your time."

She starts to walk away, then turns back toward them. She touches Jeffrey's shoulder and stands very close. "Your family's gorgeous," she says.

Ellie feels a thrumming in her stomach. Jeffrey smiles. The girl brings her hand back to her side.

Winter 2013

They're inside a club Maya hadn't known existed. It's the sort of place she's never been, or meant to go: dark lights, loud music, young, lush people. They walked past the line straight through the door. Laura nodded at the doorman. "I sleep with him sometimes," she muttered. And then here they were.

Maya's hips move as they wait at the bar and order drinks from the hardly more than adolescent bartender. She's tattooed all down both arms and her belly is bare before them, flat and firm and covered in some liquid that makes it catch the light.

Laura gets them martinis. Maya's feet wobble underneath her—there have been two bottles of wine in addition to the one they had before leaving her house. Her knees buckle beneath the weight of all she's drunk.

She can't remember ever being out this late.

Laura leads Maya to the dance floor. Booths line the edges of the club where people sit and drink. A few of them are hidden by curtains. A cage hangs in the center over the crowd, suspended in the air by hidden lines. Inside the cage, a girl dances. Maya wants to get her out and take her home with her. She's writhing, a small roll of fat on her belly curves and twists as she throws her arms back, lowering herself deftly to the cage's floor. She wears only a sparkling red bikini. The top is oddly old-fashioned, a sweetheart cut, thinks Maya, though she can't think how she knows this term.

Laura puts her hands lightly on Maya's hips from behind her. She turns Maya toward her and Maya gives the dancing girl one final look. And then Maya and Laura are dancing together. They're dancing in a spirited imitation of the caged girl. Laura's grip gets firm on either side of Maya, and Maya lets herself dip into her friend. Her hair's out of its clip and down her back now, and strands of it catch in her mouth as she smiles at her friend. She tastes smoke and her shampoo, and she's enjoying not having hold of anything. It feels as if she's finally been let loose.

The music gets louder, faster. She likes the feel of Laura's hands on her. She wants to fall into her and let her hold her as she moves.

Slowly, though, Maya feels herself begin to slip. She's either too drunk or becoming not quite drunk enough. The result is nausea, nausea and wanting to get out. She puts her hands on top of Laura's shoulders, which are slick with sweat right through her shirt.

"Bathroom," she says and then screams it twice more before Laura nods that she's heard. They walk determinedly toward a bright red EXIT sign. The bathroom's nearly empty. A girl, so young Maya thinks a moment she should scold her, is leaning close to the mirror, lining her eyes in black as a girl in the one occupied stall yells to her about "that fucking assface Ross."

Maya avoids the mirror. She closes herself quickly into an empty stall. She puts down the lid of the toilet and sits, slipping her feet out of her shoes. She stares at her long, unpolished toe-nails, the little hairs on each toe. Black lines are smudged around her feet from the boots' leather and her sweat.

She breathes slowly, sits back against the tank. The porcelain clunks once against the wall and Maya keeps her eyes fixed down-ward. She listens to the girls. They're talking about someone else now, another girl whom they seem to hate.

"Her dress, though."

"I know."

"Like it's the fucking prom."

They're both laughing. One high and sharp. One hoarse.

"She's really skinny, though. I could never wear a dress that tight."

"Coke." Maya hears the toilet flush beside her.

"Really?" The door of the stall opens with a creak.

"I know." She imagines that they're looking at one another in the mirror.

"Well, I guess it works."

Heels clank against the concrete of the floor. Water runs.

"I love that lipstick." Maya thinks of Ellie's thick broad lips.

"Here."

"Thanks."

Maya looks at the freckles on her knees. She can still make out the lines of her quadriceps from all the mornings up over the bridge. She still has the knot of something certain pulsing thick and tight between her shoulder blades. She's no longer drunk, but does not feel sober. Her mind pounds hard and crooked from the music and the alcohol. She thinks, briefly, of texting Stephen. But she can't think what she would say. She thinks maybe instead she will just never leave this bathroom. She will stay here, eavesdrop-ping on young girls, pretending that they're hers.

"You okay, Ma?"

Her eyes are blurry and she can hardly make out the shape of him. He's in boxers still and an old tournament T-shirt. Maya sits up and runs her fingers down under her eyes. "Fine," she says.

She fell asleep still in her dress (Laura's) in Ellie's room, without ever checking in with Stephen, without brushing her teeth or washing her face. Now Ben has found her, under the covers with mascara smudged beneath her eyes.

"Where were you last night?"

"Laura," she says, hoping this explains things.

"Right," Ben says.

"What'd you do for dinner?" She should've been here cooking for him, talking to him, loving him.

"Dad made pasta," Ben says.

"How was it?" she asks. They were supposed to make up. Stephen was supposed to tell Ben he was sorry, prepare him for Ellie.

"Fine, Mom."

"Benny . . ."

"I know. You don't know what that means."

"You feel better about things?"

"He's still pissed."

She's quiet. She should have been here. She stares at her son's face and then looks down.

"I know he just wants . . . you know, he's Dad. He wants us to achieve, right? To *enact ourselves upon the world*." Ben raises his shoulders and lowers his voice when he says the last part. Maya smiles.

"Benny . . ." She wants to say something to prove she loves him, to show him she'd still do anything on earth to keep him safe. "You want breakfast?"

"Nah," he says. "I think I'll run."

She doesn't want to get out of bed with Ben still watching. There's a large black *X* on her hand from the doorman at the club. There are still lines of grime along her feet.

He lingers a little longer, toeing the carpet, running his fingers through his nearly nonexistent hair. "Okay," he says.

"Tonight, maybe?" Maya asks him. "Dinner?"

"Sure," he says. He looks up at her. Maya holds the comforter up close to her face and breathes in the smell of cigarettes.

She needs to talk to Stephen first, to clear things up, to remind him to be careful with her children.

"Dad and I aren't coming," Ben says.

Maya's only holding on to bits of what he's saying to her. She sees the pounding music, the caged girl.

"To Florida," he says. "To get El."

She will not react here in front of him. She will wait until she sees Stephen to respond properly to this. She must figure out, in the meantime, what responding properly might be.

"It's fine, Benny," she says. "If you don't want to come, it's fine."

"I want to," Ben says. "But Dad . . ."

She looks out the window of Ellie's room, down into Stephen's garden. He could not ever quite make sense of who their daughter was. He understood and responded well to *goals*. He never fought with Ellie. Instead, he just slowly wandered further from her. She was, he seemed to believe, of Maya's making, and therefore Maya's task most of the time.

It was messier than this: He kept trying sometimes. He took Ellie for walks, gave her books, cooked her favorite dinners. He took care of Maya so that she could take care of their girl. He was busy trying to be the consistent, steady parent—organizing, scheduling, keeping their lives going—while Maya flailed and grasped for whatever might finally save Ellie.

"Ma?" says Ben.

"Yeah, Benny."

"You're a mess, you know?"

She drops the comforter and smooths the front of it over her lap. "I know, Benny." She laughs, swinging her legs out of the bed and walking toward him. "I know," she says.

Summer 2011

It's Annie's one day off and Jeffrey is still down the street with clients. Ellie comes back from the beach and walks barefoot into the kitchen. Her feet are speckled with sand and her ears are still half clogged. Her head feels blurry and the skin along her cheeks smarts from the sun. She hasn't eaten since the morning. She went to swim before anyone else had risen and stayed at the beach until after five. There's no one in the kitchen and Ellie thinks the place is empty. She's wearing a T-shirt over her bathing suit, but she's left her shorts in the car. She makes a sandwich, slathering hummus on the bread and cutting big pieces of the cheddar cheese Jack likes. She's taken on many of his eating habits as her own. She's not sure how she knows to do it or what about Annie's voice signals to her that she's on the phone with Ellie's mom. She might have picked up the phone only because she hears Annie on the other end in her bedroom and her fascination with Annie has no end. Because she's not used to landlines any more. It's jarring, though, suddenly hearing her mother laughing. She's someone else when not talking to Ellie. There's none of the worry, none of the terror muddying up her words. She seems so young and comfortable, talking to Annie about her classes. They chat a while longer. Annie complains about one of the busboys who always comes in stoned. Ellie listens to her mom get quiet. She knows now she's begun to think of her.

"How is she?" her mom asks; Annie gets quiet. Ellie wonders for the millionth time how much Annie knows.

"She's such a sweet girl, Maya. She's really good with Jack."

Her mom's silent again and Ellie sees her sitting in her study with her feet up on the desk, holding a book in one hand, the phone held to her ear with her shoulder, rifling through the pages with her other hand as she talks. "Is she?"

"She seems good. I'm not sure what else there is to say. She doesn't say much about herself and I don't want to push."

"Of course," her mom says. Annie said she didn't want to tell her mom about the sailing. She didn't want Maya to worry when there was no need.

"I'd tell you, you know, if there was anything else. But she seems all right. She swims every morning. She's a sweet girl, Maya." Ellie thinks she hears her mom set her book down.

"I don't know who she is." This is her mom again. Ellie cups the phone more tightly. "When I think about her down there, I can't think of a person so much as a reason to be afraid."

Annie whispers something inaudible to Jack.

"I mean, I remember her as a child. And then I remember all these years of never knowing what to expect. She was always so unpredictable. When I think of missing her, I always think of the little girl I miss. But I'm not sure who she is now. I'm not sure I'd even know what to do with her besides be afraid."

Ellie still has hold of her sandwich. She's squeezed the hummus out of the bread and it's now smeared along her palm.

Her mom continues: "I can't say that out loud too much. I hate how it feels, even thinking it. But I've been relieved since she went to you."

Ellie stays very still and waits for Annie's response.

"She's figuring it out. I really think she is."

There's a noise behind her and Ellie almost drops the phone; she sees Jeffrey standing in the kitchen, watching her.

He holds a finger up to his lips and shakes his head. Ellie's been crying and she hopes that he can't see it. She has her fist held tightly over the phone's receiver and she knows that he must know that she's been listening in. He's wearing what he wears to work, jeans and a button-down shirt that he usually keeps untucked. He has hold of his hair behind his ear and nods reassuringly at Ellie as she carefully places the phone back in its cradle and walks past him to her room.

The next morning Jeff and Jack come to her door together, early. Ellie's still in bed. "Nor," she hears through the slats. It's the two of them calling her in unison. She's quick out of the bed. She pulls on shorts and ties her hair up. "Hey, guys," she says. She comes out the door instead of opening it to them. She thinks Annie must be somewhere close.

"We're going on a picnic," Jack says. His hand is wrapped around his dad's shoulder, he's high up in his dad's arms as he talks. "To the beach, Nor," says Jack. "You have to come."

Ellie looks down at her bare feet, eyes Jeff's ankles, then his shins.

"We already made your sandwich," Jack says.

Ellie feels Jeff smile.

"Sure," she says.

"I told you we could get her," Jeff says to his son.

They bring sand toys for Jack, a surfboard, towels, an umbrella under which only Annie sits. Made sloppily by Jack and Jeffrey, wrapped in tinfoil that's too loose, all the sandwiches are soggy and wet from melted ice that's leaked through by the time they unwrap them. Jeff takes Jack out on the surfboard, paddling behind him like Cooper's done the few times they've gone out with him. Jeffrey's easy with his son, strong and confident in the water. Ellie watches Annie, who is smiling, watching them. Annie wears a simple orange one-piece. She's pulled her hair back and has sunglasses perched atop her head. She has a dimple in her left cheek, but not her right one. She has freckles on her nose and three along her jaw up to her chin.

The waves don't so much break as roll steadily to shore. Some of them get white and frothy before they trickle in, but mostly the water's calm. The beach is almost empty. There's a man fishing by himself about five hundred yards from where they sit, but otherwise they have this space of sand and water to themselves.

"I never thought . . ." she says to Ellie. She turns toward her briefly, then faces the boys again. "I never thought all this was an option for me, you know?" Her face is almost never bare. She wears a little lipstick, some sort of concealer underneath her eyes, mascara, or a thin line of black at the tips of her lids. Ellie loves the look of her like this, though, completely clean. She squints into the sun. "That's absurd, right?" Annie says. She pulls down her sunglasses.

Ellie stretches her legs out and buries her feet into the sand, her hands dig in as well. She keeps her eyes fixed on the water. The sand is warm and heavy over her toes and fingers, and she wishes she could do the same with her whole body, straight up to her head.

The surfboard flips out in the water and Jack and Jeffrey fall.

Annie leans forward, her knees up by her shoulders, her hands grabbing her ankles, then reaching up to place her sunglasses back atop her head. Dad and son are up as quickly as they went under. Jeff holds Jack up over his head, then sits him back on the board. They both wave to Annie before turning out to start paddling again.

"Should we join them?" Annie says. She's put her glasses on the towel and stands, holding out her hand to El.

Ellie slowly pulls her hands and then her feet out from under the holes she's dug and reaches up for Annie's hand. She places her own sunglasses on her towel and they walk together, almost brushing shoulders, till the water's deep enough that they both push forward, not walking any longer, and dive down beneath the lumbering waves. They're close to Jack and Jeffrey, and Annie breaststrokes toward them. Ellie lingers, scissor-kicking, treading water, then heads in the opposite direction of the three of them. She stays under for as long as her need for air will let her, then comes up again, far enough from Jack and Jeff and Annie that she can't hear the things they say.

She watches Jack swim between his parents. Annie dives down deep and comes up again, her son in her arms. Ellie swims out farther, farther. She thinks maybe if she could stay out here. If she could just stay always two hundred feet from the people that she loves, maybe then she won't hurt them. Maybe then they'll all stay safe.

Winter 2013

"Where were you, Maya?" Stephen's there as soon as Ben has left her. He's already dressed for work.

"I went dancing," she says. It's strange, saying it out loud.

"Seriously?"

"Seriously," she says.

"With whom?" He is a man with perfect pronouns.

"Laura."

He nods. As if this is just as he expected. As if, of course, she'll continue to do all of it wrong.

"Ben tells me you're not coming?"

He reaches his hand behind his neck and looks past her to the street.

"May—"

She will not let him say her name. "Stephen, you will not not be there."

"I'm staying here with Ben."

"We should all go, Stephen."

He shakes his head at her. "She doesn't want me there."

"You don't know that, Stephen."

But he does.

"Maya," he says. This time she lets him talk.

"Daddy," his daughter said. She was nine; he was in London. She was back in Brooklyn, though he could see her perfectly. She would be sitting in the shelf close to the floor that they kept empty just for her. It took up a corner of the kitchen, just below the phone, and though the phone was cordless—when Ben or Stephen or Maya talked, they often paced or sat comfortably on the couch—Ellie always sat, her thighs up to her chest, inside this small child-sized shelf.

Maya'd been a mess from the moment that he'd met her, hardly functional some days, but the smartest woman he'd ever known. He'd been brought up to believe in that, the intellect. He figured every other part of life could be managed if they both had that.

"Daddy," their daughter said now. She seldom called him Daddy. She sounded desperate. She seldom called him at all when he was out of town. Ben was at his first sleepaway camp for soccer. It was the first time, for such a long stretch, that it was just Maya and Ellie all alone.

"I can't take care of her all by myself," said Ellie.

He should have gone to her immediately. He knew, of course, what she meant. "What's wrong, El? What's she doing?"

"She's just . . ." She was disappearing. She was folding in on herself.

"El, go get her, baby, put your mother on the phone."

"She can't. You can't. You'll make it worse," said Ellie.

"Elinor," said Stephen. "Now."

He heard her stay still a minute. He imagined her unfurling her small body, her wrists reaching for her ankles as she rose.

"Can you just come home, though?" she said. "She'll be fine, I think. We'll be okay if you come home."

"El, I have commitments."

He should have gotten on a plane.

He should have worked less hard to take care of all the practical endeavors for her. He should have tried to meet her where she so often went. It was absurd, of course: what might have been done differently.

"Elinor, go find your mother, please."

He yelled at Maya when he finally got her. It was exactly the thing Ellie had begged him not to do. He was far away and feeling helpless. She was the adult. All she had to do was to be present for their nine-year-old.

"Maya!" he said, and she cried without speaking, and he stayed on the phone until she stopped and promised to go outside, to take Ellie to the park. Sometimes, if he just got her outside, she would be better. If he could get her within a close enough proximity to Ellie, she would have to suck it up and be functional again. After this, he only ever left her if Ben was with them. He didn't trust his wife, but he was unerringly dependent on his seven-year-old son.

He knows that she resents his stridency. She, much of the time, infuriates him. But oddly, maybe obviously, they have largely created these qualities in one another. They've spent twenty years nurturing and shaping the exact things in one another they have now grown to resent.

"I can't come, Maya," he says. "I called the lawyers. I checked in with the doctors. I've kept you steady enough to get you to her. I don't want Ben to have to be there. I want to take this time to be with him."

Fall 2011

"Best part of Florida," says Cooper. "All the old people in pain."

Ellie keeps her eyes free of the rearview mirror, where she knows for certain Jack's trying to catch her eye. They've had another surf lesson. Then Cooper asked if she wanted to get high. He's posturing, pretending. He's not at all the boy he was at the fish restaurant.

Ellie wishes she hadn't made him this instead.

The house is only a couple of miles from Annie's. Small and flat-roofed, with grass dying in the front yard, the driveway cracked, stained orange and yellow concrete with weeds growing right up through.

Cooper parks on the street and leads them to the side door that opens into the garage. Ellie tempers the desire to clamp a hand over Jack's eyes. He stops her as Cooper knocks the first time.

"Nor?" His small round face is scared. He holds tight—damp

and cold, his short fingers hardly reaching past the base of her thumb—to Ellie's hand. "I want to go home, Nor," he says.

She looks down at her feet, tan and slipped in flip-flops, her toes speckled with sand.

"Don't worry," she says. "Soon, kiddo." She tries to smile at him but turns back toward Cooper when she can't. He's knocked for a second time and is now looking impatiently, a bit nervously, toward Jack.

He mutters something. The door opens: a very thin old woman in black stretch pants, yellow rubber clogs, and an oversized pink Hello Kitty T-shirt. Ellie stares at the thin veiny skin that covers her hands. The woman winces when she sees Cooper, not greeting any of them, just moving aside so they can come through the door.

Ellie tries to ignore the tingling covering her whole body, the excitement, the knowledge that if she wants, she's only minutes from relief. She keeps hoping for the guilt to override it, for the fear of falling back or the anger at herself. But all she manages is to work hard to temper her body's elation, the knowledge that there's something certain to look forward to.

They enter the garage, which is thick with humidity and the smell of sour chemicals. Large and small pieces of thin glass shapes scatter the floor and the aluminum shelf that runs along the opposite side of the room. The glass is in all sorts of sheer sparkling colors; a single piece flows from red to pink to yellow, shaped like a massive trumpet, narrow at the bottom and rising into a wide round top. It could be a tulip. There are smaller pieces that are more intricate, animals, and twisting crooked shapes. Ellie wants to go to hold one. They seem too delicate, like they would shatter in her hands.

Ellie squeezes Jack's hand.

"You like 'em?" It's the first time the woman's spoken. She's standing close to Ellie. She smells like must and cigarettes, and the mold that grows in sheets left in the wash too long.

"I do," says Ellie, turning toward her. "They're very beautiful."

The woman nods. "Thanks, yeah. It's my real passion."

Cooper looks at her and she shrugs and nudges Ellie, leaning in close so Jack won't hear. Her elbow sticks sharp in Ellie's rib. "And it helps cover the other business I do."

Meth, thinks Ellie. Fuck. Her fingers itch, but she can't mention it. She's never tried meth, can't admit any agency in this whole thing.

She looks quickly, nervously, at Jack.

The stench of chemicals is making Ellie dizzy. She stares hard at a purple glass alligator, wondering at the tiny perfect scales. She tries to think of how to not get high. She tries remembering how she got here, tries forcing herself to accept that she chose to be standing in this place, that she chose to bring Jack with her, that she is stupid and fucked up.

"But that's not what you all want," the woman says, looking back at Cooper and then at Ellie; she has not once looked down at Jack. There's a large gray plastic chest of drawers and shelves across the back wall of the garage and the woman very methodically goes through a drawer at waist level that Ellie sees is separated into lots of small glass-covered squares. The woman pulls out a plastic bag and nods toward it, facing Cooper.

She looks at Jack for the first time, "Sciatica, sweetie," she says, winking. "The boy and I both got it bad."

Ellie pulls Jack to her.

Ellie counts, one, two, three, four, five, six through the clear plastic. Six. White-clean, one inch across, an eighth of an inch thick. She can see the stain on Dylan's parents' ceiling perfectly, the browns and blacks, the way they stuck to, settled down into, her eyes. She thinks of asking just to hold the pills. She doesn't have to bring them with her. If she can see them, feel them close to her, that will be enough to keep her good.

She keeps counting as the bag moves from one hand to the other, as Cooper steps farther from the woman. Onetwothreefourfivesix.

Cooper looks over at her. She knows she's grinning. She steps farther from Jack again. Cooper nods at the old woman. He reaches into his back pocket and takes out a large wad of cash. He closes the pills into a fist. The old woman begins counting out the cash. Ellie counts with her and then counts six again. Cooper's hand reopens. There's a line along it, where the skin lightens. It goes from dark, dark brown to beige. She steps one step closer to him. He makes a fist again.

"Fine," says the woman.

She goes over to the shelf and picks up the purple alligator, careful, and hands it to Ellie. The glass is as thin as Ellie thought it would be, almost weightless, but it doesn't shatter as she holds it in her hand.

"It's a present," says the woman. Ellie smiles, worried that she'll cry.

"Thanks," she says. "It's beautiful."

The woman reaches up and touches Ellie's cheek. The feel of her skin: cold damp wax paper. "Be careful, baby," she says.

Ellie shudders and steps back. She looks again at Cooper's too-tan fist. She runs her thumb along the alligator's scales.

Winter 2013

It's dark out and cold. Maya puts on tights and shoes, her windbreaker and a band around her head. Stephen's out and so is Ben. She brings a Metro and a credit card. She always does this when she doesn't have a plan for where she'll go or when she'll feel like stopping, though she does, tonight, have an idea of where she might end up. She retraces the run she did with Ben just days prior. It's different, though, in early evening. People, almost every one of whom looks younger than Maya, walk in packs of twos and threes down Smith and Court Streets. Smokers stand outside of restaurants puffing slowly, their hands chapped from the cold. The smells are different also. It's dinner: instead of bacon, it's french fries and grass-fed burgers, pizza slices, Thai spices, and the bitter stench of beer. She brushes shoulders with the groups that take up the whole sidewalk. She runs out into the street, hugging the parked cars along the bike lane, the cars in the street going past so close sometimes that she could knock their rearview mirrors out of place with her elbow or hand. Once she's crossed the bridge, she goes east. She heads uptown through Chinatown, not willing to get close to the water yet. More smells, more people: raw meat, salt, lo mein noodles, the screaming of the street vendors as she reaches Canal. In SoHo, she gives up on Broadway. The packs of people walk in swaths of six and seven, shopping bags over their shoulders, tourists not paying attention, standing in line for street food and stopping to take pictures of lights and stores. Maya heads farther east to Lafayette and then to the numbered, almost to the lettered, avenues. She's at Astor Place before she knows for sure where she'll end up.

She wants to knock on Caitlin's door and be taken in; she wants to talk about her book, to pretend, just very briefly, that she's hers.

She's at a stoplight, legs still moving, toes bouncing off the pavement; it's just behind her, quiet, at her shoulder: "Maya?"

It isn't Caitlin, though.

The voice is timid, unfamiliar. Maya almost runs the other way. She knows it's her only because the hair is there still, falling in her face a little, thick and knotted behind her ears. There's no baby this time. Maya looks quickly for her, underneath the coat Alana wears, but Alana's bundled up and looks much smaller, though as she comes up closer to Maya, she's retained her height and must turn her head down to look Maya in the eye.

"Alana, hi," Maya says. She is suddenly painfully aware of her shoes and tights, her too-thin legs. She's not used to seeing people when she's running. She's used to, those few times she does recognize someone, running fast enough, averting her eyes soon enough, to avoid having to interact.

"I was running," Maya says, because Alana still looks down at her but doesn't speak.

Alana nods.

Maya watches two girls behind her share a cigarette. They hold the tip close to their lips in the exact same way, deliberate, pretending, long drags and short puffs out, playing at a thing they can't quite shape.

"I just left her with him," Alana says. She's crying now and shakes her head. "I just couldn't take it and I left."

"Oh," Maya says. She wants to tell her that she's sorry, help her, lead her back to her apartment, and hold the baby to her chest.

Alana grabs hold of her hair, one heavy chunk held with both hands. "I wanted. Fuck. I don't know. I needed to be a free a while, you know?"

"Do you want . . ." Maya stops. They're standing in the middle of the sidewalk. People brush past, and Maya feels them look. "Let me buy you coffee?"

"Yeah," she says, shrugging. "Sure."

They duck into a place on the corner of Ninth Street. It's dark, with small round uneven tables. A cappuccino machine whirs. "Coffee," Maya says.

Alana orders tea.

They sit far from the counter, in the back corner, farther from the door. Alana places her elbows on the table and lays her face, briefly, in her hands. Maya waits and sips her coffee. There's a small line of sweat down her back from running, and she feels a chill run through her as she waits for Alana to look up again.

"Honey," Maya says again. "Your baby's fine, okay? Just breathe."

Alana cups the shallow mug with both hands and holds the steam up to her face.

"I'm not sure he even knows how to heat the breast milk." Her chin drops to her chest.

Maya laughs. "He'll figure it out."

"The problems of the privileged, huh?" Alana says.

Maya smiles, doesn't answer.

"I just left," Alana says again.

"It's rough," Maya says. "At first, especially. It's really rough."

Alana pulls her tea bag from the water and wraps the string around it, wringing it, then placing it carefully beside her mug.

"Bryant traveled the first couple weeks we had her," says Alana. "I mean, he was there for the delivery and everything, and then for a few days after, but then he had some conference. And he just went. He got all weird about how little money he makes. I mean, we're fine, you know? He'd never cared before, but he's a not very widely read writer with an associate professorship. He's been in the same rent-controlled apartment for thirty years."

She has patches of red beneath her eyes; they're parched and swollen.

"So, all of a sudden, he's completely freaked out that he's not rich. And he just leaves me there to figure out how to keep this kid alive."

She flicks the tag at the top of the tea bag's string until it rips, holding the now-split halves between her fingers.

"I remember thinking I'd made a mistake maybe."

Maya holds her coffee with both hands. She blows lightly into her cup so that the steam rises up and she breathes in. She nods and hopes Alana sees.

"I mean . . ." Alana grabs her hair again; her hands fall back to her mug. "I'm sorry to do this to you," she says.

Maya shakes her head. She wants to tell her how grateful she is, to feel like she might help.

"I just stared at her and thought, people make mistakes, you know?" Her thumbs line the edge of the table; hands, worn raw-rubbed cuticles on every finger, reach again for the mug. "I'm a capable, functional human. There has to be a way out of all of this. I thought maybe I was doing it wrong or something, that it couldn't be as hard as it felt those first few weeks."

Maya shakes her head. She has known well this need to leave, but it was tempered, most of the time, by the slightly more immediate need to stay.

"I don't know anyone who has kids." She looks again into her tea; her nose is long and a little crooked in the middle, almost bumps against her mug. "I'm twenty-eight. That's old for where I'm from, but here I'm like a child bride. My friends feel too young to get married, much less have kids." Her eyes are big and full, still splotched with red.

"But *he's old*, you know? It felt so urgent when we met, to make our lives right then." She shakes her head. "It felt like it was this inevitable union. It felt like . . ." She stops. She looks past Maya to the door. "I'm supposed to be a fucking writer," she says.

Outside, people who all look like children walk past the large windows fogged at the edges, lit up by headlights and the overhangs and night-lit signs of bars and convenience stores, the antique shop next door. The kids are pierced in unexpected places; some wear heels and clothes not warm enough for the cold. They laugh in packs, walking quickly, bumping into one another, looping elbows, clutching hands.

"You know, I used to pity her," Alana says. "Caitlin." She stops.

"She was always so awkward, the way she used to follow Charles like some lost pup."

Maya has an image of Caitlin, cowed and crying in her office, then of Charles, his hand along her back.

"And now . . ." Alana says.

"Now . . ." Maya says. She looks past Alana; CUSTOMERS ONLY, reads a sign hanging from the knob of the bathroom door. "She has a book."

"And I have this person," Alana says. "I'm in charge of a *person*."

She raises her hands, up out of her hair and in the air a moment, like she's not sure where she might put them next. "How the fuck did I do that?"

Maya laughs; so does Alana. She reaches for, then briefly holds Alana's hand.

"It gets better," she says. She knows this is inadequate. She wants to give her more.

Maya left once too, like this, much worse than this, she'd gotten on a plane. And not just for a day. She'd left for weeks. She'd just packed her bags and booked a flight. The kids were older. El must have been four, Ben two. Stephen left all the time, for conferences, for meetings, to see his parents on the Cape when Maya didn't want to pack the kids up and drive eight hours for a two-day stay. But she'd never left them. She'd never spent a night away. Ellie was in preschool in the mornings. Maya was teaching three courses a semester and was home with the kids besides. The semester had just ended. Ellie needed from her always to be held often, even at that age. She would regularly crawl into their bed at night. It was the constancy that Maya needed to get free of. She'd told Stephen as she did it, but she'd not given him the option of asking her not to go. It was early May and the Florida house was empty. She'd rented a convertible and swum and read and ran and drove around. By the third day she'd been desperate for both her kids again, but that had only reaffirmed her need to stay. She called daily and talked to both children. Stephen seemed too afraid to ask much, what she was doing or when she might be coming back. She wanted to prove to all of them that there were parts of all of them that belonged to no one but themselves. She'd eaten almost every meal at a tiny local restaurant close to the house that served simple pastas and salads. She sat alone in a back booth and ate the same bland spaghetti with massive meatballs that she separated and cut up on a separate plate, dipping the warm rolls into the sauce that pooled beneath them on the plate. She was thirty-two and the same waiter, who must have been in his early twenties, would come and flirt with her each night, and she hadn't disabused him. She'd smiled and laughed at his awkward jokes and halfhearted attempts at gleaning information from her, about where she lived or how she spent her days. He complimented her legs, and in the second week he complimented her tan. She realized she could have had this whole other life. That she could still have it if she chose. This had felt both imperative and terrifying.

She thought of her mother more than ever, where she might be now. She'd met her once, the year she'd left Florida for grad school.

She'd found the information in her dad's stuff while she was cleaning out the house. All those years, he'd been in sporadic touch with her. There were letters, a few emails. She'd asked about Maya, but had never asked to speak with her or sent anything for her to keep. Turned out she lived in New York. Turned out those months Maya had been there already and, possibly, in all the years that followed, she was never more than a few miles away. But this was the only time they'd meet.

They met at a restaurant close to her mom's apartment. Maya thought and thought about what to wear and then wore jeans and a plain T-shirt, not wanting to look as if she'd tried too hard. She wore sandals. It was June. She'd walked from her apartment west, then north, and waited half an hour. She was twenty minutes early, her mom walked through the door ten minutes late. Her mom wore three-inch heels, crisscrossed two straps—they slapped her feet as she walked toward Maya. She wore a long black skirt, a yellow tank top, her beige bra strap slipped out against pale freckled skin, and Maya stood, thinking, *Mother, Mother, not.*

"Maya," she said. Her voice was wrong somehow. Her eyes were large and darkly lined. She leaned in to kiss her. Maya pulled back, then leaned in too late.

"Sorry," they both murmured. She'd placed her hand on Maya's shoulder. It was cold and Maya shuddered. She pulled it away quickly and Maya sat back down. Her mom pulled out a chair and held her hands on the edge of the table. Maya unrolled her silverware, placed her napkin on her lap, and ran her index finger down the handle of her fork.

"Maya," her mom said again. She wore bright red lipstick. A thin line of it rose above her lip on the left side of her mouth. Maya wanted to tell her to stop saying her name—she hadn't earned the right yet. Her mother grabbed the saltshaker. Her arms were thin, her fingers short and nubbly, and her nails cut close to the quick.

"How's . . ." she tried again. "How are you?"

Maya nodded. "Okay."

"I thought. I guess I'd stopped expecting."

A waiter came and took their drink order. Maya got water. Her mom ordered a white wine.

The whole thing took less than an hour. Her mom asked awkward questions Maya didn't want to answer. Maya asked her about painting. It was what she'd done when she'd left them, what she'd said she'd left to do. She said she "cobbled," said she didn't paint much anymore. Maya didn't ask her why she'd left. Once she'd seen what she was, she didn't feel the need to ask. When the check came, her mom waited a long time without looking at it. She sipped slowly on her third glass of wine. After an infinity of time passing and neither of them speaking, Maya finally paid the bill while her mom looked past her to the restaurant kitchen. As they left, her mom had once again moved to hug her and Maya had pulled away again.

Maya tells Alana none of this. She holds her coffee near her face again and sips; it's turned tepid since either of them spoke.

"It's completely terrifying," Maya says. "It's also . . ." A thousand million other things.

When she'd finally come back from her time in Florida, it had taken her weeks to get Ellie to forgive her. Ellie was sullen and quiet, spending more and more time close to Stephen or alone in her room. Maya had the summer free and worked to court her, taking her for days alone in the park and around town while Ben was with Stephen or with friends. Her daughter, like her mother, loved the subway and wandering the city. They filled whole days finding new and different ethnic restaurants, pastry shops. Maya dragged her to run her hands over the spines of books at all her favorite shops.

"When El was tiny . . ." Maya says to Alana, "She was probably six or eight months old—I was hardly leaving the house still, except to go to work—a friend of mine forced me out to go with her to MoMA." It was Laura, always Laura, reminding Maya how to live. "We drove up there with Ellie screaming in the car seat and I was already regretting trying to do normal grown-up things too soon, wondering if I ever would again. I had her in the carrier." She laughs. "She shit all over herself within the first five minutes." She feels Alana smile. *This is right*, she thinks. "She was facing out, strapped to me again, looking at the paintings. My friend . . ." Laura was so young then and surprisingly comfortable with Ellie, taking her from Maya for an hour or two when Stephen traveled, for long walks, letting Ellie lie on her in Maya's bed while Laura read. "It was Jean Dubuffet, you know?" Alana smiles. "This sort of accidental warmth and joy." She stops, remembering the paintings, the texture of them up close, the disproportionate portraits, the burnt reds, the blacks and browns. "And El just lost it," she says. "She started squealing." Maya laughs, remembering, the feel and weight of Ellie wriggling, strapped to her. "People stared, thinking she was crying at first, that I was this awful person, disrupting the sanctity of these great works. But she was squealing with this incredible *joy*, you know? Like whatever he was doing, she understood it. I realized she could teach me. That even from the beginning, she would see the world in ways I'd never even thought to see before."

Fall 2011

They're outside again. The bag has gone from Cooper's hand to the front pocket of his pants. It forms a small, almost imperceptible bump below his waist. Ellie wants to be free from him. She wants to take the alligator and the onetwothreefourfivesix.

"Shit," she says. She takes her phone out of her back pocket. It hasn't rung or vibrated, but she looks down at the black face and then over at Jack.

"Annie texted." Jack looks at her, then back toward the old woman.

Ellie says to Cooper, "We have to go."

"Seriously?" he says.

Ellie shrugs. "Sorry."

"Listen . . ." His eyes wander to Jack, then back to Ellie.

"We really have to go," she says.

She starts walking toward his car.

"I can pay you for some of those," she says, nodding toward his pocket. She says it quietly, leaning toward him, hoping Jack can't hear. He turns away from her, unlocks the door. She helps Jack up into his booster seat.

"Nor?" Jack asks.

"Jack doesn't think you should." His car is old and the locks don't work. Cooper has to reach across the seat to open Ellie's door.

"It's fine." She grabs Jack's knee a minute, but he pushes her away. "Just, since you bought more than you would have."

Cooper laughs. "I'm sure you feel bad."

She pulls on her seat belt, stares down at the purple alligator that still sits in her hand. She reaches into the back pocket of her shorts where she has stuffed a wad of cash. She was planning. She's been trying not to look it in the face. She puts the alligator on the dashboard, hands the money to Cooper; she rubs her other hand up and down along the side of the wet sandy canvas of the seat.

"Enjoy," he says, handing three pills to her and pocketing the money.

She doesn't say anything about the other three. She looks briefly in the rearview mirror, but Jack turns his face down as she looks at him. She sees his dad in the way his face has flattened out.

She thrums her thumb quick and careful on the alligator. The scales of it sting briefly each time her hand hits it.

Back at the house, the pills are in her pocket. Jack looks like he's about to cry. Ellie leaves Jack in his room with his bugs while she slips back into her room and stuffs the pills to the bottom of her lowest drawer. She calls to Jack and for a while they sit together silently on the couch. Ellie Googles the cockroaches Annie bought him last week and starts reading different random facts out loud. Jack doesn't mention where they've been, so Ellie doesn't either. She picks the pieces of sand off Jack's feet and drops them on the floor.

The clouds come quickly, covering the sky all at once, and the first crack of thunder comes just as she gets up to find the Nutella jar. They pass it back and forth, and Ellie swipes big mouthfuls with her index finger and licks the remnants from underneath the nubs of her fingernails. Another crack, and this time the power goes out. The house is dark and the TV switches off. The roof is tin and the rain is loud against it. Jack grabs for the Nutella jar. "Can we go outside?" he asks. Ellie can smell the rain through the screened porch. She's kept the door to the house open and when Jeffrey's gone they keep the air conditioner off. "Now, Jack?" she says. He loves the storms almost as much as she does. Often, they sit under the overhang that covers the front door and stick their feet out as it pours. Ellie looks at him, taking one more swipe of chocolate for herself, then licking her finger and cleaning a smudge off his chin.

"Now," he says.

Jack leads the way to the backyard. There's a hammock hanging between two trees and a small brick patio that holds four chairs and a table, all made of wrought iron that has just begun to rust. The rain's coming hard now, and Ellie can barely see to the fence around the backyard. Jack holds tight to her hand and they step out underneath the downpour. She looks over at Jack, who has his head tipped back just like her, his eyes shut tight, his nose scrunched up. They walk out past the deck and lie down in the dirt that's turning quickly to a muddy slush. The palm fronds whip back and forth, lashing loudly, Jack laughs as the mud squishes underneath them, and the thunder cracks again.

Winter 2013

Maya holds tight to her coffee. "Sorry I'm late," she says.

"You're not," says Charles. He's wearing slip-on shoes that are lined with fleece, no socks, a dark blue crew-neck shirt under a brown suede blazer, no coat. His hair falls over the tops of his glasses. He's beautiful, she thinks. He's beautiful in the way he moves and talks, in the way he has hold of his brain. If there were a way to simply have him always fifty feet away and living his life, that's what she'd want most. She wants to give him small things and ask for nothing from him. She wonders if it would be possible to make herself so small he doesn't notice when she's close.

Jackie enters, and then three other students. Charles sits, and Maya leans back against the desk.

"I . . ." he says. "The other night."

She holds her hand up.

She turns back to the desk and holds her *Mrs. Dalloway* close to her chest. Woolf today. Clarissa. Septimus. Isabel and Shake-speare. There is still that.

Halfway through class a hand from the back of the room rises: a boy who hardly ever speaks. He wears a black skullcap, pulled back off his forehead so bits of blond hair peek out from underneath.

"Seriously, though, Septimus, dude's crazy, right?"

Maya stares at him. She's afraid to look at Charles.

"I mean, what's he there for? It's this story about this woman and her party, then all of a sudden, dude kills himself."

Maya nods. She's not sure she can answer. She picks up her copy of the novel, the edges furred and softened, the back cover ripped. The students stare at her, the lot of them. She feels Charles's eyes right through his glasses. She opens the book, close to the end, begins to read.

She can see perfectly, her first, her second, her seventeenth time inside these sentences. The breathlessness with which she's always read.

There was an embrace in death, she reads.

She thinks maybe she won't look up at them till they've all left.

"I think we're done today," she says, still facing the page. She listens to the shuffling of bags and papers. Charles murmurs something to them as they scurry out. She keeps reading through, quietly to herself now, to the end of the novel, ten more pages, before she looks up to see Charles standing there.

"Are you okay, Maya?"

She can't remember if he's ever said her name.

"You want to sit down a minute?"

She shakes her head. "I need to get out."

He tries to help her with her coat as they walk toward the exit.

She sloughs him off, walking quickly, clutching the handle of her bag with both hands as he holds the door and she walks through.

Overnight, they've hit a warm spell. The sun shines on her face. She wishes it were still cold and cloudy, that she could stay more bundled up. "What happened to winter?" she says. If he hears, he doesn't answer. He walks with his large bag slung across his torso, the weight of it flapping at his hip.

"I live on 111 and Amsterdam," he says.

She nods.

They walk briskly down Broadway. They go east at 112th Street, past the bookstore. Across Amsterdam is the huge cathedral Maya's always loved, the garden in front, the spires, the mounds of steps. He leads her past the Hungarian pastry shop, unlocks a heavy metal door, and heaves it open hard with the side of his shoulder; they're in a small dark vestibule, six silver mailboxes line the wall. He leads her up the steps and she tries hard not to think.

Fall 2011

"Annie's getting jealous."

Ellie breathes in one sharp breath. They're having dinner. Tourist season has swept the town full suddenly, and Annie's hardly home at night.

The pills are in her drawer. Every night, before she goes to bed, she lays them out on her desk and counts them.

Jeffrey nods toward Jack, who has climbed up onto Ellie's lap as they eat take-out Indian.

"We finally found someone he loves as much as her," he says.

Ellie burrows her face into Jack's hair. Jeff gets plates and forks and spoons and lays them out, and Ellie takes a bite of her biryani, eyes still averted down.

Jeff pours two glasses of wine. "I'm a little jealous too," he says.

Ellie helps Jack serve himself food, then holds her wine glass. She lets the weight of it settle in her hand

"You two surfing."

Ellie laughs, turns to Jack. "We're pretty awesome, aren't we, Jack?"

"And your boyfriend?" Jeffrey asks.

Ellie stops a minute, wonders what Jack might have said when she wasn't with them. She looks briefly toward her room.

"So he is, then?"

Ellie looks back toward Jack. "Of course not." She pulls her cardigan more tightly to her. Rain falls in violent heavy drops and pounds along the roof.

"Didn't work out?" asks Jeff.

Ellie looks down into her wine and helps Jack cut his lamb into smaller pieces. She takes a long sip of the Syrah before she speaks again.

"It only rains like this here," she says.

He shrugs. "I wouldn't know."

"You . . ." She just assumed he's traveled as much as his wife has, but watching his face now, she thinks, *Of course*.

"I love it," she says, her eyes fixed on the rain.

"Of course you do."

He says it like he knows her, like he knows exactly what she's always been.

Spring 2013

His apartment is a single room with a bed, a desk, two chairs, and two small windows; a galley kitchen runs along the wall. The bed is tightly made, with a dark blue duvet cover with two red-and-white-checked pillows on top.

"Cozy," she says.

He pulls the larger chair that's leather and on wheels out for her and sits primly on the bed.

"Septimus," he says.

She shakes her head, crosses her arms, sits back. "He's always been my favorite."

"Of course he has." Like he knows her.

He looks past her out the window. "Communication," he says.

"It's all he wants," she says.

His back straightens. "Except it's so much harder than he thinks."

"Fucking doctors." She smiles and uncrosses her arms, walking over to his bookshelf. He stays where he is. She fingers a Marguerite Duras, a Nabokov, picks up the Evan S. Connell.

Maya opens the book and keeps her eyes steady on the small, careful paragraphs. She closes the book again, runs her fingers up and down the dark blue cover. "You like the sad ones," she says.

He shrugs. "I guess." He pushes his glasses up and pinches his nose with his thumb and forefinger. "I'm not sure I've read much that isn't at least a little sad."

"At least a little sad," she says, walking back to the desk, and touching a stack of papers that sit on top of it: his dissertation.

"How is it?" she says.

"Who knows?" he says. His back rounds again. His hands rest on his knees. "It's almost finished."

She looks at him, then back down at his work. "You're sure?"

"It's as done as I can do."

"What does that mean?" She's trying to drag something out of him, something that will show her what he's capable of.

He eyes the papers, then puts his palms behind him on the bed. "I'm not sure I care if it's any good. I think I want to teach high school."

"Oh?"

"I've been teaching up in Hunts Point. An after-school program. It's just so much more active, you know? Instead of all these useless papers no one reads."

Maya laughs and begins flipping absently through his chapters. She's a little hurt that he didn't tell her, that she didn't already know that he'd been teaching someplace else. She wants to ask if Caitlin knows.

"You know my life is those useless papers, right?" she says.

"Oh. No," he says. "You're not like that. You're not one of those teachers who's just here to publish and get some useless appointment."

"Some would consider that one of my problems."

"But it's so absurd," he says. "To want these accolades that mean nothing to the world."

"And Hunts Point? Means something more?"

"Yeah," he says. "It's actual engagement. I can see it, you know? What I'm giving every day."

She stares at him: of course, she knows. Her students, reading; it's the one thing she's felt capable of giving properly.

"Well, I guess then you should do that."

He nods. "But I have to finish, you know. It's been too many years of my parents patiently awaiting my arrival at an *Actual Career.*"

"Where are you from?" she asks and can't believe she doesn't already know the answer. She has an image of a pear-shaped mother somewhere in Ohio. She angles her knees farther from him in her chair.

"The Bay Area," he says.

"Far," she says. "They must be proud."

"Maybe," he says. "They like to say *Columbia*. They like to say *PhD*. The fact that it's in literature, I think, they keep to themselves."

Maya laughs. "I'm sure they're proud."

He's so close; she could reach her hand out and rub it slowly back and forth over his head.

"Maybe," he says.

"I tell them about you," he says.

Both of them look straight ahead.

"How much your help has meant to me."

He turns toward her. She can't look at him. If she looks at him, she'll cry. "Thanks," she says.

His hands hold tight to his knees.

"You should be easier on your parents."

"Maybe," he says. "They're just not very interesting."

"Interesting or not. They must have done some good things, making you."

"You say it like I'm a loaf of bread."

"Of all the analogies."

"I like to bake."

"You bake," she says. She laughs, holds up her hands, acknowledging defeat.

"We make ourselves," he says.

"And some of us make bread."

He smiles. "They loved me as well as they could."

"And it wasn't enough for you."

"It was fine."

"I wonder if there's ever more than that."

They're quiet a long time and she looks out the window. She watches the cars out on the street, people walking, talking on their phones. His eyes are full of too much expectation. He leans toward her, but she stays far enough away that they're touching only at the knees.

Fall 2011

The television plays on low and Jeffrey leans in toward Ellie, who holds Jack. He loops his arms around Jack's waist, the back of his hand and then his forearm brushing Ellie's waist. He smells like the wine they've shared throughout the evening. The second bottle he opened silently, refilling the round thin globe of Ellie's glass each time it got below half full. Besides a lamp lit in the far corner of the room, the lights are off. They've been watching a movie, a movie Jack chose and to which Ellie has stopped paying attention. Jeffrey leaves the room, carrying his son and smiling at Ellie, smiling at her in a way that she thinks might be different than each time he's smiled at her in the past.

She should leave, she knows, sitting here alone, no matter the sort of smile he just gave her, no matter what she might do once she gets to her room. Whether the smile was meant to be more intimate, or meant to simply thank her for being so in love with Jack, she should get up, walk out to her slatted door, and close it.

If she turns her head in just this instant, she could see the door, and that might be enough to get her to get up.

She wonders if he's ever wondered what she does when she leaves them.

When she leaves them, the three of them are nearly all she thinks about.

He's slow returning. Waiting, she thinks, hoping she'll be the one to decide to keep things as they are. Let it stay just a thing that happens, moments that pass between them, that they can keep without losing anything of what they already have. Him: the family, the whole grown-up life he's built with Annie. Her: the pieces that she gets when one or more of them is somewhere else.

She doesn't leave, though. She's too young to walk to her room and close the door behind her. She's too desperate to be touched. She's too hungry for the looks he gives her—the looks that have become more and more frequent, have begun lasting longer, that she thinks about when she can't sleep at night—to be made manifest across her skin.

Perhaps, though, she thinks, he'll simply sit and ask her what's happened in the movie since he left. And she won't know and she'll have to mutter something about nodding off or she'll just pretend to know and make it up. And he'll give her an easy out. He'll say, *You must be exhausted, Nor.* And then, chastely, she will leave him, unfolding her legs from beneath her and folding the blanket that now sits atop her and placing it back on the couch. She'll walk toward the door that now she cannot bring herself to look at. They'll nod at one another. She'll say, *Good night, Jeffrey.* She'll go to bed with one of her mom's books.

Spring 2013

What happens next: They're sitting, both of them facing the window, and then he turns toward her. His hands, which up till now have sat chastely at his sides, reach around her waist; they're both lying on top of the covers, their legs still hanging awkwardly over the edge. He's slow and careful, silent. His size seems to disallow him the use of all his strength.

She wishes she were slightly less sentient as it happens. She wishes she were able not to notice the way he fumbles too long with the condom, the way he squints as he comes close to her, his glasses set on the table by the bed. She wants to stop him to ask him what he's gaining from this. If he could teach her something. If he could promise her when this is over something fundamental will have shifted from either him to her or her to him.

Fall 2011

What happens next is far less formal, far messier, far more terrifying, and the whole time she wishes she didn't already know that only bad things will come in the end. Because even during and then after, even when the first intimations of what must be pre- and then present and then post-coital bliss settle in to dull the sharp edges of her brain, she still knows what she's done.

They fall slowly into one another. He slips underneath the blanket with her. He—by more degrees than her, with more deliberate force, though she also comes toward him—reaches up to touch her face. His hands aren't as warm as they've been in all the moments leading up to this one. They create in her a sharp intake of breath; her limbs loosen. His hands climb up under her shirt and she gasps as they reach under her bra and latch onto her breasts.

The whole thing happens in the same room where they've just sat with Jack, where they've been eating, where soon Annie will sit when she comes home. All the windows are still open and the rain pounds on the roof, the AC pumps. Outside, a palm frond cracks free of its tree and slaps hard against the window, and Ellie startles underneath him and Jeffrey doesn't stop to ask if she's all right.

He's less gentle than she expected. He's quick and as he comes she wonders if he hasn't timed the whole thing perfectly, to be sure his wife doesn't walk in, to be sure he still has time to shower. To be sure that he has Ellie fucked and safely put to bed before his wife comes home.

Spring 2013

She brings her face up close to his, hoping he'll wake up and also grateful for his sleeping. She gets up quietly and pulls her pants back on. She puts on her bra and shirt and coat. She lets herself out of the apartment with one more glance at Charles naked, half of him under the covers, half of him twisted on top of them.

She goes straight down Amsterdam, block after block. At some point, she crosses through the park. She heads east, not thinking where she's going. She has on boots, her too-big bag slung over her shoulder; her feet start to ache from the pounding, one foot, then the other, the whole right side of her body stiffening with the extra weight of all her books. She stands on Broadway and watches the rows of lights change from green to yellow to red, then back again. Around Twentieth Street she decides that she needs water, more air. She covers the last few avenues to get to the river and finds a bench. She watches the water move and the moon bounce off it in bright patches. She's close to Caitlin's, thinks of calling her, realizes she can't.

Fall 2011

"I don't want to hurt anyone." She winces as she says it. She sounds like a little girl.

He stops smiling. He turns his legs off the couch and reaches for his boxers. Her hand slips from his. The weight of the cushion shifts up on her side as he stands.

She stands up, but she's not sure where to go. She pulls her clothes on. Her sweater reaches down to the middle of her thighs and she stands on tiptoes, wanting to seem larger than she is. She shakes her head and her hair's a mess around her shoulders. She gathers it with her free hand and ties it on top of her head.

She looks at him once more before she escapes to her bedroom. There's something cruel and a bit sad that she hasn't seen before in the way his eyes are set. That's where Jack is different: he has something better in him. That's where Annie is.

Spring 2013

"I got an apartment," says Stephen. Maya's been walking around all night. This is the second morning in a row that she's come home after sunrise.

She wants to ask how long he's been looking. Where else her husband's been while she's been with Charles. She feels comfortable and calm next to him for the first time since long before their daughter left.

He tried at first, right after, when she hardly spoke, when she took leave from work, only answered when Ben called. Stephen would come and bring her back to bed with him when she'd wandered into Ellie's room; he'd wake her carefully, knowing that she startled easily, rubbing a foot or shoulder while whispering to her that it was him, that he'd just come to bring her back to bed. He would take her hand and lead her back under the covers. Sometimes he would even hold her briefly, staying silent as he did. Other times he sat and talked, his body very close to hers, about nothing, really, just to keep her from brooding. But in the weeks or maybe months that he kept trying, Maya simply refused to listen, to feel better, to feel anything at all.

He'd made her laugh once, too early. They'd just had sex. She hadn't meant for it to happen. It was two months after Jack died. Stephen had reached for her and they'd both undressed. She'd felt him moving, slow and careful, the familiarity: his face, his hands, his mouth. She'd been relieved by how untouched she remained even as she felt herself start coming: her underwear still hanging on an ankle, her camisole still covering her chest. He'd slipped it up and kissed her stomach. She'd reached her hands up to his face and held it still. He came quickly. It had been so long. He'd dipped his forehead into her chest, still inside of her, "Like a fucking teenager," he'd said.

And the way he'd said it: like he was sorry, embarrassed. Before she realized it, she'd laughed. And she'd been terrified by this, this moment. By feeling like all that had happened hadn't happened after all. She'd been terrified by the implication that they might somehow have moments when they didn't remember, that they might still get to live. She'd slipped out from underneath him, quickly, not willing to look at him. She'd pulled her clothes on, gone into Ellie's room. It would be months before she allowed herself to lose control like that again, to laugh, to smile accidentally. She wouldn't, in all the months that followed, let him reach for her like this again.

"Where?" she says now. They are New Yorkers. All that's happened, and she's curious about his choice of real estate.

"Broadway and 122nd." Across the street from work.

She nods. "Easier commute."

"I think it's better, Maya."

She holds her hand up to her mouth. "Yes."

She reaches up and places her fingers softly on his cheek, just above his chin.

His chin is warm, clean-shaven.

He reaches up and takes her hand.

"We'll be okay," he says.

She purses her lips and then turns them up at the corners. "Stephen," she says.

He pulls her close to him. They can do this now, she thinks, now that they don't have to anymore.

That Day

They go in the evening when the beach is almost empty. It's never too cold to swim. The water's like a bathtub, it's so warm. The sun sets behind them. The sky is pinks and blues and purples. Ellie wants to be inside it. She wants to climb up over the dunes and dive into the clouds. She's taken all three of the oxys. There's no point any longer in pretending: she's fucked up now; this is who she is. Jack is with her, as he always is now. If anything, his presence makes her feel capable of more, not less. He's smiling at her, all slightly crooked teeth and short round limbs. He's excited to go swimming in the evening—his mom is at the restaurant; his dad is with clients until nine—laughing at the faces Ellie makes as they drive to the ocean. Both of them are barefoot. She has not put on a bathing suit and neither has he. It's a thrill for him; he seems as high as she is. High on wearing his shorts into the ocean, on not being forced to put on sunscreen or a hat or the long-sleeved SpF 50 shirt. Ellie wears shorts too, an oversized T-shirt. She wishes briefly it were the four of them.

She's just stoned enough to fantasize about the family they would be: her, Annie, Jack, and Jeffrey, forgetting for a minute how she might not fit. They've also not brought towels. They walk barefoot over the hot asphalt of the parking lot. Jack squeals and Ellie lifts him up and twirls him in circles. An older couple sits at one of the picnic tables on the wooden platform that leads out to the beach. They have a small basket that folds open and they smile at Jack and El as they twirl past them. They wear sun hats—red for the man and yellow for the woman—Ellie stares a minute at the spots on both their hands. Such great colors. She tries to take a picture with her eyes so she can paint it later when she's back alone inside her room. Swim swim swim, says Jack. There's a sign up on the lifeguard stand that says NO LIFEGUARD ON DUTY: swim at your own risk. Swim swim swim, says Ellie back to Jack. She lifts him high up in the air and her mind is calm and clear and happy. The moment her feet touch the water she thinks, Yes, this. She puts Jack down so they can run out to where the shore drops and the water gets deep together. They race, and water splashes up over their ankles, then their calves, then up their knees, and then the sand drops down quick and both of them tread water, big drops splashing, Ellie wishing they could always always always stay like this. She dives down under, chasing Jack. He flails and gets free of her. She dives down deeper and he swims, quick and sure, outside her grasp. The waves are lolling in. Those big soft mounds that hardly break, just building into blue-green mountains, then sloughing back before they make it in to shore. It's so warm under the water, but not the awful stifling hot that it is back on shore. Ellie only comes up because she remembers oxygen is necessary, because she hears Jack laughing and wants to have hold of him again. "Jack!" she calls. She has his ankle. He splashes hard in her face and he's free again. Her eyes sting. She closes them and dives down deeper. Her mind clears. She doesn't think of Annie or of Jeffrey. She doesn't think of Ben or of her dad. She lets the water rush all through her. She feels warm and full inside. She reaches the bottom, runs her hands along the sand, and then burrows her face in. She plants her palms and pushes herself back up to the surface, kicking hard, in awe of her legs' strength. When her head breaks up—she breathes in one full breath—she's facing west and sees the pinks and oranges and purples. The clouds are thin strips through the colors and she calls to Jack to look.

The Next Day

Stephen had itemized what happened in as clear and certain terms as he could. There had been a riptide. These came often, especially that time of year. The tides were highest, least predictable, in September. The water often deceptively calm. The boy had been pulled out and under. He was small and must have struggled, panicked. Ellie'd swum in the opposite direction and hadn't seen or heard him. By the time she'd gotten to him: his brain had been too long without air.

M,

He was so wet right after. I used to carry him some-
times. He'd fall asleep in the car, or on the couch, and
I loved the feel of him against me, warm and quiet,
as I brought him to his bed. But he was heavier than
he'd ever been.

The water tried to pull me down as I dragged
him. It was windy and the tide kept pulling me back
out. As we came in to shore I got hit with a wave and
I remember thinking if I could just stay standing he
would be okay. I kept looking forward to the moment
he'd be fine again.

I think she tried to think it wasn't my fault. She
held my hand in the ambulance at first. I was crying
and I wouldn't . . . I couldn't let go of him. But as
she watched him and once she really looked at me—I
couldn't focus, couldn't get warm, couldn't make
sense—she just turned away and didn't speak to me or
look at me again.

Sometimes I think I want to call her. Sometimes I
try to write it down. But I don't think there's language
for the sort of sorry that I am.

Every day I see the therapist. We all see him every
day, between the self-serve frozen yogurt most of us
subsist on and avoiding talking to one another, the
walks around the grounds that are too pretty, like
they're trying to make up for all the awful shit that
we've all done with perfect plants. The therapist says
I have to re-imagine the experience. He says I have to
take account of my actions, understand my culpabil-
ity, situate myself within the context of this thing I've

done. He has masks along the wall of his office, big dark angry pieces of wood that I stare at when I can't look at him. He sits with his leg crossed over his knee like we're just talking about some small gripe I have with you guys, like I'm just some wayward girl who likes boys and drugs. What I want is for him to scream at me. I want him to tell me how to fix it, to fix me, even though I know he can't. I sit there staring at those masks and think fuckyoufuckyoufuckyou for not making any of it better. And then I think, fuck me.

The other day I laughed at something. This guy made a joke in group that wasn't even funny, but I laughed. It was like my body wanted to remember what it felt like, to make that sound, to move that way. I felt awful after. I hid in my room in case anybody noticed, in case anybody here cared what I did, or what I've done. But sometimes now whole minutes pass in which he isn't all I think about. I think about you or Dad or Benny. I think about a book or a TV show, random, stupid shit. I think about all the time I might still have in which I have to figure out how to keep on living. It feels almost totally impossible. It feels like all that's left.

El

Ellie has on jeans and flip-flops. She looks young to Maya, far too thin.

Ellie's mom looks scared.

Maya grabs tight to her daughter.

Ellie stands very still and breathes in the scent of *Mom*.

They drive out to the beach without anybody talking. Maya stares at El at every stop. Twice: the blare of horns behind them as the light turns green and they still haven't gone. Ellie turns to her the second time. Same eyes, same nose, but Maya's still afraid to look at her too long. She almost grabs her daughter's hand, but stops. They park at the least-used beach access Maya knows: two worn dirt spots for cars, no shower, a path straight through the dunes. Both of them are barefoot. The path is overgrown. Large flaps of leaves slap their thighs and shins. An errant branch gets caught in Ellie's hair. The ground levels off up by the dunes and then dips steeply. The water's soapy, choppy; whitecaps form and trickle in. A long time, Ellie and her mom stay far from where the water meets the sand.

"El," says Maya. Her daughter wears a tank top and Maya watches as her shoulders rise and fall. Maya grabs her hand. She loops an arm around her daughter's waist and pulls her to her. She brings her back against her chest and holds her still.

Acknowledgments

THANK YOU to my parents, who've loved me, always, who love so much our little girls.

To my agent, Amelia Atlas, brilliant reader, prolific emailer, extraordinary listener, thoughtful talker-off-a-ledger, most trusted lovely guide.

To my editor, Katie Adams, who knew exactly how to make this book what I'd always hoped that it could be.

To Cordelia Calvert and Peter Miller, for your meticulous thoughtfulness.

To my teachers: Rob Devigne, Lecia Rosenthal, Victor LaValle, Deborah Eisenberg, Christine Schutt, Heidi Julavits, Ben Metcalf, Richard Ford, for your boundless stores of generosity.

To Steven Luz-Alterman, for saving me.

To Bryant Musgrove, most constant trusted reader, writing soul mate, first ever champion, dear, dear friend.

To Elena Megalos, Sanaë Lemoine, Eliza Schrader, Natasha Suelflow, and Yurina Ko, baby holders, playground goers, sidewalk chalkers, subway sharers, couch sitters, dinner makers, apartment lenders, ice-cream bringers, endless versions of the first ten pages readers, the best talkers, who taught me all community could be.

To Tara Gallagher and Rebecca Taylor, fellow drowning girls.

To Willa Cmiel, for thinking fear is useless and absurd, for how very strong you are.

To Catherine Boshe, Buggy holder, other mother, second partner, the best listener, always a place that we can stay.

To Cheryl Fabrizio, teacher trainer, constant reader, Faulkner shower, long text sender, I'm proud of you too.

To Osvaldo Monzon and Mauricio Botero and Heidi Rich.

To Ricardo Lopez, Marisa Strong Baskin, and Kara Steger.

To Mimi Fry, for beach dates, such great mama conversations, for showing up and always bringing extra snacks.

To Shannon Carthy Curry, for walks and runs and mulberries.

To Emily Joanna Bender, dorm bed listener, first book sharer, best mom friend always, one of my favorite brains.

To Kayleen Rebecca Hartman, for all those years of almost everything.

To Alejandro Strong, for calling and talking, and walking and talking, and driving and talking. For the Trachtenbergs.

To Scott Steger, who always tries.

To Kenny Strong and Cristina de la Vega, who saved our lives a million times and stuck around and made us cake, who held our babies, took our trash out, made us dinner, hugged and listened, all those rich and lovely hours talking in the kitchen, who give our children so much love and care.

To Peter, who is steady, careful, confident, who is generous and kind, who is my favorite conversation, my favorite couch or walk or dinner partner, my most trusted teammate; who taught me love, who taught me fun, who gave me a whole world.

To Isabel and Luli, who taught me joy.